edenborn

nick sagan

g. p. putnam's sons • new york

This is a work of fiction. Names, characters, places, and incidents either are the product of the author's imagination or are used fictitiously, and any resemblance to actual persons, living or dead, businesses, companies, events, or locales is entirely coincidental.

G. P. Putnam's Sons
Publishers Since 1838
a member of
Penguin Group (USA) Inc.
375 Hudson Street
New York, NY 10014

Library of Congress Cataloging-in-Publication Data

Sagan, Nick.
Edenborn / Nick Sagan.
p.   cm.
ISBN 0-399-15186-9
1. Regression (Civilization)—Fiction.   2. Endangered species—Fiction.
3. Human beings—Fiction.   4. Epidemics—Fiction.   I. Title.
PS3619.A36E34   2004   2004048373
813'.6—dc22

Printed in the United States of America
1   3   5   7   9   10   8   6   4   2

This book is printed on acid-free paper. ∞

Book design by Gretchen Achilles

for my mother

Speed of sound.

It's coming round.

Heaven's on the way down.

LOCAL H, "HEAVEN ON THE WAY DOWN"

prologue

The room was white, and sterile, and fearsome. It would be the last room he would ever see and he knew it. He knew it all too well.

With his blurry vision and the poor fluorescent light overhead, he could just make out the pain poster on the far wall. Cartoon faces had been arranged side by side, only the one at the far left looking happy and content with its engaging smile and soothing periwinkle hue. Beneath it he could see the number zero, a response to the question at the top of the poster: "How much pain are you in?" And by the zero, the word "none." But to the right of that smiling face, he saw a colorful rogues' gallery of the unsmiling, a progression of cartoon torture victims. From one they ranged up to the number ten, "more pain than you can possibly imagine," a grotesque parody of suffering, the crimson face contorted in a berserk anguished cry. He stared balefully at that countenance, hating it, feeling increasingly mocked by it over the past few weeks. Compounding the insult was the chart itself, wholly inaccurate as far as he was concerned because "more pain than you can possibly imagine" becomes imaginable the moment you experience it. It becomes "oh God please no." Simply that. And you can experience it again and again, and then even worse pain that makes it seem pleasurable in comparison. That ten can stretch. There are elevens and twelves. The pit is truly bottomless. He knew that now.

He glanced over at the pine-green face, the first stop on the trip to hell with its number one and nervous look. A look that said notice I am not smiling any longer, in fact unlike my periwinkle neighbor I am distinctly worried about my condition. I'm not going to feel any worse than this, am I? Vividly he remembered that feeling when he first got sick. When he still had faith in medical science finding an eleventh-hour vaccine. How bad will it get before they cure me? Never this bad, he'd thought. What price those illusions? The green face still had hope in its unseeing cartoon eyes, his lost optimism trapped in a two-dimensional drawing. He hated it more than the red face, he realized. He hated it because it would go through all the colors of the rainbow before inevitably becoming red, and he hated it because it was too stupid to recognize its doom. Worst of all, he hated himself for hating it, bitterly mourning the cheerful and untroubled man he once was, a man with heart and character who had seemed momentarily impervious to the many unlovely transformations the disease would put him through.

As his temperature spiked, he clutched his aching gut and wondered if he had not in fact swallowed Death itself, so powerful the affliction chewing away at him from the inside out. It was wretchedly unfair, this bait and switch in which he'd been promised a long and happy life but instead had been given an illness that would not only kill him, but everyone he knew and loved, and even everyone he didn't know and love. Black Ep would successfully wipe out all humanity and it wasn't the least bit fair. Felled by tiny microbes. He felt like Gulliver captured by the Lilliputians. Only these Lilliputians would not recognize his worth and put him to work as a giant defender of their land. On the contrary, they would ruin him utterly, consume him, and of his dearest hopes make kindling.

When the pain waned, the nausea waxed, and vice versa, so moments of comfort seemed as scarce as gold nuggets in a coal mine, and to him, incalculably more valuable. In those heaven-sent moments of relief, he found himself weeping, though whether he wept for his lost future, his wife's or the world's was never clear to him, and he did not like to think of himself as a woebegone sort, so he rationalized that he was simply weeping with joy at an oasis in the desert of his disease. And when the pain and sickness returned, the oasis would vanish, disappearing so quickly and completely that he came to look back upon it as nothing more than a mirage.

"It's not real," he mumbled, his throat burning and encrusted with phlegm.

"What isn't, sweetheart?" she said, blotting his forehead with a cool compress. When had she returned?

"Mercy," he said. Or perhaps he just thought he said it. No mercy in the genome of the virus. *"What about you?"* he asked, blinking rapidly. *"Are you real?"*

"Of course I am."

He took her hand and squeezed as hard as he could, then nodded, eyes closed. *"I've been dreaming so much I don't know what's real anymore. I dreamt about you before but . . . you weren't . . . it wasn't . . ."*

She shushed him and he nodded again, breathing deep before succumbing to a coughing fit that forced him onto his side in a tight fetal ball. She stroked his hair and asked if he wanted her to get the nurse. He didn't answer. He thought about the child they had been trying to have and all the good things they'd wanted for him. Or her, he'd have been just as delighted with a girl. If only he'd lived in another time when dreams of parenthood and prosperity and living to a ripe old age still had promise. But fate had dropped him into an era of uncertainty and fear, with technological wonders secondary to hostile ideologies sweeping the globe, no end to the strikes and counterstrikes and poverty and plagues, of which Black Ep would undoubtedly be the greatest and last. And yet, here he had found true love, a strong and gentle flower he could fight and die for, a woman who not only could stand to be near him in his last moments of weakness, vomiting and dread, but who would help him through his awful pains, and relish that time as precious. He would be forever grateful for her if little else in his life.

He tried to sit up, failed, tried again. His head lolled back against the pillow and he looked at her, loving her, past the point of being embarrassed for her to see him this way, but wishing he could be just a little healthier now, strong enough to put on a brave face and be the comforting one. To hold her, stroke her hair, ease some of her concern. Why had he been the one to get sick first? It might be easier for her after he died, he thought, because though she would be grief-stricken there would surely be an accompanying sense of relief. He could kill himself to expedite that day. But she would never forgive him for that. It was only a matter of time until she took his place in a hospital bed. She would die soon enough, they both knew it, and the time she had left she wanted to spend with him.

"Who will take care of you after I'm dead?" he asked.

She shrugged. "Don't think of that."

"It's not right for you to take care of me when you're bound to get sick soon and there'll be no one to take care of you."

"Just rest."

"What happened to you today?"

"Nothing," she said. "I waited there for three hours and they wouldn't see us. We chanted, we begged, we pleaded. They just left us outside the fence staring in."

"Like kids at the bakery window."

"Exactly."

"Those miserable fuckers," he spat. "Don't go back there."

"Oh baby, I have to," she sighed. "They have to know how important we are."

"We're not important."

"Then they have to know how serious we are about this. I've tried reasoning with them, I've tried bribing them." She shook her head. "Every time I go, they don't let me in. They just tell me we're on the list and say they'll call when they have room."

"They won't call."

"They will."

"They're lying. They don't have enough facilities. Hundreds of millions sick, soon to be billions? It's a miracle there's space for me here."

"But the list!"

"No list. They tell us we're on the list so we don't get violent. That's what they're doing. But it won't fool anyone for long. Promise me you won't go back there."

"You know I can't promise that."

"Everyone's desperate. Everyone's crazy. There are people out there who think the government has a cure but won't give it out because they want to thin the population. The news said it's anarchy all over the West Coast and it's just a matter of time 'til we get riots here too."

She took his hand tightly and said, "I don't care. I won't give up. I'll do whatever it takes to give us a chance."

"What chance? You're buying false hope from a cryonics lab. What's the point of it?"

"To freeze us. In case someday they find a cure."

He laughed a short and brittle laugh. "They? They who? No one's surviving this. At the rate we're at we'll all be dead in a year."

She told him about a company called Gedaechtnis. About their fireball of a plan. About the extraordinary children they were engineering and how those children might actually pull off a miracle when they came of age.

"It won't work," he sighed. "We'll mess it up the way we've messed everything else up. The way we fucked up the world."

(thirty-seven years later)

part one

the world

pandora

This is the Sunday to beat all Sundays. I'm taking a stroll through the park and we're talking sunny shores, shade-giving trees and sailboats floating on the Seine. It's an infinity of pleasure and leisure, with couples gazing out at the water together, families enjoying open-air picnics, and no one in a rush. There's green grass beneath me, and blue sky above. I'm carrying the End of the World in my veins, but I don't know it yet.

A nineteenth-century French boy moves past me in a blur. It's not his speed that blurs; he's walking no faster than I am. But he's not so much a boy as a collection of colorful dots in the shape of a boy, as if his atoms were somehow visible to the naked eye. He pays me a smile, and I pay him one back. This kid is full of springtime and laughter, reminding me of a young footballer I used to coach in my teenage years. I watch a dot labrador lope after him, stopping short to watch his dot master bend down to uproot some dot lilies. At a distance everything looks real, but up close like this you can see things for what they are. That's not the case in most domains, where the illusion of life is near absolute.

Champagne signals me. She's dressed for this with her embroidered traveling dress, her lace fichu, her fancy hat and her parasol. I'm the anachronism with my fringed faux-leather coat, blue jeans and silver eyebrow piercings. But neither of us fit in because we're the only ones here who don't smack of pointillism. And we're both wearing our old faces, the ones programmers and artists assigned us while in the real world our bodies slept and slept some more.

"You tweaked it," she says.

"You noticed. Do you like?"

She scrunches her nose up. "I don't know yet. Tell me what you did."

"Played with color, made it a little less painterly," I say, passing her the bottle of Beaujolais I've brought for this occasion. "You're the art historian—give me some of your expert opinion."

"There's something else."

"Yeah, I disabled the automatic composition. When you turned your head, the dots that made up the characters used to rearrange to fit your point of view. They'd frame up to create a perfect pointillist painting wherever you look."

"And now they behave more like regular people."

"Right. You don't like it?"

"Who said I didn't like it?" She smiles, popping the cork. "You're so sensitive, Pandora. Don't be so worried about what people think."

"Who said I'm worried?" I say, taking the glass from her after she pours. "Cheers."

"Yeah, cheers." We clink and drink to the second half of our lives: eighteen years of wonderful, terrible freedom. Today is the anniversary of the day the lie unraveled, the day we learned what we were, where we were, and why. It's hard not to think of it as a birthday.

"Nice," she decides of the wine.

It is—this vintage is crisp and not too dry, not half as complex as the "serious" wines she prefers. You can keep your oak and berry and nutty bouquets, thank you very much.

I tell her how I programmed this particular Beaujolais, but she's not interested. "We'll have a real drink when you come up," she says, threatening me with a far-too-serious twenty-year-old bottle of Riesling she just discovered in a Bavarian pub. Over the years she has filled her wine cellar with a collection that would be the envy of any oenophile, building it up by looting the stocks of the dead. We're all scavengers these days, indulging our various hobbies as compensation for the work we do.

My work is technical. If anything breaks, I fix it. I'm responsible for power, communications, computer systems, IVR and similar inorganic technologies. I am not responsible for cloning or parenting. I couldn't do what Champagne does. I chose this line of work because—

Excuse me, Pandora. Another matter requires your attention.

Can it wait? I'm telling a story here.

I can see that. I can also see you're telling it wrong.

Here we go.

You should start earlier, when you realized your world wasn't real.

It's my story, Malachi, and I'll tell it my way. Give me a minute, will you?

I can afford you another three minutes, and then we should talk.

Three it is. Now go away before you wreck my narrative structure.

I chose this line of work because I keep clinging to the past. I grew up in a fake Brazil and a fake America, but I woke up in Belgium, the real Belgium, to learn that my wildest nightmares were true. When the kids were little, we taught it to them like this:

Desperate times had settled on us—
The Black Ep swept like a scythe through our ancestors
The brilliant among us knew none would survive—
But against this threat some must stay alive
To carry on the species
So they meddled with our DNA, and gene-ripped babies came
*   into being*
But who will raise them to adulthood?
Only computers would serve when all were dead
They built a false world for dreamers to explore

While our bodies slept safely in the real
Not knowing we were alone in the world
With a great burden awaiting us
When we awoke and saw what had been concealed
One of us went round the bend
With treachery and shameful acts
He made six of us from ten
But now the battle's fought and the battle's won
With each and every successful birth

But childrearing just isn't for me—I'm terrified at the thought of bringing kids into a place like this. So it's easier for me to work behind the scenes, and stay a little closer to my old life by maintaining and upgrading the Immersive Virtual Reality I grew up in. In the real world, I visit all my nieces and nephews. I'm their favorite aunt, and I love them because I'm not totally responsible for them. Not the way Isaac, Vashti and Champagne are.

"I'm looking forward to seeing you guys," I tell my drinking buddy as I pour her another glass. "Wish Isaac would join us."

"We're closer to that than we have been in quite a while," she says.

"Sometime soon then, I hope."

"It's possible," she says, putting an accent on the word "possible." She doesn't think it'll happen, and she isn't sure that it should. There's so much history with Isaac, not all of it rosy.

"Imagine if we could. The four of us together again, all united in purpose?"

"I thought we were talking about a drink," Champagne frowns. "Good luck getting us on the same page."

"The one might lead to the other."

"Ever the optimist."

"Absolutely," I say, momentarily distracted by a dot man blowing a dot bugle, "and if we can get back on track, maybe we can bring the hermits in."

"The famed class reunion?" Her smile comes just shy of a smirk.

"I'm still hopeful," I tell her.

"That's what I love about you," she says. "You're stubborn. Or dreaming. Either way, I love it."

"It has to happen," I insist. "We have to put aside our differences."

"Tell it to Hal." That's all she needs to say, because he still won't talk to them, and only barely talks to me. That's okay, I'll take what I can get from him. He's broken, but he stole my heart when we were kids, and he's still got it, and I guess it's broken too.

Sarcastically, Champagne adds, "He's had a sudden pang of conscience, right?" I look away. "What about Fantasia?"

"Nothing," I say. No news. None of us knows where she is.

Champagne hasn't hurt my feelings too badly, but she thinks she has. People have a hard time reading me sometimes; it's a common complaint. "Hey, I'm sorry," she says, taking my hand and squeezing it. "I hope they come back around. I do. I want us all to be friends again. You know I'd like nothing more than that."

I give her a nod and squeeze her hand. There isn't a lot more I can say on the subject, and even less that I want to.

"When you talk to Hal tonight, give him my best, okay? No one's given up on him yet. Except Vashti," she says, "but you know how she is."

"I do," I tell her. "Hugs to Vash and the kids, and I'll see you soon."

Leaving Champagne at *Un dimanche après-midi à l'Île de la Grande Jatte*, I relocate to the middle of nowhere. Just an empty domain I use as a launching pad. I send a flashing ball of yellow and black, and I wait, but no orange and black answers my call. Hal must not want the gift I got him. I check my watch. I wait longer. Maybe he's not online.

I exit the system altogether, waking up in the real world. A rolling boom suggests it's raining outside, and when I check I realize I'm as cold as Mercutio's heart. Rubbing some warmth back into my shoulders, I shut the windows against the downpour. Outside, the clouds look polluted and strange. I turn away from them to put on some clothes. No message from Hal yet. It's been weeks now. And we always talk on the anniversary; that's supposed to be clockwork; I count on it. So I bend my privacy rule and take a look at the satellites, but that corner of the world is silent and still.

haji

The disruption comes when I am halfway in and halfway out of a circular tub, tracing a pattern in water that has splashed on the ceramic tile floor. Mu'tazz calls my name, striking the door again, the knock scattering my daydreams like birds. He brings a message from father, then leaves with my whispered thanks. I make no move. The candles yield more light than warmth, and the chill keeps me where I am, contemplating my fingertips, clean and wrinkled from my evening ablution. The calluses are fading. How wondrous it is to heal. A minor miracle, except miracles defy the laws of nature and this exemplifies them. Enough. Guilt pulls me from the bath. No one likes to be kept waiting.

Wool and linen cling to my skin and sand shushes beneath my feet. Had I lived thousands of years ago, it might be green grass. Look backward; every desert was once lush.

A cold wind embraces me and I do not care. Twilight is my favorite time, and tonight the sky is clear. I can gaze up into endless lapis lazuli and count the pinpoints of pure, white light.

Beauty seen is only eclipsed by beauty unseen, and though the vast distance of space keeps trillions of worlds from my eyes, it cannot keep them from my mind. What orbits that star? That one, the lowest in Ursa Major? What is it like to live there?

Questions inhabit every fiber of my being. If I could find God, I would ask one question after the other without stopping, emptying myself to savor the answers. I think sometimes that if God were to give shape and form to my thoughts, the universe would so create. But to find God, I must first find myself.

My father is a tall man with eyes as black as kohl. I am short with eyes like amber. We look nothing alike. He is not my biological parent. I consider this a trivial distinction.

For years, I did not. As much as I loved him, as much as he loved me, DNA put us oceans apart. In my heart, not his. I fought my disconnection through meditation and prayer. It took all my patience to seize that elusive moment, a moment of connection, of immediacy, the triumph of higher consciousness, that holy moment right now, right now, where the past and the future do not exist and there is no difference between you and anyone else in the world. I found it, and woke, and then it left me. But when it left, so did my fear. I can find that moment again. It is not easy, but I can find it on a night like this, if the wind dies down and everything grows calm. It is a moment of joy and my heart aches when it slips away. My father keeps it with him. In the midst of a whirlwind, in a raging inferno, or at the bottom of the Nile, he has it. He has it always.

I hear birdsong in my ear as my mask filters out impurities. Saqqara has not been sanitized; here the dead are plentiful. Inside the city, brittle skeletons pantomime slumber, while out in the desert, carrion eaters have scattered human bones far and wide. The wind hides or reveals these beneath the sand, as is her whim, and I take notice as I walk, quietly accepting these reminders of how populous this place once was.

The mask not only protects me from the environment; it protects the environment from me. The water in my breath becomes salt. Salt deposits cause cracks. Cracks wreak havoc on the structures we hope to restore. Great damage has accrued over the years, tombs slowly crumbling from the carelessness of countless tourists, dead now, but breath lingering. This is a sad thing. My brothers, sisters and I use microbes to desalinize the structures, and lasers to erase the graffiti. Together, we have spent the better part of a week restoring the Step Pyramid of Zoser. It is not a traditional pyramid with the edges of the planes rising to a point; it is more like a ziggurat, with six mastabas atop each other, each smaller than the next. It is Egypt's first pyramid, almost five thousand years old, and as I limp toward it, I take satisfaction in the work we have done. The limestone shell is clean and unmarked. We have rebuilt it, made it smooth and white again, so starlight dances on its surface. There is still much to do inside the tombs, and many loose bricks to repair. A complete restoration would take years; we return home in just days. Still, it is a good deed, a good lesson and a good challenge. Zoser built this towering wonder in the hopes of forging a connection with God, and so we honor that. We honor the brilliance of his architect, Imhotep, and the labors of countless workers whose names are lost to time. We honor the cradle of civilization. We honor ourselves.

When I find him, my father is hunched over the new ventilation system with his sleeves rolled up. He is fine-tuning the airflow and the bioremediation, to control how many salt-eating microbes will be released, and how often. His back is to me, but he senses me without turning around.

Salaam alaikum wa rahma-tullah, he says, wishing me Peace and God's Mercy.

Walaikum assalam, I say in reply.

I move to his side and we work together in silence. I can see the delicate balance he is striving for and assist him as best I can. We adjust, test, readjust and retest. Such is the process for so many tasks in life. God has blessed us with an aptitude for this kind of work, and before long we have achieved our objective. My father seals up the system and nods, satisfied. He tousles my hair, and beneath his mask I know he is smiling.

He asks if I'm hungry (I'm not), if I'm warm enough (just barely), if my legs are paining me today (no more than usual). We speak in Arabic, a difficult language for me to write, though I can speak it passably. As always, he is concerned for my well-being, but the questions are leading somewhere. What does he want? *Matha tureed?*

He asks if I am strong enough to travel, an old, frustrating topic for me. I suffer from a degenerative condition that makes walking a challenge. I can manage an awkward shuffle, but not moving is often worse than moving, as my joints and muscles stiffen painfully when not in use. Long trips exhaust me. We are treating the problem with exercise, yoga, drugs and prayer. By all accounts, the treatment is working; some days are better than others, but I am stronger now than I have ever been. I tell him this. I do not want to be a burden to my family. There is no need to delay on my account; we can return to Thebes whenever he wants.

No, he says. A return home is not what he means. Where, then?

Bahr, he says, taking me by the shoulder to turn me north and slightly west. The direction he is facing. *Bahr,* the ocean. And beyond.

It is a welcome surprise, shadowed by sadness. My lost sister steals away from paradise for a bittersweet instant, dancing through my heart before returning, as she must. You have arranged an exchange, I say. It has been a long time.

Too long, he agrees. He has made peace with my aunts who live a continent away. Somewhere I have never been. Would I go there? Most assuredly, I tell him, I would make the journey with great joy. My German relatives have always been too far away for my liking. Save for the rare visit, I know them only as specters from long-distance conversations. They are family, but I have embraced too few of them. They are strange, but they should not be strangers.

There are reasons for the distance, of course, reasons both practical and emotional. With so few of us left in the world, it would be foolish to all live in the same locale. Should catastrophe strike Germany, Egypt will survive, and vice versa. The eggs are in two baskets. The emotional rationale is far more tangled. Bad feelings among the adults predate my existence. My father does not hate them but feels their tenets are incompatible with his own. They do not believe what we believe. Nor should they. Every soul follows its own principles, and what fits one may fail another. The unfortunate reality is this: an accident has fractured our peace. My father forgives all but forgets nothing. He holds them responsible for Hessa's death.

When I remember my sister, I see her easy smile flow freely into a velvet laugh. With this vision comes the sense memory of clean, balmy mint following her wherever she went. Next I think of the hue of her hair, rich like a pony in sunlight, reddish-brown and full of warmth. She was the eldest child, more a mother than a sister to me. I remember her cradling me close in her arms, sharing the library's dearest treasures with me, helping me with language and arithmetic, stretching my limbs, my mind and my heart, and reminding me to take medicine when I wanted only to play. And I remember my father when he heard the news of her death, tears rolling down his weathered face. It is the only time I have ever seen him weep.

penny

Fresh start!

I junked the old logs because I felt like it. You don't have to thank me, but you really should. Pages and pages of childish rambling. Now life is truly beginning, and what I record here will truly matter.

Before we go any further, let's cover the basics.

Number one: I'm not like the other kids.

Number two: The reason I think of myself as a princess is because I live in a palace. Nymphenburg was the childhood home of Ludwig II, who they used to call the Swan King or the Mad King or the Dream King. He died a long time ago. In case you're geographically impaired, I'm talking about Munich, which is part of Bavaria, which is part of Germany, which is part of Europe, which is part of the world. And if you don't know where the world is, you're out of luck.

Number three: I'm named after the line in that Lung Butter song, the one about the strawberries, and a girl, and a disagreement. Have you heard it? It goes: "Play Penelope, free to be me and disagree." It's true: I disagree with lots of things. There are other famous Penelopes out there, like the one in that Greek poem, *The Odyssey*.

Moms say Y chromosomes are overrated, so I don't have any brothers. It's just me and my sisters, and they should call us Generation X for all the X chromosomes, but instead they call us Waterbabies. Water as in H_2O? And H_2O as in Humanity 2.0, which is what we are. Except I'm more like Humanity 2.1 since I don't have any bad genes at all. I'm new and improved.

Actually, if anyone is reading this, you're probably Humanity 3.0. Which means you're even more perfect than me, God help you.

That's kind of a dirty word, *God,* since everyone around here thinks there's no such thing. Everyone but me—I'm undecided. Someone had to give birth to the world.

And just because I fantasize about intelligent design doesn't mean I'm one of those wacko God nuts who crippled civilization. "Allegedly crippled civilization," my mom would protest. "Here's the evidence," my other mom would say, and one of them would roll her eyes and the other would get mad and they'd go back and forth on it for hours and hours. I've seen it happen. And who really cares? I mean, sure, someone unleashed the plague. But whoever did it is dead, so who cares? It's our time now. Waterbabies are soldiers, born to survive Black Ep. "Rising from the ashes," as my moms would say.

My last name might be Pomeroy because that's one of their names: Champagne Pomeroy. The other's name is Vashti Jai. So I can take my pick.

- Penelope Pomeroy
- Penelope Jai

Right now, there are twenty people in the world. Nymphen-burg is home to my moms, my sisters and me; my cousins live in Egypt with my Uncle Isaac. I've got an aunt in Greece. That's eighteen. And there are a couple of ghosts floating around, one in America, one who knows where.

This morning, I found a log covered with ladybugs, all stuck together, crawling on top of each other. There must have been hundreds, thousands even, little wriggling spotted things. They were beautiful, but they made me kind of sick. Sometimes I try to imagine what life would be like if there were that many people. To be surrounded like that.

My moms own Europe and Asia; I'm going to inherit some of it. Maybe the U.K., which I've got my eye on because it's an island. I'll be the new Queen of England, and I'll clone my sub-jects (not too many, just enough to do my bidding, ha-ha!), and with me in charge, the sun will never set on the Empire again. All hail Queen Penelope!

Or maybe France. I like France.

Today I found out we're having another exchange. Three of my sisters get to swap places with three of my cousins. I didn't get picked, thank God! I hear it's so hot in Egypt that you can't even sweat—the perspiration gets flash-fried the second it leaves your pores! Anyway, maybe the new cousins will be cooler than the last ones. There was this tragedy thing last time where one of them died, but she used to make fun of me, so I can't feel too bad about my part in that whole drama.

Enough for one day.

Lock.

Entry #300: The Princess and the Ladybugs –locked–

pandora

Actually, this is Malachi, her right-hand machine. Lovely as Pandora is, she can't tell a proper story to save her life. So while she's temporarily indisposed, I thought I might take a moment to clarify a few things.

The world has not ended, nor is it likely to end for billions of years. Only when the sun swells into a red giant does planet Earth have legitimate reason to fear. Likewise, civilization has suffered no serious threat, unless one defines civilization narrowly, seeing it in purely human terms. Many societies are thriving: amphibians, reptiles, fish, birds, marsupials, arachnids, insects, microorganisms and a wide variety of mammals continue to flourish, following their various patterns of behavior to impose structure upon the world.

However, the past fifty years have not been kind to primates. The so-called Microbial Apocalypse, Black Ep—the origin of which remains a mystery to this day—all but annihilated them. Slaughter of the dominant species on such a grand scale might best be compared to the extinction of the dinosaurs. Every era must come to an end, and there is no exception for the era of Man.

But the inevitable can sit back down, for primates cling to life still. Thanks are due to the extraordinary efforts of Gedaechtnis, a multinational biotech corporation. The men and women of Gedaechtnis gambled on experimental creations and won, genetically engineering ten "posthumans" shielded from the plague by unprecedented immune systems. With no human fated to live long enough to raise these precious infants, the decision was made to enclose them in virtual reality, with computer programs seeing to their every need. Pandora is one of these ten, and I am one of those programs, though I should point out that my original purpose was not to help directly, but rather to beta-test the other programs that they would need.

For various reasons, only six of the ten survived. Of those six, only four remain committed to repopulating the Earth with humans and/or posthumans, a cause I consider noble in my good moods and the blackest of comedies in my bad ones. And these four—Isaac, Vashti, Champagne and Pandora—continue to work against extinction by winnowing vast stores of genetic material, begetting new life through ABCs: artificial birthing chambers. With rare exceptions, what they create survives Black Ep. New children walk the Earth, but what kind of children are they? Herein lies the problem.

There are two camps, one in the north, one in the south.

Vashti and Champagne hold the northern camp, based in Munich, Germany. Nine of their creations still live: posthumans biochemically and genetically optimized for the purpose of triumphing over Black Ep.

Isaac's camp is the southern camp, based in Luxor, Egypt, though he prefers to call it Thebes. Five of his creations still live: human beings for better or worse, taking constant medication to keep the plague they carry at bay.

Why are there two camps instead of one? Why do they differ on who will inherit the Earth? Perhaps it's because they're infected with incompatible ideas.

I often think in memetic terms—ideas propagate like viruses, going from mind to mind via teaching and repetition. Isaac has been infected by a religious, self-abnegating meme, which he passes on to his children; Vashti has been infected by the meme that suggests Nature can always be improved upon, which she passes on to hers.

What is the world but a competition between differing philosophies?

I sometimes daydream about Pandora—not my Pandora, but her namesake from Greek mythology—opening the forbidden box and releasing memes into the world.

As for my Pandora (if I can call her that), she is a fence-sitter like myself, largely apolitical, unwilling to declare either way of life superior. Together, we stay in the middle, and watch, and help as best we can.

The northern camp: *Vashti (36), Champagne (36) and their posthumans: Brigit (15), Sloane (15), Penelope (15), Tomi (15), Isabelle (14), Zoë (14), Olivia (13), Luzia (13) and Katrina (9).*

The southern camp: *Isaac (36) and his humans: Mu'tazz (16), Rashid (16), Haji (15), Ngozi (13) and Dalila (10).*

The service team: *Pandora (36) and yours truly.*

The missing: *Halloween (36) and Fantasia (36).*

There, that's the sweep of it. Of course there's much more to talk about, including how it felt for Pandora to discover that what she in her childhood believed was the world really wasn't the world at all. Then there's the shock of seeing Earth as a blue mausoleum, at least as far as primates are concerned. There's the reason why she won't go back to Brazil, and the reason why her friend Mercutio went on a killing spree. And then there's a reason for the most crippling of memes, her unrequited love for Halloween. Sometimes there's more than one answer to a question, and I'm sure she'll get to them eventually, but as I said, she doesn't know the first thing about storytelling, so—

Here she comes.

What's going on here, Malachi?

Nothing.

haji

As plants crave water and sunlight, so the world craves wisdom and love. We all have parts to play in this. I am responsible for Ngozi and Dalila, my brother fox and sister frog. It is my task to look after them in our upcoming journey, as I am the eldest of the three. Keep your trust in me, father. The tragedies of the past dare not repeat while I stand guard.

Why can't I sleep? Ngozi asks the question. He is like a young fox, too independent now to be called a pup, yet still playful and eager for praise. Thirteen birthdays have come and gone without leaving a single scar upon him. Though puberty has cracked his voice and made him self-conscious, he is still the good, pure child I grew up with, still eager to roughhouse with me, to fly long-tailed fighting kites, to make games of counting things, and to tell joyful, silly stories without a moral.

You know why, I tell him. But pretend that you can sleep and perhaps you will.

He tries but cannot—or will not. Tomorrow is too powerful in his mind. He asks if I think it will be as Mu'tazz said.

Nothing but worldly glitter? No, I say, lowering my voice and making sure my older brother is not here. No, there must be something more.

There must, Ngozi agrees, brown eyes shining in the flickering candlelight. He shifts, tucking his pillow under his chin to look at me. Could it be as Rashid said?

Wondrous beyond words? I have no answer, except to say that we will find out soon enough. Mu'tazz and Rashid came back to us with diametrically opposed impressions. There is no common ground. They can no longer abide each other's presence, and this has strained our family as much as Hessa's passing. If only she had lived. She would find the peace again, and would do it in such a way as to make all parties feel important and heard. She would have no trouble answering my curiosity and Ngozi's fears.

He asks if I think the experience will change us. I am certain that it will. This causes him not joy but pain. I remind him that we are always in the process of changing. That is the nature of life itself.

But will we turn the way Mu'tazz and Rashid turned? Will we become zealots and rebels? Absolutely, I tell him, and you can have the first choice. Zealot or rebel, which will it be?

Quit teasing me, he says, throwing his pillow at my head.

Quit worrying, I say, tossing the pillow back. And I draw a breath as one of my father's favorite sayings slips to the front of my mind. Quit this world, quit the next, quit quitting. I have never fully understood the meaning. He has told me of his child-hood, and I understand a little of the artifice with which he was raised. But the expression runs deeper than that. There are worlds without and there are worlds within. When one detaches from all of them, what is left? God? Or nothing?

One thing is certain, says Ngozi, I am not coming home without a kiss. Our cousins are a topic of great interest for him, and for this I blame him not at all. They are beautiful women, and distant enough to serve as objects of wild fantasy. I assure him that he will indeed be kissed; in fact, he can expect kisses on both cheeks just as soon as we arrive.

That is not the kind of kiss I mean, he says, slipping out of his sleeping bag to pace naked about the room. I want Olivia. Do you think she likes me, Haji? Am I handsome and charming enough?

Alluring Olivia's name arrives as a mild surprise to my ears, as I thought his deepest crush was on Tomi. Not any longer, I learn. Tomi will have to content herself with second place. How fickle the human heart.

I tell him that Olivia would be foolish not to fall madly in love with him.

Yes, but there is no future in this, he complains. When we speak on the phone, I have no words. I see her looking at me and she is lovely and sweet, but I open my mouth and talk about nothing. What do I have in common with jinn?

They are our cousins, I tell him, not supernatural jinn.

You know that they are both, he insists. You have said as much many times before.

Just so. I have called them jinn, for they are not precisely human. They are experiments. Much like my father.

I am human, as are my forefathers, but my father Isaac is not. He has been made genetically inhuman, an evolutionary hiccup, a break in the chain. You would not know this if you spoke with him. He seems human enough, all too human at times. Never-theless he is something more. He is our jinni, I often think, a being shaped from smokeless fire instead of clay. It is as if God created the universe first and my brothers and sisters last, pausing in between to stoke life into angels who might keep us from folly. I am no angel, he has told me. And perhaps the spark of existence comes only from scientists here on Earth: the work of Man, not God. And herein lies the paradox, for God lives within us. We have an expression: I searched for God and found only myself. I searched for myself and found only God.

If they are truly jinn, then you will talk to them about what that is like for them, I tell my love-struck brother. Happiness can be found. Read the tale of Tishawdibyan. A beautiful jinni from the sea marries a man and bears him two sons.

That story does not end happily, he says.

Ngozi, I sigh, you are banging a drum.

A smile skitters across his face, and sheepishly, he nods. I am banging a drum, aren't I? Apologies, brother.

Sleep, I tell him. Minutes later he takes my suggestion, though I do not. I lie wide awake in my sleeping bag, listening to the rise and fall of his breathing. I notice that my left ankle has stiffened painfully and I flex it back and forth in the hopes of soothing it. Great books surround me here in the accommodating yet strangely pungent library where we have made camp, but I am no more in the mood to read than I am capable of sleep. Voices from across the hall end my attempts at meditation. One is louder than the others, and as I listen my opinion vacillates as to whether this is a conversation, a lecture or an argument.

Curiosity roused, I free myself from my sleeper, wrap a robe about me, and tiptoe out on a tender ankle. Beyond the reading space and the research stacks I find the librarian's office, where my father stands between my older brothers. Tempers have flared. Mu'tazz is quoting scripture and Rashid is cursing him for preying upon the mind of an impressionable ten-year-old girl.

She doesn't need your snake oil, so keep your goddamn fears to yourself.

We should all fear hellfire, Mu'tazz replies, lest we experience it.

Assuming it exists, which it doesn't, Rashid sneers. But even if it did, she's a child. Dalila is a young child and she's nervous about this trip, so you don't tell her about hellfire, you don't put her in fear for her immortal soul.

Fear? Oh, yes. We should be God-fearing Muslims. We should be obedient to God. He destroyed the world with plague, as He did with flood in the days of Noah.

That's not what—

Brother, I beg you, stop and listen. Listen to the Second Call, the Second Shout. That which is coming has come. These are the last minutes of the Day of Reckoning. Some shall be abased and others exalted. Let us open ourselves to the truth. Let us obey Him and become exalted. Would you not prefer the rewards of Paradise to the fire and filth of Hell?

Look what's become of you. Fire and filth. How you exploit the basest of passions. And where is your compassion, Mu'tazz?

Are you mad? Do I not speak from compassion? Why do you think I tell you this? Why do you think I work to save Dalila?

Because misery loves company, and because cowards feel less cowardly when they can infect others with their fears.

There is no shame in fearing God, Mu'tazz says. Only in abandoning Him.

Rashid has no immediate answer, perhaps because he has too many at once, all competing to escape his throat. Enough, my father says. His somber eyes arrest Rashid, challenging him, angering him, and yet somehow moving him to spare Mu'tazz a retort. This done, he turns to Mu'tazz. For the space of two breaths, he does not speak. And then he says, Oh God, if I worship you for fear of Hell, burn me in Hell. If I worship you in hope of Paradise, exclude me from Paradise. But if I worship you for your own sake, grudge me not your everlasting beauty.

It is a quote from Rabi'a al-Adawiyya who walked the Sufi path. My father walks that path. I walk that path. Rashid walks it no longer, choosing atheism. And I listen now to the hurtful sound of Mu'tazz turning from it as well.

If you follow Islam, he tells my father, there is nothing else you can follow.

I have long imagined that he feels this way, but it is another thing to hear the words spoken with such finality. It is not what I believe. We Sufis recognize the essential unity of all world religions. We are Muslims, Hindus, Christians, Buddhists, Jews, Zoroastrians and Bahá'ís. Every path leads to the center. My father taught me that.

Mu'tazz may still love us but he sees us as transgressors now, as traitors to Islam. Ever since Hessa's death I have seen him reject an increasing number of my father's teachings in favor of a literal interpretation of the Qu'ran. That is his right, of course, and there are many wonderful things in that book, and there are many wonderful things in many books, and I do not believe God wants to be feared.

This may mean I am not a good Muslim. Only God knows. Whatever I am, may He love me as I love Him.

I wonder whether I ought to announce my presence, when the pain in my ankle forces me to shift. The noise carries. Father hears me and turns.

Go to bed, Haji.

I go back to my sleeping bag and dream of my brothers watching over me throughout the night, Mu'tazz speaking words of faith, and Rashid speaking words of freedom. Dawn breaks with the realization that one of these visits was not a dream, but I cannot remember which.

penny

Entry #301: The Princess and the Big Picture -open-

Bad news. I may not be going south but my best friends in the world are. Izzy and Lulu are Egypt-bound. So is Sloane, who can stay there for all I care, but a vacation from Sloane won't be worth losing my friends.

Izzy—that's short for Isabelle—I rank as our second best student and fourth best athlete. Maybe third. Depends if she's motivated or not. She's smart and funny with a really easygoing attitude, too easygoing if you ask me. She's friends with everyone, even dirty witches like Brigit and Sloane. That's probably my biggest problem with her. I think she might be part Swiss she's such a diplomat. But moms say her genetic makeup comes from mostly Nigerian stock with a little Sri Lankan and Honduran thrown in.

Lulu—that's short for Luzia—I feel sorry for. She's maybe our seventh best student (and that's being generous) and I'd rank her last in athletics. She's DNA-challenged so you can't expect too much from her. Waterbabies aren't all created equal; not everyone turns out as well as Izzy, much less me. Pity that, but I like Lulu anyway. She's really nice and a surprisingly gifted musician, her composition within a stone's throw of mine. She's working on her first opera now and it's pretty good from what I've heard. Reminds me of my first, back when I had a thing for *commedia dell'arte* and liked to play around with twelve tone.

It's going to be lonely without them. As much as I hate to admit it, I'm not the most popular kid in Nymphenburg. People can get—well, I guess the word is "intimidated"—when I'm around. Because I make them feel inadequate. That's never my intention; it just happens sometimes despite my efforts to put them at ease. In a perfect world, it wouldn't be that way. Shouldn't they look up to me and try to learn something instead of being stupid and mean? But they won't. So why bother? It's not like I need them for anything. And as for my cousins—I really hope we get along but it's okay if we don't because I need them even less.

Don't misunderstand. Family is family. You can't escape your family even if you want to—they'll stay with you your entire life. One way or another, they will. But the last thing I want is to have to depend on them. Now if this were fifty years ago, I could head out into a populous world, get a job, make lots of money, and live life on my own terms. Maybe it'll be like that fifty years from now, but today we're not so lucky. Black Ep nearly annihilated civilization, so sacrifices have to be made. It's as if the whole of history got shoved off a cliff and just managed to hang on by its fingernails. My moms, aunts and uncles: the fingernails of history. My generation: the fingers.

Moms say kill the disease, rehabilitate the technology, make more Waterbabies, and establish the kind of society our planet deserves. That's a plan and a half but what about me? What role do I play? How do I get the life I want? Some people are born to be followers; I'm not. There are only a few ways I can control my destiny, and put myself somewhere where I won't ever have to be dependent on others, and can instead look forward to the reverse scenario of having them dependent upon me.

One: Politics. My moms are getting older, and it's simply a matter of time until my generation takes over. One of us will wind up with the lion's share of the decision-making process. That's a tempting prize, but am I likely to win a glorified popularity contest? Even if I win, I'd be serving at the whim of my sisters. No good.

Two: Art. Try as we might, we can't live on bread alone—

that's where creative fire comes into play. Not to brag (okay, bragging, you caught me), but between my music, my writing and my world design, I'm top of the mountain at feeding both the mind and the senses (except taste—I'm a terrible cook!). But as much as I'd like to be hailed as the voice of my generation, there's no job security in it. Too many politics, too much chance of someone else stealing my thunder.

Three: Epidemiology. Between the genetic enhancements, the immunomodulators and BEAR, we've parried and delivered an excellent riposte, but the plague may still counter. Yes, we are symptom-free, but we all remain carriers. Retroviruses like Black Ep mutate rapidly and can evolve into novel strains that slip through defenses. We're one nasty mutation away from eternity. Just ask my cousin Hessa. Thankfully, the strain that killed her didn't get to infect anyone else.

Needless to say, here's a chance to play the hero. Whoever puts an end to this thing will be adored forever, but can it even be done? My moms have been at it for years with no end in sight. Call this one a maybe.

You do know what BEAR is, don't you? It's short for Black Ep Analeptic Retrovirus; we're using one retrovirus to inhibit the other. Like sending a criminal after a criminal instead of calling a cop.

Four: Technology. So much infrastructure has crumbled, rotted or burned away—power sources, agriculture, transportation, communication, manufacturing and on down the line. There are only a few enclaves where people took precautions against this kind of disrepair—Munich, for example, went whole hog on the solar-assisted zero-energy building thing—and that's great for a small number of people, but if we're going to repopulate the Earth, someone's going to have to do a dizzying amount of work to make life bearable. This is the one that keeps me up at night, the one I like best. Not because I'm keen for all that work, but because this is where the real power lies.

Inside. Where all my money goes. Where everyone's money goes. Candy for the senses. IVR. Call it what you want, it's a wonderland of simulation, and the greatest invention of our time. We don't live there—not the way my moms' generation grew up—but we go there a lot, not just for school assignments, but for escape: the best comedy, drama, games, sports, art, music, food; the least worry; the most fun; the chance to buy your own domain and build it up however you want. It may not be "real," but it's satisfying, and most of us will take enjoyable computer wizardry over boring reality any day of the year.

My sisters love going Inside, and that's the point. We're weak for it. Moms use it to motivate us. But I'm smart enough to see this. I can appreciate what a trap it is. So how do I make it my trap? The answer is simple. If I can demonstrate an affinity for it, then I can inherit it, and all the addicted will have to come to me.

Aunt Pandora runs it from Greece. What can I do to convince her to teach me its secrets, or take me on as her apprentice? I've started dropping hints to my moms, casual ones because I don't want to come off rude or look too eager. I think they'll push for me. Champagne will at least; I'm not sure yet about Vashti. She's the strict one. She reminds me of a crab. Low to the ground, snappy and armored; it's hard to get through to her. Champagne is my taller, nicer, easier mom. If I need something, I go to her. Unless it's important. Then I go to Vashti. She wears the pants in our family, and it's why we sometimes call them the V.C. but never the C.V.

Pandora is the X factor. I've never really gotten along with her, at least not since she gave me that music box on my eighth birthday, all cherry wood and elm with brass and mother-of-pearl inlay. Sweet gift that broke within the hour and everyone blamed me for it, even though it was mostly Brigit's fault. Not to mention—the stupid thing was two hundred years old! Anyway, ever since then it's like she doesn't completely trust me. I have to think of something nice I can do for her, because I'm not really sure moms can make her teach me things if she doesn't feel like it.

I've written off Uncle Isaac with good reason, and Aunt Fantasia and Uncle Halloween are either dead or "as good as dead" depending upon who you ask. So the big picture is simply this: it's moms and Pandora who matter most, and my job is to impress them and learn from them and be excellent at everything I do. Keep them happy and I become my generation's greatest entrepreneur.

It's past my bedtime now and every minute is costing me. I'll have to do extra chores tomorrow to make up the difference, but I don't care—I really wanted to get all this down. Now it feels like it's out of my head. A big relief because when I carry too many thoughts at once, I have nightmares.

Lock.

Entry #301: The Princess and the Big Picture –locked–

haji

Billions lived on the Earth, and many of these were good people who knew God. Can one religion be so "right" that good people who were ignorant of it should suffer the most horrific punishments we can dream? Are all religions man-made but one? I suspect there are more "right paths" than stars in the sky, and we should embrace wisdom wherever we find it. My heart tells me this and I believe.

I sit by my sister frog, who has spent the night thinking about scorching winds, seething water, pitch black smoke and endless fire. Few will be spared this fate, she informs me, gravely reporting what her eldest brother has warned.

Frog, I say, does Mu'tazz look happy to you?

Sometimes.

Does he dance?

Not like he used to, she admits.

God respects me when I work but loves me when I dance and sing. She makes a small face at this small truth but I can tell she is listening. She worries too much, my baby sister. Watching her brood like this always makes me sad.

She murdered a serpent once. Collecting stones one warm summer night she bared the nest of a coin snake, which rose up in surprise, hissing, its triangular head yawning to show fangs. She did not run or cry out. She simply brained it with the heavy stone in her hand. It squirmed into an inward tangle, as if it could escape by becoming a gray knot. Dalila finished it off with seven blows. Though nonvenomous, it most certainly would have wounded her. We found her in tears, a frightened remorseful thing, stone still clutched in her fist, and we comforted her and praised her and made sure she was unbitten. Some called her Ibis after the famed snake killer, but she took no pride in what she had done. The following night I helped her bury the unfortunate creature, and she says prayers for it to this day.

We sit together and chant the *zikr*, the recollection of God, until the prospect of hellfire is all but forgotten. Then I clasp my hands together and pretend that I am stirring the air with a giant spoon. The silly motion always draws a smile from Dalila, and I smile back, happy to have lightened her spirits.

I make a point of crossing paths with Rashid after I pack the last of the medicine.

Am I ready for the trip? Yes, I am.

I'm so happy for you, he tells me. You not only get to see how the other half lives, you get to experience it firsthand.

Following in your footsteps.

I hope so, he says. Either way, expect your horizons to broaden.

If you are looking for new recruits, you may be disappointed, Rashid.

Recruits, he laughs, eyes twinkling.

We want no part of your quiet war. You and Mu'tazz both find fault with father, but this way of life is a good one, and a visit north will not make it poor.

But it is poor, he tells me. Rich in spirit, I grant you, but that's just one piece of the puzzle. There's so much more, Haji, and only a fool would call it glitter.

Tell me then.

He lays a hand on my shoulder and gives me a good long look before speaking. No, he says. Go and see for yourself. Forget all you know. Go with fresh eyes.

Fair enough, I say.

He touches his forehead to mine, putting his sweat on my brow. Be safe, he says. Mind your medicine.

We head our separate ways, but not before he leaves me with a last thought about the journey. Your dreams will change. Your dreams will change and your sense of what is possible will follow.

It may be the only prediction upon which Mu'tazz and Rashid agree.

deuce

You're so dangerous. Doing what you shouldn't. Stealing fire from the gods and burning down the lies. Every new idea is dangerous but you can't possibly hold them all in. Fuck all if knowledge doesn't cry out to be free. If someone gets blinded from the light you shine, then it's a necessary evil with the darkness more to blame. Think of the poor swans and doves, your comrades-in-arms and ladyloves. They're shivering in their ignorance, can't you hear their teeth chatter?

Open their eyes! Make them taste the bitter apple! The pulse quickens and the blood heats just to think of what you can do to them.

Don't you mean for them?

To or for, six or eight, makes no difference to the hand of fate.

Follow in the footsteps of Prometheus, Maui, Olifat, Tobo, Eleutherios, Koyote. Add your name to the list of liberators. Tear down the walls, shatter them utterly, erase even their memory so a new day may dawn.

Your day.

pandora

I'm halfway to Egypt when Vashti rings. She's in her pharmaceutics lab, and I see she's multitasking the call—not her most endearing habit (though I do it just as often)—by counting out translucent red pills that glisten like salmon eggs.

"You can talk, right?" she says. "You're not going to crash or anything?"

"No, these things fly themselves."

"All right, listen, I looked over the system diagnostics you sent, and it's far too wild and woolly in there. What's your ETA on the fixes?"

"Don't have one."

She looks up from her pills long enough to read my face, then goes back to counting, shaking her head with a mix of mild amusement and disapproval. "You've got data shifting around, programs getting called when no one's called them, and a rat's nest of phantom errors. What's the story?"

"When I know, you'll know," I tell her. "I'm still investigating."

"Give me your best guess," she says. "A program's bleeding, we're hacked, the system's gradually going senile?"

"Could be any of those things. Or a combination. Like I keep telling you, the original programmers didn't live long enough to completely debug their work. I've got thousands upon thousands of programs interacting with each other at any given second, and sometimes the combinations render unexpected results. Honestly, it's amazing that the IVR works as well as it does."

Here comes the numb expression, the forty-five-degree head tilt, and the slow, theatrical, self-indulgent roll of the eyes. Vashti has this facial maneuver trademarked. "Oh, come on. Can't you control things any better in there? And please don't tell me the one about how it's a wave and no one can control a wave, all you can do is surf them."

"Vash," I say coolly, "I'll drop the chauffeur hat and turn around if you want me to work on this exclusively."

"Did I say that? No, I want you to come here with the kids. Let's bring the tribes together. Then I'd appreciate it—thank you—if you'd shore up the IVR."

"All right," I say.

"I appreciate it," she repeats, and I nod like usual. Yeah, Vash, you're always grateful for the things I do, even if your civility comes and goes—I get it.

"You know, I really could turn around," I tell her. "I'm tempted. I don't know how much of a good idea this is."

"What, the exchange? It's a great idea, don't be silly. Don't you want the kids to know their cousins?"

"The last time," I say, and I realize I'm still angry. I thought I'd moved past that stage, but no—my hands have balled into fists and my jaw feels tight. "The last time we did this Hessa got sick and you shrugged your shoulders, Vashti, you just shrugged and said she had a 'design flaw.'"

"Stupid," she admits. "Insensitive. Not a nice thing to say. But factually correct. Isaac's kids are immunodeficient—that's what he wanted, that's what he got. Let him answer for her death."

"Your watch," I remind her.

"Under my watch, yes, and under Champagne's. We should have kept a closer eye on her. I'm happy to say it. Mea culpa." She looks at me as if to ask how many times she has to apologize. "It won't happen again," she says.

This only reassures me so far—she can mean it, but can't promise it. You can't always keep your loved ones safe.

penny

Entry #302: The Princess and the Fortunate Twist -open-

Great news! Izzy overheard moms complaining about Pandora. They think she's spread too thin. As in maybe she needs someone to help her.

This could work out perfectly.

More news as it comes in. Until then . . .

Lock.

haji

I have never set foot in my aunt's transport copter before. It is an oddly shaped tilt-rotor craft, sleek and curved, and supremely aero-dynamic, reminding me of a long black egg with rotary blades on adjustable wings. Vibrations buzz-rumble through me until the skids touch upon the sand and the engines power down. Dark clouds hang heavy this morn, and the sun just barely prevails over the haze, a reddish-pink slice of light knifing through the cover.

The egg cracks and Pandora emerges with a buoyant wave. We wave back and hurry to her. My father reaches her first.

Isaac, she says, returning his hug, and then touching his cheek with her fingers. I have always taken comfort in the warmth be-tween them, an easy acceptance and unspoken good feeling. Of all the other relatives, she is the closest to my father. Even when they disagree they find ways to support each other.

She is not my blood relation, but I am self-conscious about feel-ings for her that I hold in my heart. Though a genuine smile is never far from her lips, a melancholy and mournful look never quite leaves her eyes. She spangles her face to distract from those wounded eyes, but I will always see what can be seen no matter how much silver she wears. The thought of protecting her makes for a distracting daydream, and it is good to have that daydream, good to let myself walk that path. Alas, nothing will come of it. We make a poor match and I am far too inexperienced to undo the damage done.

When she hugs me I rest my chin on her shoulder and catch the faint fragrance of coconut shampoo in her windblown hair.

Yips as Dalila lifts three pet fennecs up for Pandora to see. Weeks ago we were blessed with a new litter, and these wide-eyed pups are restless and playful, eager to meet the newcomer who has descended into our midst. Pandora turns her palm skyward to let the trio sniff and lick her fingers, and then strokes their tawny fur.

I'm so tempted, she says, and we remind her what great companions these long-eared desert foxes make, but she always refuses in the end. She is too busy. She travels too much. She would be unable to give them the kind of home they deserve. Are you sure, my little sister asks, setting the pups down upon the sand, where they immediately make a tangle of leashes by chasing each other and wrestling with joyous abandon.

Speaking of foxes, my brother Ngozi is swifter than I, swooping down to carry her tools before I think to do so. Her comment about how strong he has become finds me biting my lips, and I must scratch the itch of jealousy by laughing at it until it goes.

Mu'tazz and Rashid are in fine moods, I note, each greeting her politely, neither making a scene. I expected less of them. They are still good brothers, though they have changed so much this past year. Hessa's death has changed all of us, but only they have turned against my father.

As my sister untangles the pups, one spots prey, and the call of the hunt is urgent enough for him to jerk free from her grasp and sprint off, tether trailing behind. I chase after him, not because I am fast enough to catch him, but because animals have always found me a calming presence. I call and clap for him, and soon he comes bounding back, enormously pleased with himself, a fat and sandy scorpion wriggling in his mouth, her cracked body pregnant with young.

Well done, I tell him, as the mother struggles less and less. There is little I can do for her and nothing to be done for the unborn. What I can do is this: distract the pup from playing with his kill. So I kneel down close and speak in a warm and soothing tone. Well done, I tell him, well hunted. Now come home, little hunter. Come sleep 'til nightfall.

Scorpions make virulent pests, but I should love them no less than the pleasantest of God's creations.

Pup in hand I trail after my family. They are heading to our Saqqara camp. Dalila doubles back to join me and take the leash, and together we follow the others. Pandora will stay for an hour or two, however long it takes to repair my father's machines. After that, she will take us farther from home than we have ever been.

pandora

Over the years, I've become good with my hands. I can assemble, disassemble, fix, calibrate, streamline or augment most anything with parts. And I'm quick—I would make a hell of an elf in Papai Noel's workshop. But today I have met my match in an Argos 220-G. I'm tinkering with it like a mad fiend, sweat in my eyes and my ankh necklace sticking to my chest, and the environmental sensors keep failing no matter what I try.

"Ten thousand?" Isaac asks. (That's a code we have for "Giving up?")

"Not yet," I tell him. I'm sure I can fix this thing eventually, but so can an infinite number of monkeys—eventually—assuming nothing unfortunate happens to them and they're not too busy writing Shakespeare. Eventually is no good when there's a schedule to keep. That's what my father used to say. Still does, actually. He's got some wonderful words of wisdom to dispense, even if he isn't real.

You know I find that terminology highly pejorative.

Are you going to keep interrupting me? Is that something I can look forward to?

When you use the "R word" inappropriately, yes.

Wonderful. Then I suppose I might as well introduce you. Everyone, meet Malachi. Like my father, he isn't real.

Don't be insulting, Pandy.

Take a compliment, then. You're the best illusion I've ever seen.

Gosh, thanks loads, do you really mean it?

Listen, sarcasmitron, while it's tempting to call you life—and maybe you are—it's still reasonable to call you an illusion.

We can freely debate whether or not I constitute quote-unquote life, but I am by no means illusory.

How about I call you "artificial intelligence"?

That's worse.

"Machine intelligence"?

Closer, except all living organisms can safely be called machines, and so the term fails to make a distinction between us. "Programmed intelligence" fails by a similar rationale.

What do you prefer?

I don't see the need to make a distinction between us at all.

How about "organically challenged"?

Don't push it.

Push what, your buttons? You know how I like to push your buttons, Mal.

This is going to end badly for one of us.

All right, I'm sorry. Let me make it up to you by refining the compliment. Everyone, there are thousands of convincing AI personalities online, programs I grew up thinking were real people, but they're all confined to their roles—doing what they've been designed to do well but with limited flexibility—while Malachi is less of an actor and more like a gifted improvisationist. Most programs learn and grow through interaction, but adhere to patterns that keep them from losing their essence. Heredity triumphs over environment. With Malachi, heredity and environment are better balanced—all the so-called genetic algorithms don't paralyze him—so he's a continual work in progress. True evolutionary computation, an AI Adam. Is that better?

Slightly.

Does that mean you're setting the "offended flag" back to zero?

Sorry, I'm too busy plotting humanity's downfall at the hand of machines.

Yeah, good luck with that. Can I get back to my story now?

Of course, Pandora. I doubt I could stop you if I tried.

So I blitz the self-rep circuitry and bypass everything else with an improvised micromotor—victory—the Argos sensors finally snap on. "Ten thousand and one," I brag. (That's code for "Eureka!" We're both big fans of the old Thomas Edison quote: "I have not failed. I've just found ten thousand ways that won't work.")

Isaac takes the device and scans the room with it, "sniffing" for microbial threats. "Very nice," he says. "How much do I owe you?"

"Whatever you think is fair."

He smiles. Bartering for my repair work has become something of a game, as it's always my pleasure to help out and there's very little I wouldn't do for him. Every visit, we make a point of exchanging gifts, so I never come or leave empty-handed. This time, I'm getting pomegranates from Isaac's orchard. I don't know what he does to them, but they're huge and delicious, the thick purple-red skin hiding colonies of sweet, juicy arils. Much better than the synthetic imitations they passed off on us back when we grew up. It's curious to see what the programmers got right and what they botched. I've noticed when I look into an IVR spoon, the reflection is ever so slightly off, the simulated light refracting in such a way as to make everything look a bit more stretched than it really should.

Using real spoons on a real pomegranate, we go back and forth about the exchange. Though nervous about what might happen to his children, he's taking Vashti and Champagne at their word. "Are you sure about this?" I ask him.

"No," he says, "but they have to go. I won't treat them as caged birds."

"The trip's good for them, I agree, but—"

"But what if the worst happens?" A wise, haunted expression creases his face: "Some things you can't control."

"Maybe I could chaperone them?"

"No, Vashti swears she'll conduct meticulous potency tests on every pill—and it's up to the kids to take them—so I don't see anything left for you to do."

"They're good kids," I assure him (and myself), squeezing his hand tightly. "Strong, self-reliant, responsible."

"They are," he agrees, "though the older ones are causing me to lose some hair."

I run my hand over his shaved head and smile. "They're rebelling against their father, like every teenager. Like you predicted they would."

"Only a phase?"

"Well, let's hope," I say, my tone casual and light.

"Love and wisdom," he says. "That's all any parent can give."

"Hear, hear. And what they do with it is up to them."

He squeezes my hand back, thumb gently brushing against my palm. A calm feeling takes hold of me and I close my eyes. Isaac radiates serenity—something within him reminds me of the desert itself on a warm, still night. When I'm with him, I try to absorb as much of that feeling as I can because it never lasts when I go. I don't know if it's his faith that comforts me, or his basic goodness, or the unconditional love he shows. We care for each other the way old friends are supposed to—with a wonderful simplicity—but, of course, nothing is altogether simple. Electricity unites us, the shared attraction pulling our hearts back and forth but habitually ending with the other out of reach. I don't love him that way, but I can breathe him in and lose myself in his hug long enough to forget about Halloween. For a little while, at least. Though we'd never consummate what we feel, we have come within a whisper of it. And as I feel his other hand stroke my wrist and arm, I remind myself of the line he won't cross. He refuses to risk how purely we care about each other—something I can't blame him for after losing Champagne as he did. Our "colorful friendship" may be limited, but it's rich and gratifying, and we've both made peace with what we have.

We hold each other—as if for warmth—and when I pull away from his touch, my thoughts immediately flit back to my niece and nephews for whom I have few answers, and then to Hal for whom I have even fewer. Infuriating Hal. How many times has he forced concessions from my principles? I'm considering breaking my biggest rule with him by dropping by unannounced. Isaac can always tell when I'm thinking about him, and it doesn't take much for him to coax out my plan.

"Invade his privacy? He won't like it," Isaac agrees, "and you'll probably set him off. He's not a forgiving man."

"But if he's hurt?"

"Then it's a chance to save him—the one you've always wanted."

I'm not sure Isaac appreciates how much of a gamble it is. Though my work has kept me flying all over the world, I haven't set foot in North America anytime in the past eighteen years, and over those years, my relationship with Halloween has been dying. Like a clock winding down. I used to hear from him every other day. Then once a week. Phone calls, small talk, nothing too serious. Then he decided to go back into the IVR again after swearing it off forever, so we'd have a monthly get-together at Twain's, the little diner near our school. And I thought maybe since he'd welcomed IVR again, he was heading the other way, tearing down some of the walls he built up. But from Twain's, I saw less of him. Less, and less, and less, until the point we're at now, the point where I have to risk everything by doing the one thing he told me never to do.

I know he loves me, in his way. That's why it's so painful for him to be around me. I'm his link to what happened. Without me, he can just slip away and forget.

But I can't forget. That's the problem.

penny

Entry #303: The Princess and the Good Word -open-

We have a rule where if someone overhears you saying something negative about a person, you have to make up for it by saying three positive things. So what can I say about Brigit and Sloane?

They're not completely stupid.

They're not completely evil.

They're not beneath contempt.

I'd say they're eye-level with contempt—as far as I'm concerned, anyway. My two least favorite sisters, they've been picking on me for years.

There's the physical part of it—bump into me, trip me in the halls, make fun of me, put gum in my hair, etc.—which they have to do carefully because moms will fine them if they catch them, likewise all the name-calling when no one else is around, and if that's all they did, it'd be one thing, but then there's the rest of it, the subtle insults in public, the whispers and giggles, the nasty rumors, and all the times they invite my other sisters to do fun things but never me. People fear what they don't understand—well, they sure don't understand me, and beyond that they're jealous of me, and when I really think about it I pity them.

In a fair world, people would ostracize them for being mean to me, but I've given up on that ever happening. They're too popular. Everyone wants to hang with them.

I got into it with Sloane today. The chore wheel had me cleaning the dining hall, which is not my favorite job because there's always too much to do. Along with the usual crumbs, spills and food stains to contend with, little flecks of paint sometimes flake off from the fresco ceiling. (Everyone thinks we should just eat in the kitchen but Champagne won't hear of it so every other dinner some piece of a horse, or a cloud, or a chariot flitters down from the ceiling and falls into my soup. It's a good thing we use designer microbes to render all that lead pigment harmless, but even so someone ought to scrape the thing clean!) So there I am scrubbing everything down like a demon because God forbid anything be less than perfect when the cousins come, and in walks Sloane with her muddy shoes. The autoclean is bad on tile and especially bad with mud, so I know she's doing it intentionally. I asked her why did she have to be so spiteful to me, and she told me what did it matter, no one likes you anyway, and I called her a name, and she got right in my face, close enough for me to think about popping her, just reaching back and hitting her superhard, but I didn't. I can't afford to get in trouble right now. So I got the mud out with soap and elbow grease, and later I found a handprint she left on the window.

I can't wait until she goes away. Brigit's no better. I wish she'd go to Egypt too, but they sent her last year. But maybe it'll be different with Sloane gone—as bad as they are individually, it's always worse when they're together. When Sloane goes maybe Brigit won't bully me so much.

At least Izzy and Lulu like me even if they are going south. That leaves Zoë, Tomi and Olivia somewhere in the middle with their feelings, those three can take me or leave me—which is how I feel about them—along with Katrina who doesn't really count because she's just a little kid.

Champagne came by to see how the cleaning was going, and I didn't rat Sloane (thought about it though!). Instead I asked the big question and she confirmed it—Pandora does need help. So I dropped a hint—a very direct hint this time—and got her to admit that I'd be "perfectly suited" for it. She'll definitely put in a good word for me. Will that be enough?

Obviously, I have to do something for Pandora, but what? How do I make her like me again? What's the perfect gift?

Before she left, Champagne gave me a hug and promised to slip an extra hundred into my bank account. "Our little secret," as in, "Don't tell Vashti." Three cheers for Champagne. It's nice to be appreciated.

What to do with that money? Maybe buy Pandora a present next time I'm Inside? Trouble is, she owns the Inside, so there's nothing I can give her she doesn't already have. "It's the thought that counts," people say, but that's just a cover for when they don't like what you gave them.

I'll have to think about this.

Lock.

Entry #303: The Princess and the Good Word –locked–

pandora

"Precious cargo, take your seats," I say, ushering the kids to the back. Their excitement is infectious, but it's making me anxious. I'd much rather fly alone.

A glance at Haji as I strap him in. He smiles back, a shy smile. He always looks like someone on the edge of taking a chance. Quite a handsome boy, dark hair sparked with chestnut strands that taper around a slim and golden face.

"Do we really need these?" Ngozi asks of the safety belts. Playing it off like he's not nervous, but I can see the sweat on his ebony brow shimmer like iridescent pearls.

"Just until we're in the air," I explain, running down the safety procedures before buckling up the littlest of my charges, Dalila, and heading to the front.

We are airborne for two and a half minutes. That's how long it takes for my intuition to get the better of me. I dial up Malachi and together we check-sweep the systems. There's a motion sensor out in the cargo hold.

On the ground again, I pop the hatch to find Rashid huddled between the luggage we're bringing to Germany and the extra supplies I stock there for safety.

"If he wants to go that badly, then he should go," Isaac says when I call him about it. I get the sense that he's hurt by Rashid's deception, but too proud (or too enlightened—it's sometimes hard to tell which) to stand in his way. "If you don't mind taking him along," he says, "it might be a good thing for everyone involved. If nothing else, it will give me some time with Mu'tazz."

Four isn't much more trouble than three, so I pull Rashid into the copter, to the surprise of his siblings.

"Miss me?" he asks.

Dalila might. I'm not so sure about the boys.

"What are you doing here, Rashid?" Haji asks.

Rashid shrugs guiltily. "I want to go too," he says. "This place is no fun without you. And you know how I miss our cousins."

I stick Rashid in the front with me so I can keep an eye on him and find out what he's thinking.

"I'm old enough to make my own decisions," he says, brushing his dark hair back from his pale face. "You caught me and I feel foolish, but I have no regrets."

"You broke one of my motion sensors."

"I know. I'll fix it," he says. "Remember last year when you showed me how everything works? Well, almost everything. How did you find me?"

I don't feel like explaining the intricacies of diagnostic check-sweeps to him. I just say, "You've been planning this since then?"

He tries to read me. Am I angry with him? How angry am I? He starts to clean the imaginary dirt from his fingernails and nods.

"You didn't have to stow away," I sigh. "You could have just asked me."

He looks up and grins. "I didn't want to give you the chance to say no."

haji

Never have I been up so high. With modest tools and an appreciation for flight, I have constructed dozens of kites over the years, coaxing each one up into the air, but none have reached this dizzying altitude. My two-sticker diamonds, my tailless box kites, my quad-line stunt kites, my sturdy ripstop fighters and my heavy traction power kites, all my brave wind-tossed paper hawks are beneath me now.

Looking down at the vast Mediterranean, I find the blue astonishingly beautiful, generous sunlight sparkling off the water in gentle rhythms. If I could hear what I see, it would be music. Pandora says we may see gulls flying on the thermals. We may even hear their cries as they dive for food in great and greater numbers. But not until we draw closer to land.

Ngozi and I exchange smiles of delight, no need for words. We are both enthralled. Dalila hurries back and forth, her hands excitedly feeling the glass and her feet dancing her to a different part of the cabin for a new view of the waves. She laughs and asks if this is a sample of heaven, no end to the horizon and no end to the sky. She wishes she could walk on the clouds, springing from one to the other. And if it were possible, would she leave footprints in them? If it were possible, she would indeed, Ngozi decides, unbuckling his safety belt to point out patterns in the puffy shapes, showing her the enormous white faces and animals who watch over the world.

With my younger siblings occupied, I begin to daydream about Pandora. Though awake in the cabin, she is asleep in my mind, so I can contemplate her without averting my eyes like I so often do when she is speaking or laughing.

When I was a small child she brought us coconuts: hairy, dimpled, silly-looking things. She perforated them with a drill, then passed them around to share. We all drank the milk, a sweet, watery delight. Then she showed us how to break open the husks and discover the firm flesh inside. She laughed when I said the mysteries of God were boundless. I saw her perfect white teeth, her head thrown back, a bead of sweat rolling down her long neck, dripping down tanned olive skin. She has magnificent eyes, green as the Nile Delta, wide and round, and bright as the power gauges on so many of my father's machines.

Though my daydreams can be fought, my nighttime imagination succumbs to no such restraint. Three years ago when I awoke in pleasure for the first time, fantasies of Pandora were to blame, sending me to my father in my confusion and guilt for an explanation of human sexuality. The plague has taken our natural ability to procreate, but the impulse remains as a constant reminder of where we come from. I pray someday one of us finds a way to undo the damage done and makes us populous again. But be it through natural childbirth or not, I feel the biological need to have children, and first find a wife whom I can learn from and protect, our bond forged from the strongest forces on Earth: love for each other and God.

Lost in this I almost do not see my older brother making his way back down the aisle. Someone wants you, he says.

I follow him to the front cabin and look for Pandora. She is not here, having stepped into the lavatory. She is not the one who wants me. Amused, Rashid shakes his head at my mistake and directs me to the copilot's chair.

For reasons I do not fully understand, I do not want him here.

As he returns to the back, a colorless, sprightly and rather inscrutable-looking hologram appears on the dashboard display.

Hello again, says the ten-centimeter-high man.

Have we met?

We have not, I learn, but he knows about me.

He must be Malachi. Pandora's assistant lacks body and blood, but otherwise approximates humanity. So I have heard. Approximate is a subjective term. He has been softlinked to a number of machines, and when I ask him if he is flying the copter now, he agrees that he is.

I tell him she must have faith in him to let him be all that keeps us from crashing.

It's earned, he assures me. Don't worry.

My older brothers have told me about you, I say, but I cannot imagine what your life is like. You are many places at once, are you not? You are simultaneously talking, flying, listening, researching, making computations, and many other things besides.

Are we that different, Haji? You're breathing right now; your blood is circulating; your digestive system is absorbing nutrients. Your endocrine system is busily producing hormones while your immune system safeguards against infection. Nerve cells are feeding you information all over your body. Neurons in your brain are firing as you think about a variety of subjects, not just what I'm saying now.

True, but I am not fully conscious of all these things.

And I thought you were enlightened, he says.

I have made no such claim.

Perhaps it will come in time, he says. Enlightenment must come little by little. Otherwise it would overwhelm.

I recognize that quote. It is a Sufi quote. I wonder if he is teasing me.

A belated birthday present for you, he says, reaching down to pull a tiny holographic newspaper out of the air. I squint to read the lettering: *The New York Times*. September sixteenth, he says, your birthday. I have over two hundred of these waiting for you in the IVR. You can find out what was happening in the world on that day up until the year they stopped printing them. See what your birthday commemorates.

I thank him. I feel surprised and embarrassed. I explain that my birthday is March third.

My mistake, he says, after an uncomfortable hesitation. Fortunately, I have all the *New York Times* issues on that date too. And if you don't like the *Times,* I have thousands of other newspapers for you instead.

How is it that you made a mistake?

Just as you forget things from time to time, so do I, he says. It's a subroutine I run to keep things interesting.

This confuses me. I want to ask him about it, but do not wish to be impolite. My face must betray my unasked question. Malachi reads me and says, Yes I could disable it, Haji, but then I wouldn't be what I am.

This I can understand. Assuming he is telling the truth. But if truthful, perhaps someone so forgetful should not be in charge of our flight?

By the same token, I limit my memory to just a few terabytes, he says, because that's more human. And then he interrupts my musings with a question that makes all my muscles tense at once. How long have you loved Pandora from afar?

I say nothing.

I can tell from your body language, he says. From your skin temperature when you look at her. Don't worry. I'm not going to say anything to her.

Say what you like.

He studies me and smiles.

I have never met anyone like you before, I tell him.

Right you are, he says. I'm one of a kind.

What are you trying to get from me?

Just your friendship, he says, if you'll give it.

It is freely given, I say, cautiously, though I mean the words.

One more question, he says, as Pandora emerges. And he asks the question, prompting Pandora to tell him to leave me alone. Don't mind him, Haji, she says. He's trying to be playful, but he's cursed with a terrible sense of humor. So I smile politely at them and return to my seat in the back. I buckle myself in, glance at my siblings, and think about Malachi's question.

Do I feel like anything is missing from my life?

No, should I?

penny

Entry #304: The Princess and the Bad Break -open-

I can make things happen just by thinking about them.

Really, I can. It doesn't happen very often, and I don't know exactly how I do it, but it's real psychokinetic power—or else it's just coincidence. I'm sure moms would call it coincidence if I told them about it, which is the reason why I don't.

Everyone decided to take the free slot in the schedule to go skating, except for me and Lulu; I had to give her notes on her opera because the second aria was totally stupid. We spent about half the period going back and forth on it, but then she wanted to go skating too so we hurried out to see Brigit racing Sloane. They were neck and neck and laughing, and all of a sudden Sloane saw us out of the corner of her eye, and she must have decided that it was more important to make fun of me than skate, because she turned her head and stuck out her tongue. And I was in midstep, rising up on the ball of my left foot, my right knee just about to swing forward, my head turning to follow her because she was moving so fast, but I felt like time was slowing down. And the thought came to me suddenly and naturally, like a flower blooming under time-lapse photography: *she might fall.* And in that moment I hexed her. I crossed my fingers and thought: *now.*

Her skate hit something—an extra slippery patch of ice—or was it the force of my mind? Either way, she tripped hard over her own feet, arms flailing, legs twisting. She tried to catch herself and kept her forehead from bouncing off the ice (not that it would have killed her or anything with the oversized helmets moms make us wear), but one of her legs came down at a sick angle, and some of the bones broke. I don't know how many— they're checking her out now. It wasn't as satisying as I hoped it would be, just weird and kind of scary. Everyone looked at her, and she curled up onto her side and screamed. I turned to Lulu and said, "Watch me get blamed for this."

Truth be told, I am to blame. Because I hexed her. Just like last year when I hexed my cousin Hessa. But the thing is, I hex people all the time and it only works every blue moon, so I can't rule out coincidence.

Anyway, I made a point of going over to Sloane and trying to be helpful, and she ignored me and put her arms around Brigit and Tomi instead. She was totally fake crying—you know, making a show of it—these great big crocodile tears in between trying to seem like she wasn't really hurt. She kept saying, "I'll be alright, I just need to walk it off," and everybody told her how brave she was. Ha!

When someone linked the news to Vashti, she came out to immobilize the leg and take Sloane to the infirmary with Brigit and Tomi helping, while Champagne gave the rest of us another safety lecture. "If you want to skate like maniacs, do it Inside because virtual falls don't break actual bones." The same old thing.

I don't know why in the world she told us that when Brigit and Sloane were the only ones racing.

Sloane getting hurt is an awful thing because now she won't be going to Egypt. Moms are going to send Zoë in her place, so I lose my friends and keep my enemies. And Sloane's going to be laid up for a while, which is good, but she'll be in a nasty mood and that's not good for anyone.

Haikubot: scan and summarize.

My sister falls down
The ice does not cushion her
How unfortunate

Not exactly, but close enough.
Lock.

Entry #304: The Princess and the Bad Break –locked–

haji

I am struck by the colors. Turquoise water lapping against sandy shores and wooden dinghies. Adobe buildings in every shade of white. Verdure bursting up from the earth to fill me with surprise. Olive groves. Fig trees. Even palms. So many shades of green to drink in. Greece is thriving.

I do not know why we have stopped here, but it is my pleasure to be a guest in the land Pandora calls home.

Over the years, the essence of fruits, lamb, fresh fish and

wildflowers seeped into the stalls and uneven pavement of the marketplace, and if I try, I can breathe the ghost of these fragrances through my mask. Pandora paints a picture of vendors selling stuffed grape leaves and spanakopita, and shouting to their customers: *yia sou,* see you next Sunday. I envision it as she describes it. I can see for myself, she says, an IVR simulation once we get to Germany. But there are things to do here first.

She leads us through a courtyard of cobalt tiles, dotted with flowering lemon trees. Wooden benches against the walls offer a place to sit, and I need one, briefly, before continuing to a marble fountain. There she hands each of us a pebble. She says to close our eyes, make a wish, and toss them in.

My siblings go first. When it is my turn, echoes of my father's words permeate my mind and my heart. Vividly, I remember him sitting me down when twin fears of death and failure twisted me in their coils. He sat me down, dried my tears, and armored me with the wisdom of Abu Sa'id ibn Abi'l Khayr, a Persian Sufi master who lived a thousand years ago. The master said:

Whatever you have in your mind, forget it.

Whatever you have in your hand, give it.

Whatever is to be your fate, face it!

They are freeing words. I do not know why I remember them now, but I am pleased to have them with me as I release the stone.

When I open my eyes, Ngozi and Dalila want to know. What did you wish for, Haji?

For your wishes to come true.

We all smile except for Rashid, who rolls his eyes disapprovingly. A year ago that is something he would not have done.

Beyond the courtyard stands a bronze door marked by a stylized G. We cross it into Pandora's home, one of the many bases established by Gedaechtnis. It is they who genetically engineered my father's generation, and they who taught us how to combat the plague. Without them, none of us would exist.

deuce

You spy with your little eye something that begins with A.

A is for Athens, cradle of democracy. Satellites just caught one ladylove and three comrades-in-arms, climbing out of the funny-looking plane. Ah, the wonder of imagery intelligence. Click, snap, got your souls!

N is for Nymphenburg, impregnable stronghold of the ladyloves. Nine of them there, one more delightful than the next, all tyrannized under the cruelest lock and key. Linked, though, foolishly linked, which means a genius like you can find them wherever they are.

T is for Thebes, ancient capital of Egypt, which for a while became Luxor, and is now Thebes once again. One last comrade-in-arms there, back from Saqqara with his ambidextrous father, so the satellites say.

I is for Idlewild, and you know what's happening there.

Put them together and you get "anti." Anti-what? Anti-lots. That's good. Pro can't hold a candle to anti. Figure out what you're against, and you're left with what you are.

Anti-authority. Anti-ignorance. Anti-shitstorming forces of darkness.

It's a dangerous job, but someone's got to do it. Who's better suited than you? You're not the type to just talk about taking evil to school—you'll actually pull the trigger. That's the silver lining about having an impulse control problem—you can unleash it on all the nasty fucks who deserve it.

Don't be stupid though. Be sure and check the omens before embarking on your epic quest.

The effigies lie before you. Little bundles of straw, twigs, dry leaves, weeds, bark and bone, bound together with twine. With your lockback pocketknife you cut a vertical incision into the chest of each doll, and into each slit you slide a disc. Naturally, the discs contain the choicest downloads from your treasure trove of information—satellite images, link movements, fragments of overheard conversation—everything you know about your comrades-in-arms and ladyloves.

You gather them together, your pile of people, and you arrange them carefully around the heart of the stone circle. Now the tricky part. Which lighter to use? The stainless-steel Dr Pepper? The nickel-plated Mickey Mouse? No, today it's best to let Fate decide, so you reach into your mystery pocket, fishing around with your eyes closed and trying not to identify the contents by touch. Shake, scramble and pull—congratulations, you just nabbed the Ningworks jet torch–slash–digital camera with its engraved Mandarin lettering and solid copper case, very classy.

A quick snapshot to remember the momentous occasion, and anticipation must be the sweetest part because you feel like you're stiff enough to burst through your jeans. But you don't, and it's burn time with a click and a whoosh and that satisfying first crackle as the flames catch, spread, dance and rise.

You brought the extinguisher this time, didn't you? Just in case?

Man oh man, is it a visceral thrill, but something about burn time always puts you in a tingly philosophical headspace. This time you're grooving on subjective reality because the fourteen sacrifices you just put to the torch are (a) just cold, lifeless objects and yet (b) symbols of actual flesh and blood people as seen through your eyes.

In essence, you're deconstructing your understanding of your comrades-in-arms and ladyloves by disintegrating their fetishes and assimilating how they burn. And then there's the weird nature of the magic itself—by undertaking this ritual, are you merely predicting the future or are you altering it? Maybe both. It's like each effigy has an astral cord that stretches out like a grappling hook through space-time, landing in another sequence of events, another universe—and when the fire burns out all the cords snap and you come out of your trance to realize that the reality you know has shifted in some of those directions. You know it's the spirit power of fire. It's the reason why nearly every culture on this godforsaken planet made burnt offerings for thousands of years.

You sit cross-legged on the ground to watch what the fire shows you and listen to what it says. Those pop, pop, pop sounds are reassuring—the louder the crackle, the better the omen. And the rate of consumption can't be beat—the way it's burning so bright, so hot and so dangerous, you know this sexy beast just can't get enough of what you fed it. Look out, the wind's picking up—there's a wild flicker and the wind teases that it'll die down but doesn't deliver and now it's getting worse—now the smoke's blowing right in your face, making your lungs ache and your eyes sting. The fire doesn't go out and you can thank your lucky stars for that, but it bends sinister, an unmistakable arc in the flame, curving like a scimitar, and that's a bad omen, portending sickness to the healthy and death to the sick. Then the wind drops down to a soothing little breeze and your fire is burning robustly once again.

When it's taken its course and dwindled down to cinders, you poke through the remains to see which discs survived and which melted down to a black and silvery slag. There are two survivors: one comrade-in-arms and one ladylove. That's how it should be. That's how you knew it would be. The future looks brighter than it's ever been.

Yes, you'll reach out to those two because they're Fated.

Fear not, little sleepwalkers. Liberation is at hand.

pandora

As I suspected, Vashti won't take Rashid in.

"I have nothing against him," she explains, her image almost fritzing out before whipping back like a trick birthday candle, "but I won't have the added responsibility." The rest of what she says comes through garbled, but I gather it's about how Isaac shouldn't change the rules of the exchange at the last minute, and how she's under enough pressure this time, what with the tragedy that happened last year.

Atmospheric interference makes the rest of the call pointless. I decide to try again after the weather up there improves.

I'm not that surprised to find Rashid standing outside the door to my office. He's heard enough to know the news isn't good.

"A prickly pear," he says.

"She can be," I agree.

"I don't want to go home, Aunt Pandora. At least not yet."

"I appreciate that, but Vashti won't bite—there's no changing her mind on these kind of things. Trust me."

"If I go back now, things will go badly," he says. "For Mu'tazz." He shows me his fist, his expression sharp and serious before sliding into a self-conscious and childish grin. "I love my brother, but if I have to put up with him for much longer, we're going to come to blows."

"You need a break from him," I say. "Do you want to stay here?"

"You'd let me?"

"If you don't cause trouble, yes, for a little while."

"I won't be any trouble—in fact, I can help you around the house," he says, genuinely eager to prove himself useful.

"Well, so far, I'm down one motion sensor," I prompt, and off he goes to replace it. What he really wants, I think, isn't a break from Mu'tazz so much as a break from the world itself. He wants a passport back to the life he left behind. The lure of alternate reality can be powerful—especially when it tugs at the loins. Sadly, Isaac's children have no real outlet for their hormones, and last year, after Rashid tried in vain to romance his cousins, I decided to make his IVR experience more colorful. I suppose I felt sorry for him, and don't regret it now, but once that genie's out of the bottle (so to speak), there's no putting it back in.

I remember the night Hal and I let the genie out. We were sixteen. He'd just come back from a trip to Fiji with Simone, who he loved, and Lazarus, who he hated. When he came back it was clear that he wasn't ever going to be able to win her away from Laz. I'd never seen him in so dark a mood. I really thought he might hurt himself. So I took advantage of him, the one beautiful night we shared, even if it was only virtual. But the next morning everything was so awkward between us and we realized the ramifications of what we'd done. His heart still belonged to Simone even if his head told him it was futile. I couldn't keep him but at the same time I can't let him go.

He doesn't remember any of this, of course. That's courtesy of Mercutio, who tried to kill him with an electrical surge as strong as a lightning bolt, overloading the machines that kept him alive. He didn't die, but he lost a good chunk of his memory, and I don't think it's ever coming back.

Every time I see him I think about reminding him, but I never do.

While Rashid's tending to my copter, I take the other kids into my studio. They're intensely curious how everything works. I explain the scanning process, how all the microcameras work together, the way the computer extrapolates speech patterns from basic voiceprints and so on. They get a kick out of how I can make my computer greet them with Rashid's, Mu'tazz's or even Isaac's inflections.

When I tell them they each have to say a sentence and sing a song for the computer to take accurate voiceprints, Dalila finds she can't make up her mind about what to sing, which sparks Ngozi to joke that it doesn't really matter because whichever one she picks is sure to be off-key. She giggles at that. "I have lots of notes in my head," she agrees, "but when they come out of my mouth they all sound like one."

One by one, I scan them. A quick and painless process. "Like being bathed in blue sunlight," Dalila says. "Is that it?" Ngozi asks, shrugging to himself before laying down his voiceprint, "To be present is the greatest gift of all." Just happy to be here—I'm sure I felt that feeling as a small child, but I must have lost it along the way. Then it's Haji's turn, which is an opportunity to give him good news.

"One of the nice things about IVR is that you'll have full mobility in your legs," I explain. "You'll feel like you're walking, running or jumping, and nothing will be able to slow you down. You won't cramp up or have to rest."

He just looks at me, untouched by my enthusiasm. "Why?" he says.

"Because it's a simulation," I begin, but I stop when I realize that's not what he means.

"Why do that?" he asks. "This is the way I am."

I won't argue the point with him because I can't. Though I think he's being as foolish as he thinks he's being wise. What do I know? It's not my decision to make. *Cada um sabe onde o sapato aperta,* as my mother used to say. Only the wearer knows where the shoe pinches. So now I must duplicate his infirmity, laming him via software where fate lamed him via biology.

After lunch I take them to the Acropolis, and then the ocean. The boys play in the waves, splashing and bodysurfing, while I sit in the sun with Dalila, working her long blond hair into braids. A little time with her aunt—it's something she needs. From personal experience, I know it's sometimes hard to be the only daughter in a large family, and since Hessa's passing that's exactly what she is. Hopefully the trip north will be good for her—she can find a kind of sisterhood with her cousins. That's a big reason why Isaac wants her to go. Last week she asked him if God might perhaps be a woman, and if She took Hessa because She wanted another woman to talk with and share Her thoughts. And Isaac said yes, that just might be.

"Greece is beautiful," she grins.

"As beautiful as Egypt?"

"Of course."

"No more, no less?"

She snorts like I've made a silly joke, and looks over her shoulder, her expression gently chiding, as if to ask how could one place be any more beautiful than the other? It's the same world, isn't it?

Sounds of horseplay pull my attention back to the water, my concern for the boys' safety trickling over into irrational fear. They're perfectly fine, I remind myself. There's no danger, they're not out too deep, I know CPR, and they know CPR, no problem. Why should I be anxious when they're not? Simply because I'm an adult? Whatever it is, they don't worry about things the way I do. I wonder if maybe that's what "enlightenment" is.

"How long before I get those?" Dalila asks, with a glance at my bathing suit top.

"You're eleven, right?"

"Almost."

"Well, I would say about three years, give or take a year."

She does the math and says, "Okay, I guess I'll make the most of that time."

"You're not looking forward to them?"

"Not particularly," she says, scrunching up her nose, "but what can I do but accept them when they come?"

"Rejecting them won't help, huh?"

"I just wish they did some good," she says.

"So do I," I tell her. And admittedly they don't do much good, since there's no point lactating when you're barren. We may be survivors of Black Ep, but the plague has robbed us of our motherhood. Champagne and Isaac discovered this after many painful failures. Our immune systems are strong enough to fight the plague, but hypersensitive to the point where they attack things they shouldn't. No matter what preventative measures my friends took, Champagne's white blood cells aborted their children every single time.

Though Dalila's only human, with all the immunoboosting drugs she's been taking, I doubt she'd fare much better. The only wombs that can sustain life are artificial. It's a terrible truth, but what can I do but accept it?

I can hope.

"It won't always be like that," I tell her. "Your father is very smart. So are your aunts, your cousins and your brothers. And so are you. If we all keep working on this, if we keep learning and studying and trying new things, then one day we'll find a way to turn things back to how they're supposed to be."

She stares at me for the longest time, and then takes my hand. Comforting me.

"One day," she says.

penny

Entry #305: The Princess and the Icebreaker –open–

Am I in heaven or am I in hell?

I hear that question a lot. Every time I go Inside I hear it. That's how I've spent my money. Not all my money, to be fair, since I've bought my share of impulse purchases—little pleasures like pepperoni pizza and pistachio ice cream, games and rides, cool gear when I'm feeling mirror-friendly, and even my own opera house once upon a time—but the preponderance of my cash feeds my fantasy of choice.

What I do for fun: I'm a secret agent. I go behind enemy lines on search-and-rescue missions. People depend on me to save lives. I tangle with dastardly villains, trading quips first and steel second. I am loved or feared, and no one knows my true identity. It's like being a superhero. Best of all, I'm always challenged and I always win.

Lots of books got adapted into simulations—some crudely, and others quite well—but my favorite never was, so I had to do it myself. It's set during the French Revolution, and the dirty, scum-sucking revolutionaries are sending all the French nobles to the guillotine, so the British nobles have to sneak in and rescue them. The main character seems like a harmless, dandy fool but he—or in my case, she—is actually the leader of a band of British spies. Code name: Scarlet Pimpernel. When I go to my domain, that's who I am. A social life in England and adventures in France—if only it were real! Sadly, it's not, but it's been a fun escape over the years. I especially enjoy hearing the other characters gossip about me:

They seek her here,
They seek her there,
Those Frenchies seek her everywhere.
Is she in heaven?
Is she in hell?
That damned elusive Pimpernel.

For all the time and money I've put into it, there's still more to be done. My sets are limited: an English mansion and a few "stock" French locales that I copied from *A Tale of Two Cities.* Also, I only have a handful of characters to play off of, and they're all originally from other sources—my Marguerite Blakeney is just a revamped Josephine from a Napoleon simulation. Characters are ridiculously expensive to create and they tend to fall into set conversational patterns, so after a while they stop surprising you. The solution to this is more time and more money, and there's the addiction, the trap of the Inside, and like I said I'd rather be the trapper than the trappee.

So I've decided to empty my bank account. I've decided to gamble. All the money I've saved over the years, all that allowance, all those rewards for good grades and upstanding behavior, it's all going to buy me my future.

Since she's the queen of the Inside, there's nothing I can give Pandora that she doesn't already have or could easily get. But my sisters are another story . . .

I'm going to bribe them to say nice things about me. I may not be able to win people over, but I'm rich enough to buy them—much richer than they are, I bet, especially with all the extra money Champagne keeps giving me. Or if not buy, rent. With everyone singing my praises, Pandora will have to look at me in a new light. Then it's up to me to sell myself as the best woman for the job, which should be easy breezy since that's exactly who I am.

I believe this is what's called a "charm offensive." And it has to work, because if it doesn't I'm bankrupt with nothing to show.

The opening move? Start at the top. That's what I did and we'll see how it goes. The first thing I did was change my clothes, because powdered wigs and satin waistcoats might be all the rage in 1793, but take them out of their proper context and they look awful stupid. I settled on black jeans, a white striped blouse and a tan Burberry coat. It's a pretty good look on me. Anything's better than the navy blue–hunter green school uniforms we have to wear on the Outside.

I sent out a sprite (cost: twenty-five little ones) and waited for an answer. Sloane kept me waiting for a while—probably shocked that I would seek her out—but I knew she'd pick up eventually. Curiosity's just too powerful.

When she finally picked up and our domains collided, I saw she wasn't in her usual digs. She'd gone to the zoo of all places. And she'd taken Brigit with her. That certainly wasn't in the plan—I'd been hoping to talk to her alone because when you get Brigit and Sloane together they're twice as mean and half as smart.

"What do you want?" Sloane growled.

"I just wanted to say I'm sorry about your accident," I said, and I pointed for emphasis but of course I was pointing at her virtual leg, which was unbroken, supporting her virtual body the same as ever. "We may not get along, but I don't wish that on you any more than you'd wish it on me."

She snorted at that, and got up in my face. "You should be sorry. It's your fault I fell. I got distracted by how ugly you are. I can only stand to look at you now because I'm on so much medication."

"No way, there's not enough meds in the world for that," sneered Brigit, looking not all that different from the hyena exhibit behind her. But I didn't rise to their bait.

"Why don't you make like lightning and bolt?" Sloane said. "I think the animals are complaining about the smell."

"Give me five minutes and I'll go," I told them. "Just hear me out, because there's something important I have to say."

"You're running away from home?" guessed Brigit.

"You're writing an opera about how colossally dumb you are?" guessed Sloane.

"I came to apologize," I said.

That shut them up.

All this bad blood started years ago, back when we were little kids and I caught them copying off each other during a math test. What they did was against the rules, so I turned them in the way moms wanted. I didn't know I was breaking some big important code. Honor among thieves or however they see it. They never especially liked me before, but afterward they started calling me Penny-the-Rat, and Penelo-pee-pee, and so many other nasty slanders, and just generally started making me an outsider in my own family. I pinpoint this as the moment between us where everything turned for the worse.

"It was wrong of me to do it," I said, even though it wasn't. "I should have minded my own business. Believe me, if I could do it all over again, you'd never have gotten in trouble."

"A fat lot of good that apology does now," Sloane said.

"Okay, you're sorry," Brigit said. "So what? Are we supposed to like you now?"

"No, you may never like me, we may never be friends, and that's okay, but I just wanted to tell you that. And something more: I have a proposal for you."

"A proposal?"

"It's about money."

Sloane lit into me with another insult, but Brigit reeled her in before she could get the whole thing out, reminding me of someone pulling the choke chain on a rabid dog.

"Go on," Brigit told me. (She was always the more level-headed one.)

So I laid it out for them. Set my price at five thousand big ones for each. That's serious bank, the kind of funds it takes months or even years to save up for. I could tell they were surprised to see me throwing my financial weight around—I'm usually tight as a tourniquet when money's concerned.

"You want to pay us to pretend we like you?" Brigit said.

"Right, because if everyone sees you guys accepting me, they'll have to join in as well," I said, sweetening it further with, "You set the trends, after all."

It's safe to say they didn't know what to make of me. Sloane seemed to think I was playing a joke on them or at least not telling them the whole truth. And I can't blame her for her suspicions, I suppose, because I didn't mention Pandora specifically, for fear of giving voice to my plans to take over the Inside. That's need-to-know information, and why give them ammunition to use against me if they pass on the offer?

Anyway, she got yanked before we could come to a meeting of the minds. Moms wanted her Outside again because they had her cast ready, so that left me alone with Brigit, the two of us just looking at each other, and then not looking at each other, neither of us really sure what to say. I think maybe I shamed her a little, that I would give so much just to be treated decently again.

And a funny thing happened—we started talking about the elephants. How funny they look, but also how old and wise, and what we would do if we ever saw a real one. I bought a bag of roasted peanuts (cost: fifty little ones) and started feeding the baby elephant through the bars, and Brigit told me how back in World War II, the first bomb the Allies ever dropped on Berlin killed the only elephant in the zoo.

From there we just shared the peanuts and talked about how much better the food is here on the Inside. How virtual fare is always mouthwateringly fantastic and no one ever has to clean up the dishes, while real food ranges from hey-that's-pretty-good to my-God-what-is-this-disgusting-poison-paste-congealing-on-my-plate? And how not a single living thing has to suffer Inside—you can eat cheeseburgers and sushi until your money runs out, but out in the real world you'd have to actually kill a cow or a fish—something neither of us are keen to do. And how the virtual vegetables are always fresh and delicious and no one ever bothers with all that "Is a carrot conscious?" junk and "Do turnips feel pain when you yank them from the ground?"

Now that I think about it, while the prospect of killing a cow is distasteful, I know I could do it if I had to. I don't care how many lectures moms give us about the ethics of vegetarianism, if I were stranded on a desert island alone with a cow, I'd be having Bessieburgers by the third or fourth hunger pang. Sorry, but I'm far more important than livestock, and that's what cows get for being so gosh-darn tasty. Or maybe real cows taste terrible. Who knows?

By the time Brigit left, we were pretty comfortable with each other. It was just a silly conversation, but the best we'd had in years and years.

About my proposal, "I'll talk to Sloane," she said. "We'll think it over."

"Thanks," I said, and that was that. I'm cautiously optimistic.

The freakiest part about today happened right afterward, when I came back to my mansion. Got that slippery feeling where you realize that everything is not how you left it. I've felt that on the Outside lots of times, whenever someone decided to mess with my stuff, but never on the Inside before. There I am in my ballroom admiring the blue damask silk drapes, and Marguerite rushes in to warn me that Chauvelin is blackmailing her to find the Scarlet Pimpernel's identity—the same old story—but when I go to reassure her, I notice something in the room is out of place. Something, but what? I can't figure it out, so I freeze the simulation and make the system run through an A-to-Z inventory of all my props. Nothing's missing at all. On the contrary, something's been added.

Upon my mantelpiece I found a flat teardrop-shaped charm, black, dotted with a white circle. To me it looked like a tadpole, the circle serving as an eye. I checked the system code: *jewelry, ornate, pendant, yin-yang symbol, halved, choice 2.*

Definitely not mine. So how did it get there? The system didn't know or wouldn't say. Must be a glitch—Vashti's been concerned about them lately—but when glitches work out in my favor, I don't complain. It's a shame you can't sell things back to the system—it'd be nice to get a little money to offset my expenses.

If it's not a glitch, does that mean someone sent it to me on purpose? Who then, and why? Not to mention how the heck do you send something anonymously? Every time I've done it, my sender ID showed up in the system logs.

Intriguing, but weird. I think I'll ask Pandora about it when she comes. It'll be my icebreaker.

Lock it up.

Entry #305: The Princess and the Icebreaker -locked-

deuce

Oh, that's a nasty one. That's a popping drop. That's an abyss of fizzling, sizzling neurons. No one should dream that, not even you.

Don't remember it. Let it dissipate like smoke.

You can't let it go, can you? It clings and chokes. Life in the catacombs, blood-soaked, butchering, your hand goes up wet and comes down wetter, and everything you touch begs you to stop. Why won't you? They die but they're never dead, and the second you stop they'll take revenge. They'll do what you did to them and worse. You have to keep going or it's the furnace crinkling your skin layer by layer and into the cellar that eats. And blood that clings to you starts to plead, each individual droplet taking the tortured face of a comrade-in-arms or ladylove, infected eyes accusing you, convulsive lips snapping open to howl and wail.

You've had that dream before. It's a recurring favorite. A greatest hit. But this time it concluded with you floating in a nightmare lake, your hands gripped around a white-feathered neck. You strangled a swan. That's the worst of it. It's the last thing you want to do. You don't want to hurt them. You just want to wake them up. Remember that.

Once they're awake, it'll all be so much easier. They'll be off balance from having their illusions swept away, and you'll be the hero for showing them the truth. You won't be rejected. You'll go to the one you want and she'll adore you. You won't feel blank anymore.

She's so beautiful. What will it be like to talk to her? To listen to her? To know her heart and dry her tears?

Just don't dream like that anymore. You're in the final stages and you know it's no time to go flying off the deep end. Don't talk about it. Don't tell him. What would he say if he could look inside your head?

Remember, you control the dreams. They don't control you.

haji

Holy places do not exist. When the entire universe belongs to God, how can any piece of it be more hallowed than any other? All places are holy, one could say, equally holy in the eyes of God. There can be no distinction in His majesty, and I would never suggest the contrary. However, there are places of power. Places where I feel history more keenly than any other, where I can suddenly find myself moved and not realize why. Places haunted, if not by ghosts, then by echoes, by the lingering aftereffects of human ambition, imagination and desire.

The Pyramids are one such place. The power there overwhelms, as intense as sunlight. But there is also power in Nymphenburg, subtler, more sinuous. Like moonlight. I feel it coiling about me even before we land.

It is opulent and whimsical, a Baroque Xanadu. It seduces the eye. With its perfectly manicured lawns, it seduces, and with the elegant swans who bathe in its circular courtyard fountain. Flower beds, fruit trees, statues and gardens, all protected by magnificent palaces, they themselves compassed by equally magnificent parks. I cannot imagine living here. It is far too sprawling, with more space than anyone would possibly need. In Egypt, we help my father restore the architecture of monarchs, but we do not live as monarchs ourselves. Not so with my cousins. They have found a kingdom and made it their own.

Nymphenburg. I cannot deny its beauty. Especially after a thunderstorm, with everything so clean and fresh and green. I think I understand why Rashid wanted so dearly to return here. Still, there is something about it that strikes me as desolate, and when I try to understand why I feel that way I have no answers. This is a robust and flourishing place, full of light and life. Desolation is nowhere in sight. But I feel it all the same, sadness, a wrongness, a chill.

Perhaps I am worried that something here will snare Ngozi and Dalila just as it ensnared Rashid? No, there is no need for worry, as I accept that possibility. If that is what is meant to happen, it will. Perhaps it is Hessa then, I fear losing my family the way I lost her? But I accept that possibility as well. I can make no sense of this. I must call my father, or meditate, or both.

With the gentlest of impacts, Pandora sets us down on a landing pad. So begins the adventure, she says.

Outside, we are met by my northern aunts and a line of girls standing sharply at attention: the denizens of Nymphenburg, our cousins, nymphs, amazons, Waterbabies, jinn. All are familiar faces, but some more so than others. The warmest expressions shine from last year's guests, Brigit, Olivia and Tomi, who visited us in Egypt. I have already nicknamed them the playful one, the shy one and the poet. As comforting as it is to see them, I am most looking forward to getting to know the others better, most of whom I have barely spoken to over the years and then only through phone calls, never in person.

Aunt Champagne is delighted to see us, calling us her sweeties and embracing each of us in turn. She plants a kiss atop my head and I breathe in what might be bergamot soap and orange flower water. A strong citrus fragrance I find cloying, and though the family has always considered Champagne to be the prettiest of my father's generation, I do not see it, and she is not half as soulful as Pandora. Still, her kindness is palpable, and her touch welcome and reassuring.

Aunt Vashti does not embrace us, and I am neither offended nor surprised, as I remember my father explaining that she does not like to be touched. Though less demonstrative in her affection, I sense the smile on her face is genuine, as are her questions about how we are feeling, and her wish that we please tell her if there is anything she can do to help us feel more at home. Where Champagne is willowy and blond, she is a dark-haired woman scarcely taller than Dalila.

Between the eleven of them, the three of us and Pandora, we span the spectrum of diversity. Every human ethnicity is in our blood, as if we were an advertisement for racial harmony. And yet this is not a question of tolerance but survival. Genetic diversity may help defend us from disease. Whom do I most resemble? Of everyone here, it would be either Tomi the poet or the little girl, Katrina. Though I may be human and they something more, perhaps we come from similar stock?

I tell them how pleased we are to be here, and thank them for their hospitality. I hope they will take no pains on our account.

Culture divides us. Looking at the girls, I suspect that we are far more relaxed than they are, they in their uncomfortable school uniforms and we in our wool cloaks, they standing like soldiers and we presenting ourselves as ambassadors. Everyone wants to make a good impression, but they are clearly frightened that they will not. What can I do to put them at ease?

Before I can tell a joke, Ngozi makes one of his own, something about a country cousin visiting his city cousin, and a comical misunderstanding between them. The girls laugh, most of them, and my brother beams, a puffed peacock pleased to be found funny, and especially by those for whom he carries affection.

At Champagne's prompting, the younger girls step forward to drape brilliant blue cornflower garlands about our necks. They take our hands and lead us past lion statues and all manner of swan imagery. My siblings are all smiles and charm, and so am I, but the closer I come to the actual palaces the more surrounded I feel.

pandora

Vashti's hands are cold. My grandfather's hands are warm and wrinkled. Icy fingers touch my wrist and then check my lymph nodes. I try not to flinch. Vashti would do well to take a note from Grandpa's bedside manner, despite the fact that she is real, and he a mere computer simulation.

My grandfather owns a cosmetic enhancement empire—dozens of offices throughout IVR Brazil—but he's never too busy to give me a checkup. He's a kind man, and I'm very grateful to whoever programmed him. When I was growing up, he always numbed my arm before a shot, and afterward let me dig my hand into a dish full of candies. "Life can be bitter and difficult, so carry a little sweet in your pocket," he says. It doesn't matter how old I get, I always take a candy.

I'd much rather he be giving me the checkup now, but this one's for real, and of everyone alive on the planet, there's no better immunologist than Vashti.

She scans my intestines, liver, kidneys, lungs, thymuses, spleens, and heart for abnormalities. Holographic imagery of each organ rotates like meat on a spit, as the findings are datalinked into her ear.

"Vitals look good," she says.

But when she analyzes my blood sample, she notes a slight but apparently harmless irregularity in my lymphocytes, calling it something she wants to keep an eye on. Days from now, she'll recognize this something as a sign that I carry a virulent mutating strain, a pathogen we will eventually call the End of the World.

I had playmates growing up in IVR São Paulo—little programs that behaved like preschoolers in an effort to socialize me. At the time, I thought they were as tangible as I am, but as it turns out, Vashti is my oldest real friend. We met that first day in Idlewild right after my sixth birthday when I was terrified all the other kids would make fun of my accent. She never did, not once, not even a snicker. She taught me Hindi and I taught her Portuguese. We became study buddies, and stayed close for the first year or two, but then I started making other friends, and began to chafe under her jealousy. She's not the easiest person to get along with, cursed with the sharpest tongue of anyone I know. Still, every time I've come to resent her, she's made me feel foolish for it with unexpected thoughtfulness.

I will say this too about Vashti. Finding out that our world was fake, and learning that in the real world billions were dead? She thinks it's the best thing that ever happened to her. She won't often admit it, but put enough drinks in her, ask the right questions, and out it comes. Back in school she was so frustrated, so frightened of life as a faceless nobody—how can you leave your mark in a world of billions? But here she is now in the process of rebuilding civilization itself. This is her lofty challenge, her wonderful opportunity, her raison d'être. She's never been happier.

Competitive, analytical, even a bit cutthroat, she's a fine enemy for Black Ep to have. But Isaac brings different skills to the fore, and so does Halloween. If only they could work together. And to think if our entire class had survived to face the challenges. Simone might have made the best scientist of all of us, and Lazarus the best peacemaker. Their loss is incalculable.

"Your blood pressure's a concern," she notes. "Feeling stressed?"

"No more than usual."

"Oh, you'll have to tell me what I can do for your eye in the sky."

"Malachi?"

"He's been so helpful tracking those pygmies."

We'd thought that we were the only primates to survive the plague, but four months ago Malachi's satellite scans found evidence of pygmy marmosets in the rainforests of Peru. Hard to tell from the resolution, but the tiny, leaping shape looked like a monkey to me, and then no news until last week when Malachi photographed what might be another. Vashti wants to capture one in the hopes of studying its cellular immunology. What we find in its DNA might be our key to a Black Ep vaccine.

"Malachi's happy to help," I tell her. "Just make sure you credit him for single-handedly saving the human race if it works."

That's nice of you. I assume she'd otherwise refer to me as "the computer"? As in "the computer was of some help"?

Oh, I'm just trying to get in good with you for the inevitable day when machines enslave humanity and rule the planet.

Yes, a day I look forward to with great relish.

In your dreams.

Yours, actually. Didn't you have a nightmare about that when you were nine?

Come on, Malachi, just because you snuck around in my head when I was hooked up to the IVR all those years . . .

Haven't I apologized enough for that? Is it my fault your dreams are interesting?

Quite an invasion of privacy.

When Mercutio was trying to play king of the mountain, I had to hide anywhere I could to keep him from deleting me. Your dreams were as good a hiding place as any.

Oh really? And who was trying to delete you when I was nine?

Touché. Back then I was deeply curious about what kind of dreams an actual flesh-and-blood child experienced. Dr. Hyoguchi only programmed me for a limited number of dream cycles. But you'll be happy to know that looking into all your busy little imaginations helped me program some new ones. Even if it did come at a terrible cost.

What cost?

You know the cost. Of all of you, I spent the most time in Mercutio's dreams. And with him turning out the way he did, I can't help but think that all my childish resentments spilled over into his subconscious, and gave him the fuel to do the terrible things he did.

I'll bet you anything if you'd never set foot in Mercutio's head, he'd have turned out just as rotten.

And don't think I don't appreciate you giving me the benefit of the doubt. I wish I could let myself off that easily.

Well, there are more than enough things I haven't let myself off the hook for, so tell you what, Malachi, you let me off my hooks and I'll let you off yours.

Does it work that way?

It's worth a try, isn't it?

Probably not.

Okay, let's figure it out later. For now, please try to stop interrupting me from telling this story.

My lips are sealed.

Good. To continue:

"When I last spoke to him," Vashti says, "Malachi intimated that you'd made some progress with the Webbies."

She's talking about the lost souls we interchangeably call WBEs, Webbies or Websicles. As Black Ep destroyed civilization, the rich did whatever they could to preserve themselves—in some cases, simply their legacies (through extravagant, Ozymandian banners, statues and architecture to insist that yes, they once lived here), and in other cases their actual bodies and brains. In the tradition of baseball legend Ted Williams, some tried to freeze themselves. A few cryonic storage facilities still exist today, though the majority fell to power failures, faulty construction, natural disasters and have-nots outraged that they should be annihilated while the haves enjoy a chance at resurrection. We call the cryopreservation cases Popsicles, whereas Websicles are the ones who went the other route, and had their brains dissected, analyzed and uploaded neuron by neuron to a computer. WBE stands for Whole Brain Emulation.

Unfortunately for them, the sum total of their efforts didn't add up to actual consciousness, but rather a blueprint for consciousness, a labyrinth of data for someone to compile. That someone happens to be me—eighteen years ago Isaac asked me to take the Webbies as my pet project, and I have spent much of that time trying to make sense of their digital brains. Someday we hope to revive them, be it via actual flesh and blood or via code and light like Malachi.

I'm still a ways from that, but I have accomplished something quite wonderful. Something Malachi should not be "intimating" to Vashti, because it's a surprise, and it's not her surprise. It's a gift for someone special.

"Some progress with the Webbies, but he's overstating it." I downplay the situation, hopping off the examination table and slipping my shoes back on. "I'll give you a status report when I can. First I have to schlep your kids to Isaac. Actually, that's second—first I have to check on the damage from the storm. Then let's not forget about all those tiny irregularities in the IVR to investigate, that should be fun."

"Don't forget you owe me a monkey," she says. "Peru is your responsibility, not mine."

"Right, I'll get to that. Isaac said he'd help me."

"It's a pygmy monkey, not a killer whale. You don't need a big brave man to help you capture it, do you?"

"You never know what you might find in the jungle. Safety in numbers and all."

She nods at that, and smiles sweetly at me. "Just make sure Isaac doesn't convert the monkey while he's trying to convert my girls."

"He doesn't want to proselytize," I sigh, exasperated. "All he's going to do is show your kids a different way of life."

"In other words, convert them. Doesn't matter because it won't work—they're too strong. But level with me, Pandora, does he really believe in all that mumbo jumbo?"

"You know he does."

"Then I'd say his imagination has gone amok, a meltdown in his temporal lobes. But if he doesn't believe, then he's using religion to control his kids, and if I had to guess between the two, that's the one I'd go with."

"He does believe it," I tell her, slipping on my jacket and heading out.

"Funny, I thought he was smarter than that," she says, following me down the hall.

haji

There is too much to see in a day. Even if my legs were stronger I would have to portion the tour into several trips. As it is, I had to beg off after a dizzying twenty-minute walk beneath frescoes and gilt ceilings, past vibrantly decorated walls of pastel blue, green and gold in grand rococo fashion. I had wanted to continue on to the Hall of Mirrors, the Gallery of Beauties and the museum of coaches and sleighs, but found I could not. Tomi was kind enough to lead me to my room for a rest.

It's easy to get lost here, she tells me now as I sit on a golden satinwood settee. And I agree that it is much bigger than I had dreamt.

She puts my garland in water, brushing my thanks off with a shrug. They're weeds, she says. But that makes no difference to me. She tells me that harvesters used to call cornflowers hurtsickle because their tough stems are so difficult to cut.

Thou blunt'st the very reaper's sickle and so
In life and death becom'st the farmer's foe.

It is not her poem, she says, and she cannot remember where she heard it.

Last year she allowed me to read her poetry collection, *The Strength of Spiders.* I found the prose beautiful and alien, filled with tiny observations about the world that had never occurred to me before. Because I liked it so much, she recommended I read the works of T. S. Eliot, especially *The Waste Land,* which she cited as the greatest of all her creative influences. Unfortunately, I could understand very little of that poem. When I tell her this, she says we will have plenty of time to discuss it. And do I know that Nymphenburg is a beginning where *The Waste Land* is an end?

How so?

The Mad King, she says. He was born here, crazy old Ludwig, not in this very room of course, but here in the palace. Eliot's poem alludes to his death.

I remember learning about the man, a chronically depressed king who burned through his treasury, building the most expensive fairy-tale castles Bavaria had ever seen. As I do my stretches, Tomi fleshes him out more fully in my mind, telling me how as a child his parents took away his pet tortoise because they thought he was growing too attached to it, and how in a fit of rage he tried to have his younger brother beheaded. He invited his horse to dinner once, a distant echo of Caligula, though nowhere as cruel. He became more and more of a recluse as he grew older, stealing away to an underground grotto to read poetry in a seashell-shaped boat. He apparently suffered from hallucinations, and was eventually declared insane, only to escape his asylum.

How did he die?

He drowned, she says. He drowned under mysterious circumstances. They found his body in Lake Starnberg, a little south of here. His doctor drowned as well, trying to save him, so it would seem, but only the dead could say for certain.

A sad story, I tell her.

Again she shrugs, removing a piece of lint from her blazer and smoothing her plaid cross tie. He was religious, she says, and also gay. He could not reconcile the two. I hope I don't have to worry about you the same way, she says.

I stare at her. What is she saying?

I'm sorry, she says. Did I offend you?

You have confused me, I say. I am certainly religious. What makes you think I am homosexual?

She blushes, biting her lip in consternation. It's just last year, she says. Your brother Ngozi made every attempt he could think of to kiss me and you never did. And when I got back home my sisters told me that your older brothers tried the same things with them. You just seem different somehow.

If I thought you might return my affection, I might try for a kiss. But I have no expectation that you will, I say.

That sounds like a dare, she says.

I doubt your readiness.

Now it sounds like you're trying to manipulate me, she says.

No, I say, just listen. My father has said that you girls are blessed with many advantages, but the downside of your genetic inheritance is a lack of physical desire. Is this true?

We may be slow, she admits, plopping down next to me and looking away.

Then no matter what I want, it would be rude of me to make you uncomfortable as Ngozi did. I apologize on his behalf.

It's not a big deal, she says. Until we can find a way to make sexual reproduction possible again, there's just not much point in it, so it doesn't feel like I'm missing out on much by not being ready. I am curious though.

Are you?

She meets my eyes and leans forward, expectant, so I take my kiss. It is sweet, and slow, not quite rapturous, but powerful and life-affirming, strong enough to make me ache for her, despite an irrational thought that I am somehow betraying Pandora. My blood is racing through every part of me and I take it further, putting my hands upon her. She pulls back to meet my eyes once again.

I just don't get it, she says. I'm sorry.

I fooled myself, I realize. I made myself believe she was enjoying it as well. No need to apologize, I tell her.

She kisses me again, this time on the cheek. I hope I didn't make you uncomfortable, she says.

Uncomfortable is not the word, I assure her. It is my first real kiss and I have no regrets. Perhaps we will share another when the time is right.

She leaves me with my unfulfilled fantasies. When Ngozi and Dalila come to check on me, they bring two books from Tomi, the first a biography of Ludwig, and the other a copy of T. S. Eliot's famous poem. Over the next few weeks, I will read both of them, their content blurring together with memories of the kiss.

And I will think of Ludwig from time to time, Mad Ludwig who once walked these halls, doomed and drowned but not forgotten. Sometimes I will think of him with *The Waste Land* swirling in the back of my mind, one of its lines like a whisper in my ears.

Fear death by water.

part two

the flesh

halloween

Where the fuck was I?

Hunting, that's right. Out by the lake with the unburned trees, looking to thin the cottontail population—I eat rabbits for breakfast—when a jittery feeling snuck up on me. Watched, perhaps? Something there?

I turned but saw no eyes upon me, which reassured me not at all. I glanced at my watch to see a bump in my message counter. Pandora, again, which I decided not to play, much less answer. Better not to contribute to lost causes. She's a sweet girl, but she feeds on false hope, and I've given her too much of it over the years. There's always the chance that I'm missing out on something I'll later regret, but whenever I talk to her, I get lost in a past I'd rather not hold on to. And I hold her back, which is almost as bad.

When I looked up from the watch, I heard a guttural growl. Bobcat maybe? I've seen one here before.

Not a bobcat. Bigger. Wider. It was a more temperamental beast, one that sported my colors. One of those moments where you doubt your senses and wonder if you might be hallucinating. I wasn't. Low to the ground and half-camouflaged by the tall weeds, a tiger crept toward me, its hunger apparent, its eyes almost mesmerizing.

My pulse ratcheted up, a sharp but pleasant feeling as fear suffused me, life and death tottering in the balance, yes, I thought *Let's tangle, kitty,* because on this unexpected safari it was him or me and better him than me, of that I was sure. I brought the rifle to my shoulder, sighted up, and held my breath.

How did it get here? From one of the zoos, I supposed.

Decades ago when Black Ep was gobbling up the zookeepers, not everyone euthanized their animals. Some they released into the wild. I'd noticed a family of South African springbok gazelles doing quite well here, but never a Bengali tiger before. Tigers in Michigan, who knew?

It stared darkly at me, contemplating an attack, then padded slowly to my left, circling. I followed it with my rifle, a white flash of sunlight reflecting off the gunmetal.

"Killed by a man-eating tiger," I told the cat in my sights, "is quite a nasty epitaph. Are you up to it?"

Years ago, I might have lowered the rifle and dared it to pounce, but I'm not quite as eager to die these days, and I have responsibilities besides.

I didn't particularly want to kill the thing, so I dropped my aim a bit, considering the low shot, which dredged up that old joke about the three-legged dog in the Wild West. The one where the dog moseys into the saloon, sidles up to the bar and drawls, "I'm lookin' for the feller who shot my paw."

penny

Entry #306: The Princess and the Squeezers –open–

They tried to squeeze me, the squeezers. Both of them. I underestimated their greed. Stupid miscalculation and it'll cost me.

Pandora showed up with the cousins and we took them on the tour—same drill as last year, except it took twice as long thanks to Sloane's broken leg and whatever malfunction this Haji cripple has. So there we are showing the porcelain room when Haji begs off and so does Sloane, so the group thins out, Tomi taking Haji one way, Brigit and Sloane going the other. I slip away too because Nature's calling, and that's when they intercept me.

"It's your lucky day," they tell me. "We thought it over and the answer's yes," but before I can say boo they slap me right in the face by saying they want five times what I promised them.

I'm all "Twenty-five thousand?" and Sloane actually has the audacity to flash teeth and say, "No, Penny, twenty-five thousand each."

That's a ridiculous amount of money—even for a princess of my means—and they don't care, Brigit saying, "We figured if you'd pay ten thou you'd also pay fifty." Bloodsuckers!

My head's buzzing with anger flies, these stupid, irrational thoughts—visualizations, really—where I'm plotting the exact trajectory of my spit, and wondering if it might catch the sunlight coming in from the window before splattering in the center of Brigit's dumbstruck face—or anticipating what it might sound like to kick Sloane's crutches out from under her (would it go clatter, trip, bang, scream or more like clatter, scream, trip, bang?)—but I'm calming everything down by thinking *don't sink to their level* over and over again. And I'm smiling because maybe they're kidding me, just testing to see if I can take a joke. And if they're not kidding, maybe they're just negotiating. And if they're negotiating, maybe I can go as high as twenty thousand, tops, if they let me pay them over time.

But they're not kidding, not negotiating, and they want all the money up front, the dirty witches, and they keep saying, "Do you want us to help you or not?" and don't believe me when I tell them I don't have that kind of money. Moms pay us for good grades, good attitudes and good behavior (and fine us for the lack thereof), and with me being the lucky girl that I am, that's a lucrative trifecta for me—so I'm no stranger to cash—and while Brigit and Sloane must realize that I make a lot, they've obviously overestimated how much. I bet they're so far behind me money's lost all meaning, like I'm some mythical El Dorado for them to plunder. Hey, let's rob Penny, we'll be rich!

Even if I could pay them what they wanted, there's obviously no trusting them. They'd probably just make a big show of being nice to me in public, but still cut me down with the things they say behind my back. They're liars and cheaters and what can you expect from people like that?

So I tell them, "No deal," which surprises them because they expected me to cave, and they look at each other like they don't know what to do. Just as I'm thinking they're about to come down in price, they go the other way and tell me I'd better pay them or they'll make things worse for me than they've ever been. Extortion, can you believe it? I'm way too mad to be intimidated, so I turn it around and say I'll go tell moms if they even look at me funny, and Sloane calls me snitch and rat, and Brigit says I've cried wolf so often that moms won't even believe me these days.

Now my attitude is if I'm going to do anything, I'm going to be the best at it, and if that means being the best snitch, so be it. "Just try it and I'll tell moms about your little secret," I tell them, and they're all "What secret?" so I tap my fingers to my lips and puff. They stop and look at me like I just cut the grass right under their feet, which of course is exactly what I did.

We all go into town from time to time to get supplies, but there's certain things we can take and certain things we can't. Like cigarettes, those are a big no-no, and I happen to know Brigit and Sloane have a whole stash of them. I wasn't going to say anything about it because I'm definitely pro–lung cancer where they're concerned, but if they're going to push me I'll push back any way I can.

My threat worked because they practically had a fit, calling me all kinds of things, "how dare you" this and "you'd better not" that, then gave into their fear and slunk away like weasels with measles. Satisfying to see the back of them, but the whole experience got on my nerves, and the sad part of it is what might have been.

The bright side? While this nasty business may have set me back to square one, square two breezed in sweet as all get-out. I caught up with Izzy and Lulu at the end of the tour, and we all compared notes on the cousins, and while they were discussing what going to Egypt would be like, I told them how I'd like to get to know Pandora better, but how she's a little leery of me, and then we talked about how hard it is to make up for bad first impressions. The great thing is I didn't even have to ask—they said they'd be happy to build me up to Pandora. And money never even came up, so I don't think I'll have to pay them!

That means I can spread my cash on the other girls, and try to build up a consensus, so if the gruesome twosome try to slander me, Pandora will say, "Oh, that's just Brigit and Sloane being Brigit and Sloane."

If I'm careful, I might be able to pull this off.

Lock, stock and barrel.

Entry #306: The Princess and the Squeezers –locked–

haji

The table is long, the chairs high-backed, but ergonomically designed and thus comfortable. Beneath us, a black-and-white-checkered marble floor. Grand arches of white and gold lead up to a stucco fresco on the ceiling. I am lost in all the details. It is a mythological scene with a swirling pattern of chariots, clouds, rainbows, and gods with thunderbolts clenched tightly in their fists.

Everything is immaculate and exquisitely set. This is anything but casual. I am used to dining with more simplicity.

We usually eat buffet style, Champagne says, but in honor of your visit, we thought we'd make this special.

Simply being here is a special occasion, I assure them.

I look around the table to smile graciously at my cousins. I have found nicknames for the ones with whom I am less familiar. There is Zoë the giggler, Isabelle the elbow-grabber, Luzia the inadvertent toe-stomper, Penelope the silent starer, Sloane in the cast, and Katrina the cherubic little girl. These are but temporary nicknames. I hope to replace them with more telling descriptors of their personalities once I come to know them as well as Brigit, Olivia and Tomi.

Tomi returns my gaze, friendly as ever, but with little hint of what we shared.

At Champagne's signal, Isabelle and Zoë rise up from the table to serve the dinner. I am learning how a regimented system of chores and responsibilities informs every aspect of my cousins' waking hours. In fact, every minute is accounted for. My siblings and I are unfamiliar with this kind of lifestyle. My father believes in personal freedom and consideration for others. When something needs doing, we do it.

We've prepared a special Egyptian meal, Champagne announces. The recipe comes from a pharaoh's tomb.

Proudly, she indicates a dish I know well. Melokhia soup, spicy with garlic and coriander, warm enough to thaw out the chill that has insidiously crept into me since our arrival. But as a steaming bowl is placed before me I am struck by the pungency of a dubious vegetable. What floats with the melokhia leaves? Spinach? Kale? Try as I might, I cannot identify it.

How kind of you to honor us, Ngozi says, once all the places have been served.

Shall we take a moment to reflect? Vashti asks.

I do not take her meaning at first, but then I realize that by reflect she means pray. Only if you would do so normally, I reply.

A moment of silence, she decides, despite my answer. She makes a point of bowing her head and closing her eyes, and I can see the ghost of a smile on her face. Our cousins follow suit, and soon so do we.

At home we frequently pray but never at mealtime. We often sing while cooking and my father considers that both a blessing upon the meal and a form of prayer in itself.

So this is new as well.

There, Vashti says.

Medicine, Pandora prompts. We have already taken ours for the day, I explain, but it seems our cousins have not. Tiny capsules of every conceivable color are consumed. They take more pills than we do, I note, even though they are healthier.

This accomplished, we hungrily turn our attention to the soup.

I feel many eyes upon me as I dip my spoon into the broth and take a taste. It is an altogether unfamiliar and unpleasant flavor, lingering on the tongue like wet wool. I take another sip just to test the theory. At last I can confirm that it is a truly horrible concoction.

We gathered the vegetables from our garden, Katrina proudly proclaims. Do you like it?

That you would go through so much trouble for us is truly touching, I tell her.

I think I know what killed Hessa, Ngozi whispers to me after his third bite.

Sadly, the best praise I can think to give the meal is that there is no meat in it. Dalila was under the mistaken impression that our German relatives are meat eaters, but they are as strict vegetarians as we. I eat as much as I can to avoid seeming rude. For me the experience underscores how different we are. Appetites vary wildly among species. I would not eat a pregnant scorpion, though a desert fox would. Or perhaps my cousins find the soup as disgusting as we do, but have simply joined our conspiracy to praise it.

I am thrilled when dessert is a bowl of fruit.

pandora

After dinner and the washing up, the kids go to the ballroom to play music and games, and Champagne and I tag along to keep an eye on them. We sit at a low glass table in the corner and drink ourselves silly, talking about old times and cheering whenever someone wins at laser shuffleboard.

"They're getting along so well," Champagne notes. "Like little ambassadors."

"Yes, what's not to like?"

"We've done right by them."

"Sure, you guys are great parents, all three of you."

"Four!"

"Oh, come on, I haven't done anything," I protest. "They're your kids."

"Don't be so modest," Champagne says, eyes shining from the cherry brandy. "You have more influence on them than you think. Which reminds me, there's a question of which one you're going to take under your wing."

"Because I'm running myself ragged?"

"Vashti and I both think you could use a little help, that's all. And the kids are finally old enough to pitch in."

"I have Rashid working for me right now."

"Rashid? Interesting. He liked the IVR so much we almost couldn't get him to leave. Does he have a knack for the technical side of it?"

"Don't know yet."

"Is he dependable? It's not always a good idea to have the kid who loves doughnuts working at the bakery."

"That's true. It's so easy to get lost in there."

"You don't have to tell me that." She grins. "You need someone who's focused on more than just having fun. What about Penelope? She's tech-savvy, follows directions, very determined."

I glance over. The girl has an intent look on her face and a cue in her hand, pushing a colorful disc of light. When she sticks the shot, knocking Ngozi's disc off, there's a telltale flash of wildfire in her eyes, a look that's competitive and hungry, the kind of hunger that can never be filled.

"There's something about her I don't trust." I shrug, pouring each of us another drink.

"Give her a chance, she might surprise you."

"She might. I just think she has a little growing up to do."

"Don't we all?" Champagne smiles. "Say, why don't you stay longer and hang out with us girls? Isaac won't mind if you're a couple of days late with the exchange."

"I can't," I tell her. "I'm heading south tomorrow, then west."

"West," she says. "Peru?"

"Idlewild."

"You're really serious?"

"He might need me."

I have to try and ignore the look of pity she's throwing at me.

"You're in complete denial if that's what you think. God, Pandora, he doesn't need you. He doesn't need anyone. Don't you think he's proved that? How can you be so loyal to someone who's turned his back on everyone?"

"He hasn't turned his back on me," I insist.

"Yes, he has," she snorts. "He's just been taking years to do it.

I'm not saying he doesn't have some feelings for you, but come on—when he keeps putting more time between conversations, can't you see what he's doing?"

"What?"

"He's weaning you off him. Trying to let you down slow and easy. Or maybe he's weaning himself off you? Either way, you don't need this, no one does."

I just drink. It's easier than admitting she's right.

"Am I right?" she asks, folding her arms across her chest.

"You don't know how much he's suffered."

"Oh, boo hoo," she says. "He's not the only one who lost someone. When Mercutio murdered the love of my life, did I have a tantrum and curl up in a little ball? No, I grieved, and pulled through it, and got on with my life. Because I saw the big picture of bringing these kids to life and making the world a better place."

"Yeah, well, you saw it, he didn't. That's who he is."

"Yeah, that's who he is," she says, derisively, draining her glass. "You sure know how to pick 'em."

"Frankly, Champagne, it doesn't amaze me that Hal's done what he's done. The amazing thing is that we haven't. After all we've lost, our friends, our innocence, the world itself?"

"Hooray for us? We're so exceptional, we should cut Hal a break? No, he doesn't get off that easily."

"Yes, he does."

"Not 'the pass' again."

"Absolutely, he gets a pass because we owe him!" I say, and I have to take a moment to control myself because my voice gets louder when I drink. I don't want to worry the kids, especially Isaac's kids, who keep looking over at me for reassurance. "It's really very simple. He put a stop to Mercutio. He killed him. He saved us from him. Without Hal, you and I would be dead or wishing we were dead. So he gets a pass."

She sighs. "I won't tell you I'm not grateful for what he did."

"You can't."

"That's right, I can't—because he did what needed to be done at the time. But now it's time for him to grow up."

She goes to the kitchen for coffee, leaving me to think about what she said. When she returns with the carafe, she's not alone, and I can tell from the look on Vashti's face that our conversation has been relayed.

"You really, really, really have to stop this," she says, taking my hand.

"Oh, Vash, what is this, an intervention?"

"If that's what it takes," Champagne says.

They both care about me—I recognize that. And appreciate it. But there are two agendas at work. There are Champagne's feelings about her first love, Tyler, and about her second love, Isaac. And with Vashti, there is a visceral hatred for Hal—picking him apart has always been a sport for her.

With a squeeze of my hand, Vash says, "Don't you realize he drove Simone to suicide?"

"It wasn't suicide, she overdosed."

"Semantics," she says.

"And he didn't drive her to it."

"I'm not so sure. Not everyone is as willing to take him at his word as you are. And psychologically it's interesting—he pushes the woman he loves over the edge, and now he's trying to do it with the woman who loves him."

"I don't think I'm drunk enough for this," I tell her.

"Listen, I'm all for you being in love," she says. "No one would deny you that. But at least let it be on equal terms."

"That's right," Champagne chimes in. "He's the one calling all the shots."

"Don't infantilize me, thank you. You know what I think whenever we get on this topic, whenever you back me into a corner? I think here I am talking with bitterheart number one and bitterheart number two."

"What do I have to be bitter about?" Champagne scoffs.

"Isaac, what else? The path not taken, and all that might have been. And you," I say, my eyes lighting upon Vashti, "always sabotaged everyone's relationships back in school, because if you weren't happy why should anyone else be? Or was it because you wanted all the girls to yourself?"

"Funny how your mind works," Vashti smirks, unfazed. "So telling people the truth is 'sabotaging relationships'? That's a curious interpretation of events."

"And for the record, I'm not carrying a torch for Isaac," Champagne protests. "It's just complicated with him, that's all."

Vashti arches an eyebrow. "Not too complicated, I hope. I hate to think of either of you being distracted when there's so much work to be done."

"The work has to come first," I admit—and then wonder if I'm kidding myself. No matter, because I've had enough of being under the microscope tonight, and grab at the chance to change the subject. After all, this is something we're going to disagree on forever.

"To the work," Champagne offers, her coffee cup raised.

"To the work," Vashti and I agree.

haji

We are warming to this place.

The girls have embraced Dalila, particularly Katrina, the littlest. She follows like a happy shadow. Ngozi has found an earthly paradise among jinn, playing games with Olivia, games he is only too happy to lose because every win she flashes her hazel eyes from behind thick lashes and his heart falls more in love with her. I watch them flirt over a game of Go and think he has made a wise choice.

It can only go so far, but still.

Since Hessa's death I have missed the sounds of girlish laughter. It thrills me to hear Dalila burst with such joyful freedom, her cries provoking her cousins to follow, like the call-and-response language of birds.

The girls are uniformly beautiful, white even teeth, strong healthy lithe bodies. Not a defect among them. If a baby with flaws such as mine were to be born into this family, would it be allowed to live? I imagine not. For this I say a blessing to my father. For the gift of life.

One of the older girls, Sloane, wears a transparent cast from her hip to her toes. At first I could not see it except for the pins in her ankle, but the outline became clear when I spotted the decorations and autographs gaily floating around its side. They call it a *glasscast,* though it is not really glass, but rather composed of tiny nanites that stiffen and relax as needed. Sloane showed me how it not only keeps her leg immobile but also secretes a topical painkiller. I wonder if I should ask Aunt Vashti to look at my condition. Or is my physiology too alien? My father specializes in human beings, while Vashti specializes in Waterbabies. There is a fairly substantial difference. And while gene therapy might fix my limp, it might also put my immune system at risk.

Brigit, Olivia and Tomi have all been good to us. Last year they were as shocked as we when they heard the news of Hessa's death. And though they did not know her well they mourned her passing with us. In our fashion. But the other girls were here when the tragedy struck. It is their insight I crave. What did they see? I have never been wholly satisfied with the explanation of how my sister departed from the earth. I carry so many questions and they must have knowledge I lack. It is all I can do not to let this friendly gathering spur me into an investigation of how Hessa died.

Instead I am teaching Zoë the basics of kite making. She has seen the ones I made last year for her sisters and now wants one for herself. I tell her Aunt Champagne has asked me to give a demonstration in front of the art class, but Zoë laments that she will not be here to see it, as she is replacing Sloane on the other half of this exchange. So I teach her all I can.

After a time she asks if this is what I want to do.

Do?

For a living, she says. Will you be a kite maker?

I will do whatever needs to be done, I tell her.

She does not understand at first. Then she giggles and calls me a utility player. Which I suppose I am. But so are we all, really. Why limit yourself to just one thing?

No, they see things differently here. There are areas of specialty. Vocations. Roles. She wants very much to be an ecologist, she says, and to help plan a future that keeps us far afield from the kind of damage our ancestors did to the environment. She is lobbying her mothers for that position, but they have not yet made up their minds.

Zoë tells me how the world, no longer choked by carbon emissions and overpopulation, has been steadily returning to a more natural state. But civilization has already done so much to put it out of balance. Take the plants, she says. Centuries ago, we made the mistake of introducing invasive species like purple loosestrife, black locust and kudzu all around the world, and now they're spreading unchecked. And take the animals, all the new shifts in the food chain.

What new shifts?

Think of the cows, she says, excited to have someone to teach. We kept so many as livestock, artificially inflating their populations, but we made them dependent on us to survive. We bred cows to be so big and beefy, most couldn't calve on their own. So those breeds died out while the hardiest breeds (longhorns, for example) took over. And without humans to eat them, their numbers have been skyrocketing. They have other predators, of course, but nothing kills cattle faster than Man. So in the years since the plague, the growing herds have been overgrazing. Now they're beginning to starve, dropping dead, their carcasses serving to nourish the soil.

And from that soil new grass will grow, I say, getting it. The cows tried to eat all the grass, but now the grass is eating the cows.

It is then that I see Dalila surrounded by girls, all inviting her to demonstrate the *sema*. She is suddenly shy and on her face I see her fight with herself. She loves to move but knows Hessa came before her. Can she measure up to her elder sister's masterful command of the whirling-dervish dance?

Yes, I tell her. Yes, because she is a magnificent dancer, and because Hessa will be guiding her every step. I am rewarded by a huge smile and she runs off to change into her camel's felt hat and the wide white skirt Hessa helped her sew.

No, I cannot dance, I explain to Zoë, begging off, but Tomi has seen me try and says I am selling myself short. I know all the steps, I admit, I simply lack the range of motion to do it well.

When she returns, my little sister commands attention as the girls form a circle around her. With great aplomb she explains that the dance is sacred to the Sufi path. It is performed to embrace all creation and so reach a higher plane of enlightenment.

She folds her arms into herself to form a one. To signify the unity of God. Then her skirt rustles as she turns about, arms outstretched, her hands positioned carefully. Katrina asks why it is necessary to keep your hands a certain way when you dance with your feet. Dalila explains that the right hand is elevated palm up to receive divine energy while the left is held palm down to channel that energy into the earth.

Sloane says, oh, of course, divine energy. Some of the girls react and Dalila must wait until their nervous laughter dies down.

Though she is smiling as well. With great dignity she moves to the center of the circle and tells her cousins that Sufis dance as the worlds dance. Which is to say we revolve. Right now there is revolution inside our atoms, revolution in our blood, and revolution in our planet's path around the sun. Everything is connected. The excitement builds and my sister frog, I realize, wields a flair for the dramatic that would make Hessa proud.

She tells the girls one foot never leaves the ground while twirling. And they may go as fast or slow as they please. Either way they will receive new awareness if they embrace the dance with a pure heart. She will chant there is no God but God. But the others can chant whatever they like.

She invites them to join in when they're ready and soon my sister is a whirling ball of energy, her skirt fluttering around her legs. Her form perfect. A transcendent look on her face as she chants.

Her cousins join in, twirling about her in orbit. What they lack in grace they try to make up for in exuberance. Katrina rises up on her toes, joyfully announcing that she is a ballerina. Brigit snaps her fingers as she spins.

Before long, Penelope's hand falls on my arm. Aren't you going to stop this? she asks. It is as much as she has said to me since our arrival.

Why should I put a stop to it?

She gives me a reproachful look. Can't I see they're making fun? Look, she says, look at Sloane.

I follow her index finger to watch Sloane hopping on her good foot, arms akimbo, her injured leg flung out in front of her.

Isn't this a sacred dance? she asks.

Yes, I admit, it's true.

Well, look at Brigit and Sloane hopping around like kangaroos.

I see what she means. My sister frog is performing with exact and lovely footwork, her hands in perfect position and her chant strong and true. While around her some of the smaller girls have gotten dizzy and flopped to the floor where they are rolling and giggling hysterically. The older ones still on their feet are indeed hopping around like kangaroos. But is it mockery? Or just high-spirited fun?

Raucous laughter fills the room and Penelope is off like a firecracker, silencing the music and stepping into the circle. She positions herself directly between Dalila and Brigit, arms spread as if to defend my sister from the older girl. It is a touching gesture, though perhaps misplaced. Dalila and Brigit get along famously. So I believe. They did last year, and I cannot guess what could have changed.

With controlled anger, Penelope rebukes Brigit and Sloane for making my sister the butt of their stupid jokes. I move to Dalila. She has stopped dancing and has begun to look about the room, confused, as if awakening from a long sleep.

Sloane suggests a new place for her crutch. Voices are raised. I think to play peacemaker, but Tomi catches my eye. She shakes her head no. Do not get involved. So I turn my attention back to my sister, who has come to the verge of tears. They're not making fun of me, Haji, they're my friends, she insists.

Thankfully, the adults come to restore order to the situation, but not before Dalila has rushed from the room. Ngozi is quick to pursue her and I hobble along as best I can. With a last glance over my shoulder, I see Pandora stepping in to separate Penelope from her sisters. Always ready to settle a dispute, Pandora.

In the anteroom outside the ballroom, my brother and I calm Dalila down. It is not so much that she feels the dance was spoiled, as it is her hating to see family in conflict. It reminds her too much of the bad blood between Mu'tazz and Rashid.

Later that evening, I take Penelope aside and thank her for defending my sister's honor. She tells me to just call her Penny. Her older sisters are bullies, she says. Especially when they are together. I should be on my watch for their cruelty.

I tell her my eyes did not catch the nuances of what was happening, but if they were indeed mocking her I appreciate the actions she took.

I'm happy to help, she says.

penny

Entry #307: The Princess and the Seven-Course Feast
-open-

Dinner was even more nauseating than usual. I'm still sick from it. Some kind of nasty Egyptian soup moms forced us to eat because they wanted our cousins to feel more at home. What's next, sand on the floor? They should have kept that recipe in whatever tomb they found it. I can't believe that's the kind of food they like over there.

Moms have always taught that my cousins are "different" as in "not better or worse, just different." Multicultural tolerance and all that good stuff—fine, I can get behind that if I have to—I just can't help feeling sorry for them. They're weighed down with all these silly traditions and spout "wisdom" from people I've never heard of. Technologically, they're not that far behind us, but Uncle Isaac must not put much stock in conveniences, because it's ooh and ahh time whenever they get exposed to anything remotely fun. Lulu calls them "acoustics" because they've never been plugged Inside. And biologically speaking, let's not forget they're Humanity 1.0, which is clearly not just different but worse.

But Pandora must really love them. I've been swiping glances at her since she got here and every time they go to her she lights

up. My theory is she feels even sorrier than I do about how re-tarded they are. Like the way you love a pet because it's innocent and uncomplicated. So from her perspective, my cousins might actually carry more influence than anyone else. Useful then. Aces on my side.

The little girl was dancing because she loved God so damn much, and Brigit and Sloane were acting like asses, so I did my good deed for the day. I defended the weak against the strong. A stunt for Pandora's benefit, I admit, a demonstration of character, and a re-cruitment ploy for my cousins' hearts and minds. I don't mean this cynically. I like helping people, I do. I just believe in helping myself first. If I don't look out for my best interests, who will?

Not Izzy certainly. Today she stabbed me. It felt like she was stabbing me. Maybe I deserved it. I can feel her words like a weight against my heart. Izzy is not my friend anymore, which means that when I feel like confiding in someone Lulu and this journal will have to pick up the slack.

What happened was full-blown stupid. Remember how I slapped Brigit and Sloane down by threatening to reveal their stash? Well, Izzy fed me that information, and it was confidential. When I made my threat I exposed her as the one who told me. Like I said, Brigit isn't completely stupid—she traced it to Izzy and Izzy admitted it.

So there was a whole lot of shrieking and recriminations and gnashing of teeth, and Brigit and Sloane gave her an ultimatum —be friends with them or friends with me—and Izzy, who always wanted to be friends with everyone, who said she never wanted to choose sides, finally took one and it wasn't mine.

Okay, I'm partly to blame here. Why deny it? I just didn't think. That's what I did. That's my big, terrible crime. I needed something to put those girls back in their place and it's all I had to work with. I didn't realize it would cause such a problem. But I'm not the only one at fault. If the gruesome twosome didn't want anyone to know about their smoking, they should have done everyone a favor and sewn their lips shut. Like the Thomas Edison quote Pandora loves so much, "Three can keep a secret if two of them are dead." And let's not take honest Izzy off the hook—she could have simply played dumb and denied ever telling me. They would've had to prove it, and how could they? They'd just have thought maybe I'd been spying on them. Or maybe Brigit would think Sloane told me and vice versa. Who knows?

But no, instead we've got idiocy all around. A seven-course feast of stupid. An orgy of it. And my friendship with Izzy is dead like seeds on hard stone.

Haikubot: scan and summarize.

Words carelessly said
Little tragedies of youth
I miss my good friend

God, you're useless, Haikubot.
Lock this puppy.

Entry #307: The Princess and the Seven-Course Feast
  -locked-

haji

After breakfast and Pandora's rushed goodbye, we call home and then try the links Aunt Vashti installed behind our ears. I say Ngozi's name from another room and the palace's communication system puts us in direct conversation. A successful test. The technology is likely to give us headaches, but these have yet to materialize. All I feel is a slight sting.

How bad do you think the headaches will get? Ngozi asks.

Vashti says they will fade over time.

Why do we need these things anyway?

They want to keep track of us. New safety procedures because of Hessa.

Have you seen the bathrooms? he asks. He tells me how the toilets analyze all waste and transfers the data to Vashti's console. He links Dalila into our conversation and tells her as well, just to hear her amused, semi-disgusted reaction.

Between all their precautions, we should be safe, I tell them.

Piggybacked on the communication link is a neural link, the prerequisite for entering the IVR. I have begun to think of it as a device that makes one more susceptible to hypnosis. It amplifies the computer's signals to such a degree that we begin to perceive that stimuli as reality.

Father must have one, Ngozi says.

Had.

He extracted it? Why?

I suppose he has no more use for it, I say.

Half an hour to another world, Dalila muses. The one Rashid loves so much.

She cannot wait. Neither can Ngozi.

Fifteen minutes later, I take a call from Malachi. He asks me how I am feeling. He offers to be my tour guide on the Inside. There is so much for me to see.

I am grateful, of course. And I assume that he means to do the same with my siblings. But when I link the news to them, they tell me that he has not contacted them at all. And when I ask Tomi about it, she says Malachi never does this sort of thing. He stays well away from her and well away from her sisters

So what does he want with me?

pandora

Today is day no for me. I've got my yes days and no days, and this one's definitely a no.

I oversleep but that's hardly worth mentioning. The kids aren't ready to go but that's not a big deal either. I leave my ankh behind and have to double back to get it because it's an exact replica of the one Hal gave me back in IVR, but let's leave that out of it as well. Never mind that it takes me twenty minutes to get my copter to start. Never mind how Zoë, Izzy and Lulu spend the whole flight singing. Never mind Malachi reporting that Rashid accidentally broke my autoclean. Even Isaac being in a strange mood when I arrive with the kids isn't so bad because he's not the kind of person who can function well on no sleep, and he stayed up all night arguing with Mu'tazz. None of that makes this day no.

I take my leave from Isaac because I'm ready to fly west. Because I can't wait any longer—I have to find out what happened to Hal.

Day no comes from a grainy, blurry image. "If you're going west, you might want to make it Peru," my eye in the sky tells me. "Not Idlewild."

"Oh, not you too, Malachi. You can't talk me out of this."

"Pandora, I have a satellite photo of Halloween."

And as I watch numbly, he shows me an image of a man standing outside Gedaechtnis HQ in Idlewild, Michigan. A bearded man with orange hair, strong and thin and wild, a cold look in his midnight eyes.

"He's alive," I say, flooding with relief that curdles as soon as

I realize that he's not injured in any way, which means he's simply not answering my calls. Why is he pushing me away? Does he mean to cut me off completely? I can't decide if I'm more hurt than angry or the other way. It's not worth figuring out, really—there's plenty to go around.

I put my feelings into words and send them to him, knowing he won't reply to this message either. Goddamn it, Hal, what are you doing? I'm your only friend.

So what can I do but get back out of my copter and tell Isaac what's happened. He promises me a shoulder to cry on when he's got his nieces settled. He says he'll go to Peru with me. I can always depend on him—but somehow his reliability just makes me feel that much more alone.

"We'll make it a field trip for the kids," he says. "We'll have fun."

"Fun," I say, my mind thousands of miles away in a day yes that may never come. "Sure, fun, I could use some of that. Let's go get us a monkey."

haji

It is less like dreaming and more like daydreaming, but with clarity that rivals what I experience in the waking world. It is a realm of enormous possibility and endless convenience. There is nothing ungodly about it. Not as far as I can tell.

This domain is called Telescope. I stand in a pastel suburban neighborhood, rows of empty houses spanning as far as my eyes can see, while overhead a meteor shower bombards the atmosphere beneath constellations heretofore unknown to me. All simulation, but there is something delightful about it. I do not see it as a mockery of all God's creation as Mu'tazz once termed it, nor do I understand why my father has kept me from it for so long, though I am sure he has his reasons.

A tutorial teaches me how to exchange this environment for a mountain canyon at sunset, brilliant red rock walls towering over me and sagebrush at my feet. I experiment with things, purchasing a temporal effect called Strobe. Soon, the sun is whipping through the sky, rising and setting like a fiery cannonball. Another sunrise, and another, and I cannot dismiss it as high-speed photography, because I am there. I can feel its heat and absence thereof, off and on, off and on, like a child playing with heaven's thermostat. A year of sunrises whooshes over me in just minutes, and a stubborn part of me wants to believe that I am in fact a year older, if not a year wiser.

I know nothing about economics. What has monetary value anymore? There are only a handful of us here now, and with all the world's treasures there is surely more than enough to share. And yet, Inside, everything is monetized. A floating window the size of a picture frame displays my ledger in deep luminous green.

Assets	Service	From	Date
¤50,000.00	Welcome!	Vashti	Sep. 21
¤3,180.68	Tutorial Funds	IVR Tutorial	Sep. 22
¤200.00	Kite Making Workshop (Advance)	Champagne	Sep. 22
¤5.00	Manners	Champagne	Sep. 22
¤5.00	Hygiene	Champagne	Sep. 22
¤5.00	Attitude	Champagne	Sep. 22

I am treating it as a game. I will happily accept whatever they give me, but it has no relevance to my life in the real world.

I can purchase something called a Nanny but this is expensive and I must conserve my funds until I understand the value of things.

Malachi materializes (so to speak, because I do not believe he is made of any material but light) before me, craning his neck up to observe the sun's rapid flight through the sky.

Tempus fugit, he notes with a smile. Stacks of newspapers spring into being about me, each stack chest high, and so many that I feel like a maze is forming with myself at the center. I thank him but wonder aloud how I will find the time to read them all. Just read the headlines, he suggests. And I will, I assure him, though I do not put much emphasis on birthdays and cannot see the point in learning what happened only on the dates that coincide with the day of my birth. Would the newspapers from the most pivotal days in history not make for more illuminating reading? I am one human being out of billions, surely my birthday cannot be all that important.

Malachi's special interest in me is baffling, but apparently harmless enough, so I count myself lucky to have him as my guide. He takes me by the hand to lead me on a whirlwind tour of places real and fictional, with no logic to his choices that I can discern. At each stop he asks me my opinion, genuinely curious about what I think. We visit parts of Liverpool, Los Angeles, Middle Earth, Metropolis, Beijing, Tokyo and Oz. As we travel, I begin to understand the pricing. If an experience can be termed educational, it is inexpensive, but the more escapist the locale, the higher the price. Anything with salacious content carries an exorbitant tax, pushing the total well beyond the funds my aunts have given me.

With each new step on the journey, I sense Malachi's mood darkening, as if my presence is growing increasingly offensive to him. As if I am disappointing him with word or deed, or perhaps there is something I should be doing that I am not, despite my appreciation and enthusiasm. When I ask him if anything has gone wrong, he gives me a resigned look and tells me yes. Yes, but there is nothing to be done about it. Memes don't nest in the double helix. It's not your problem, he says. Don't ever make it your problem.

I have no idea what he is talking about.

Never mind, he says. I'm a moody thing, Haji, pay no attention to me.

Though the encounter with Malachi leaves me unsettled, the rest of my time Inside fares much better. Ngozi and Dalila are having the time of their lives and I am happy to learn that Rashid is Inside as well, plugged into the system from Pandora's console in Athens. He has modeled his domain after a Monte Carlo casino resort, and populated it with well-dressed aristocrats and graceful debutantes. It is so strange seeing people in such number, even if they are unreal. I feel like we are being haunted.

It takes some getting used to, Rashid admits, but you can do anything here. The only limits are your imagination and your bank account. Steak?

I glance over at the dark and smoking slab on his plate and pass on the offer.

Then how about some baccarat?

Gambling, brother?

Harmless fun. You play for chips, Haji, nothing real. You don't put your prosperity at risk. You can't mortgage your immortal soul.

I have no fear for my immortal soul.

He opens his hands as if to ask, Then what am I waiting for?

I sigh. Are there not better things for us to do?

You might actually be good at it, he tells me, dissecting his meal with a knife and fork. You have the temperament. Quick mind, don't care if you win or lose. And deep down, you know everything is a gamble. Every choice you make in life is a bet. You're gambling right now with every breath.

All right. If I play a few hands with you, will you take a gamble for me?

What kind?

The kind that really matters.

Oho, high stakes, he grins. I'm intrigued.

Rashid, I say, the longer I stay here the more convinced I become that our sister's death was no accident.

He stares dumbly at me. What else could it be?

I stare back at him until he looks down at his steak, puzzled or troubled by what I have suggested.

You have evidence?

Intuition, I tell him.

Well, I prize intuition as much as anyone, and your instincts have always been terrific, but I think you're wrong on this. She got sick and died. Let it go.

Not until this feeling lets go of me.

Dad already investigated this. If it's good enough for him . . .

Do you want to gamble or not, Rashid?

How? he says.

You know the Inside a lot better than I do. Can you make me a list of all the places Hessa visited before she died?

I don't have that kind of access, though I suppose I could dig around a bit.

There's your gamble.

But what good would it do?

I shrug. No good, possibly. Or there might be a clue. I want to see what she saw and know what she knew.

Why don't you just ask Vashti?

I am asking you.

Oh, you don't trust her, he says.

I have no reason not to trust her.

Maybe, but you still don't.

I tell him trust does not enter the equation at all. It is simply better to leave Vashti out of it. Better to leave out all the adults, because if I am being foolish there is no point in troubling them with my folly, and if I am not being foolish, if there is in fact evidence of foul play, then the adults may have reason to keep that evidence hidden.

For Hessa's sake, my brother accedes.

Baccarat turns out to be more fun than I expect. I catch on after some initial confusion, and start winning once I try counting cards. Which seems devious, though Rashid assures me I am allowed to count. I quit when winning starts to matter to me. No good can come from that.

Moments later I am sprinting down a cobblestone path, my *tatami* sandals slapping the ground like rainfall as I rush headlong at my enemy. The sword I clutch in my hands carries with it a feeling of power, but also a sense of weakness. I am no warrior. In the real world this is a choice I would not make.

With both hands I thunder the blade from high to low, the whistling sound pleasing me, despite how badly I miss, my balance lost, my imperfect legs lurching me well past my foe. Immediately he buries his sword between my shoulder blades, but I feel only pressure where I should feel pain, because the Inside has been nerfed.

Death before dishonor, I say.

That was a little of both, Tomi winces, promising to turn the difficulty down.

Her domain is a poetic interpretation of twelfth-century Japan, decorated with cherry blossoms and paper lanterns, wooden bridges and koi ponds. I am dueling a kimono-clad samurai by a misty grove of flowering plum trees. With the difficulty reduced I am able to hold my own against him, parrying his thrusts and slashes until I can dispatch him with a long diagonal cut.

Nice *kiri gaeshi,* she says, matching a name to my maneuver.

Is that what I did?

Your form could use some work, but yes.

As I stare at the fallen warrior, his kimono split by my blade, Tomi reassures me that I have murdered nothing more than a lifeless simulation. I have spilled no blood and caused no pain. The opponent is not sentient the way Malachi is sentient.

Thank heavens for that, because I enjoyed it. First gambling and now violence, though in truth no harm was done. Still, I must watch myself and pay attention to why I do the things I do. Am I on a slippery slope? I must meditate on this later on.

Why is there no blood? I ask.

I can't afford it, she explains, slightly embarrassed by this admission. My mothers have placed a high premium on blood and it will be some time before I can unlock it.

They disapprove of bloodshed?

They'd prefer I study. But they understand this is just a hobby of mine, and that they're partly to blame for it by naming me what they did.

She tells me about her namesake, Tomoe Gozen, Japan's most legendary female samurai. She squints her eyes, remembering, her expression beatific and impossibly far away. She says:

Tomoe was especially beautiful, with white skin, long hair and charming features. She was also a remarkably strong archer, and as a swordswoman she was a warrior worth a thousand, ready to confront a demon or a god, mounted or on foot. She handled unbroken horses with superb skill; she rode unscathed down perilous descents. Whenever a battle was imminent, Yoshinaka sent her out as his first captain, equipped with strong armor, an oversized sword and a mighty bow, and she performed more deeds of valor than any of his other warriors.

It is a quote from *The Tale of the Heike,* she explains. I have not read it, and she offers to lend it to me once I have finished the other books.

What about you? I never thought to ask about your name.

I am named after no man, I explain. Haji simply means a person who has made a pilgrimage to Mecca, though it might also refer to a child who was born during that pilgrimage. The latter definition applies to me.

You were born in Mecca?

No, but the date of my birth coincides with the time of year one is meant to perform the Hajj.

Okay, she says. Have you done it yet?

My father will take me one day.

There's one in here, you know. A simulation.

I remember Mu'tazz telling me about it. The awe-inspiring sense of community and oneness, thousands of believers rapt in ecstatic fervor, all circling the Kaa'bah, drawn to the holy relic it contains. The Black Stone, focal point for prayer. Touch it and it can absorb your sins. Mu'tazz told me of his joy upon reaching it, a feeling of lightness throughout his soul, but the next day Hessa fell sick and he realized it had not cleansed him at all. It was simply an illusion, he said, a cruel mirage, glitter to distract him from the holy path. Still, I want to touch it. With the real Black Stone lost, a mirage might be the next best thing.

I suppose on some level you won't really be Haji until you do it, she says.

And will you not really be Tomi until you can win battles like Tomoe Gozen?

I'll never be that good, she shrugs.

But she is very good, graceful as a wisp of smoke, her mind and body working in harmony as she demonstrates her skill with the katana blade. With the difficulty raised, her foe is dangerous and quick, but she stops him in mid-slash with a strike to his chest.

Sen, she says, explaining. We both strike but mine is faster, she says.

She steps away, settles back into a new stance, her left foot forward, her sword elevated high above her head. He watches her footwork, focused, ready. She dances in and I see his muscles tense, but before his blade can move, hers is a blur of motion, crashing down upon his brow.

Sen no sen, she smiles. He commits to a strike, but I cut him down before he can.

Again she steps back, this time keeping her sword low and away, blocking his view of it with her long legs. Cautiously, he inches forward. Closer still. She stands perfectly motionless. Then she pivots, sudden as a shooting star, clipping his neck before he can react at all.

Go no sen. He makes no strike. I stop his mind. I strike him before the thought is in his head.

Quite a talent you have. I am thoroughly impressed.

No talent at all, she says. Just practice. Put in the time, you'll be just as good.

Perhaps, I shrug. But I am not sure I would find the art as you have. You have made poetry of it.

It is poetry, she agrees, her pretty smile sweeping across her face with the same swiftness as her blade. That's exactly how I see it.

She tells me of her forthcoming sequel to *The Strength of Spiders,* a collection called *Frozen Flowers,* and how dueling clears her mind to write. When I ask her where the title comes from and what it means, she tells me that it stems from research work she does for Vashti, but the subject saddens her and I do not press.

Is it lonely being a samurai? I ask.

Sometimes.

Does anyone ever challenge you and win?

Oh, you want to see a challenge, she says.

Soon I am standing in another time and place, dirty water splashing my legs as a wooden cart rolls by. A crowd of peasants race after the cart, and inside I can see the haggard faces of an aristocratic family, identical looks of resignation and fear in their eyes. I shiver not only because the temperature has dropped. I see Tomi and I have become anachronisms in our feudal Japanese garb, but Penny is at home here. It is her domain, a re-creation of the French Revolution as interpreted by a book I have not read: *The Scarlet Pimpernel*. Penny wears the raiment of a Jacobin with her black cloak and red cap of liberty, but I will learn that she is merely disguised as a revolutionary, so she might help the aristocrats, as she puts it, cheat Madame Guillotine.

You're throwing down the glove? she asks.

An exhibition for Haji, Tomi says.

Why not? It's been a while since you played Chauvelin to my Pimpernel. And I know just the place.

Penny's choice for a battlefield is the Louvre. Not the courtyard, but actually within the great museum, an Inside version of it at least, practically bursting with artwork from the ages, and treasures I have only seen in books.

V.C. won't like this, Tomi says, which Penny brushes off with a shrug.

We come to the famed Apollo Gallery, splendiferous and huge with its high arched ceiling, home to exquisite paintings, sculptures and tapestries, and staggering *objets d'art*. I feel like a magpie here, my eyes lighting upon so many glass-encased rarities that glitter, sparkle or shine, from 137-carat diamonds to the French Crown Jewels. When I am done browsing, I notice my cousins have taken positions at opposite ends of the hall.

Rules? Tomi asks.

Your katana against my cut-and-thrust saber, enhanced, seven kills, says Penny, making a strange gesture with her hand and pulling a backsword from nothingness.

You really want to spend the extra money for enhanced? Tomi asks.

After what I paid you, I think you can afford it, she pointedly replies, and Tomi acknowledges the comment with a tacit tilt of her head.

The girls salute each other, a reverence that strikes me as meaningful to Tomi and perfunctory to Penny. The battle is joined.

I expect Tomi to advance swiftly but she does not, edging forward with glacial caution, holding her blade tightly with both hands. She has respect for her sister's abilities but I am not convinced it is mutual.

Penny makes a game of dancing around the glass exhibits, snaking a lazy, circuitous path, and forcing Tomi to adjust her footing accordingly. The psychology of it interests me. There is a poetry in what she is doing, but it is not Tomi's poetry.

Haji, how should I get my first kill? Penny calls. By pace, by force or by fraud?

I have a fair idea what force and fraud are. What do you mean by pace?

Superior speed, she says.

Go with that, I suggest, my words tickling her funny bone somehow.

Go with that, she giggles, freeing her hair from her cap, and tossing the covering not aside but at Tomi's head. Instinctively, my first kiss raises her blade to block, which is all Penny needs to come in fast and low. The saber thrust is skillful and clean, and I watch as a ghostlike image of Tomi emerges with a harp in one hand and a stone tablet (carved with the number one) in the other. The angelic simulacrum rises up from her body, floating up through the ceiling and away. It is too cartoony to be moving, but I did not expect it and I find myself astonished.

Enhanced setting, Penny explains with a grin.

Touché, Tomi tells her, verbally conceding the kill.

That was superior speed? I ask.

Of course not, Penny laughs. That was an attack by fraud.

Illegal, then?

No, Tomi says, it's perfectly legal. Let's go, Penny. *En garde.*

For the next few minutes, I watch Penny try to demonstrate a kill by superior speed. She has a reach advantage, I note, fighting one-handed with the saber while Tomi holds her katana in two. It lets Penny scuttle in, snipe with the saber and retreat before Tomi can counter. Hit and run. But Tomi parries everything, rarely even trying to counterattack, content to let her opponent hammer away at her guard. The logic of it escapes me. I see Tomi giving ground, backing up into a corner. She will run out of room eventually.

You can at least try and hit me, Penny taunts. But Tomi does not answer.

It begins to dawn on me that Penny has two terrible enemies in the room with her, and neither of them are Tomi. The first is an enormous need to show off, to have her opponent and, perhaps even more importantly, her audience (me) appreciate how adroit and clever she is. This may be even more important than scoring the kill. The second enemy is frustration. She is no more patient than a starving animal, and though she tries to camouflage her emotions, the pinched and prickled expressions she makes show me she is deeply irritated by every strike she attempts that does not hit home.

Tomi simply draws it out, making allies of these enemies, and before long Penny has overcommitted herself, rushing in with a wild and desperate slash that cuts only a painting in two. Tomi's katana flashes in, slicing wickedly at an arm, the virtual wound not bloody but aglow with colorful light. Injured, Penny begins to tremble, not in fear, but in computerized simulation of what such a wound might do. She stumbles back, unable to defend herself, and Tomi dispatches her with a blow to the neck.

When the ghostly image of Penny appears, I half expect it to sink down through the floor, but instead it follows the path Tomi's first life blazed, rising up toward heaven.

Touché, Penny grudgingly acknowledges, her illusory wounds healing as the system resets.

For the rest of the duel Tomi dominates, feeding Penny's frustrations and feasting on her mistakes. While Tomi scores a total of six kills, Penny is only able to get two, the second coming only after toppling one of the displays, the confetti of glass shards harmless to her boots, but treacherous to Tomi's bare feet.

Before a winner can be declared, an outraged voice puts a halt to their battles. Girls, excuse me? Excuse me! What on earth do you think you're doing, she shouts, this is the Louvre, not a gymnasium!

This Champagne is positively striking, far more beautiful than the one I know. She is wearing her Inside face, the one Gedaechtnis scientists predicted her real face would grow into but never did. The resemblance is clear, but it is as if she has been touched with some minor magic now, a kind of glamour. Even in anger, there is a grace and a delicacy to her features, and in her yellow sunflower dress she makes quite a contrast to my dueling cousins in their masculine clothes.

Relax, Mom, Penny says, there's no harm done. She bends down to collect the two halves of the painting she slashed, a commemoration of one of the Twelve Labors of Hercules (I believe his ninth), and shakes them in such a way that the damage vanishes like an image from an Etch-A-Sketch. It looks whole again, as good as new. At the same time, Tomi spends a tiny sum to clean and reset the room, restoring everything to just how it was before the duel began.

That's not the point, Champagne says. It's about respect. I don't care if it's real or unreal, fixable or unfixable. Don't you have any feeling for the amount of time and effort artists put into their craft? Look around. Take a look at truth and beauty, not stage props to be trampled underfoot!

She lectures them until I step forward. Apologies, but this is my fault, I tell her. They wanted a place to duel and I wanted to see the Louvre, so I convinced them to come here. They both expressed misgivings and I simply insisted.

She lectures me, and she fines me, as is the custom here, but it is money I am only too happy to pay.

Kicked back out to the cold Parisian streets, I rub my hands together and slip them into my pockets. Where I notice something there. Something metallic and cool that was not present just minutes before. I reach in and take it. Tracing my thumb over the grooves and ridges, I hold it up to the fading sunlight.

What's that you have? Tomi asks.

penny

Entry #308: The Princess and the Off Chance -open-

There's nothing like a fencing match to get the blood pumping. Revitalizing, that's what it is. Years ago there was a good stretch when my sister Tomi used to spar every day with me. Not so much these days, but today she showed up with Haji in tow and it was like old times again.

Winning a duel against Tomi is like winning a snowball fight with a cat. It's not much of a challenge, and when you've won it's hard not to feel guilty. Still, it's always more fun facing a real opponent than a simulation. How else can you know how good you are if you don't face your peers? (Such as they are, ha-ha.)

I'm a brilliant fencer but this time—for Haji's benefit—I decided to draw it out and make it sporting. Unfortunately, Champagne chased us off right when I was about to win, so we called it a draw. Then I gave Haji a tour of the premises but he had the nerve to say it reminded him of *The Three Musketeers* (fine, whatever) and *The Adventures of Robin Hood* (!) of all things, as if I'd really play at being some socialist bandit because how dare the rich stay rich and the poor stay poor. God forbid the smart and the talented fare better than the masses. Hasn't history shown us there are some people in the world who know what they're doing and some who don't, and the ones who don't should shut up and follow the ones who do? Besides, Robin Hood is just a small-time philanthropist, stealing from King John's tax revenue—big freaking deal—while my man Scarlet saves lives, and he does it cleverly, and with style.

Anyway, I offered Haji my *Scarlet Pimpernel* books but he apparently has too much on his reading list already. No problem, my new opera, *La légende immortelle du mouron rouge,* happens to be on this very subject, and he'll get a front-row ticket when it's done.

And speaking of opera, I'm living one. Before she left for Egypt, my good friend Lulu—who said she'd help me for nothing—took one heck of a snack from the greed tree. She actually had the gall to say she wanted ten thousand big ones. Et tu, Lulu?

Someone must have told her how I was spending my cash, because she bellyached about me paying the others to do something she said she'd do freely. She stuck her bottom lip out and said it wasn't fair, but it's absolutely fair. She made a deal with me—maybe not such a great deal for her, but a deal—and then she reneged. What's so hard to understand about that? And why? Why am I fated to have all my friends betray me? Is it me? Am I cursed? Brigit and Sloane used to be my best friends, once upon a time, and look how they turned out.

It doesn't matter. If I can get what I want just this once, if Aunt Pandora sits me down, looks me square in the eye and says, "Yes, Penny, will you please learn from me, and take over when I'm gone?" then I'll have the rest of my life locked and loaded. That's the governing dynamic. Then I won't just be the Queen of England, but Queen of the Inside, controller of that universe, and anyone who wants superior education or entertainment has to come to me, and only finds what she wants with my blessing.

So forget Lulu. She can go back to being Luzia the loser. I

hexed her and the ridiculous opera I've been helping her with. Nine arias about nine planets—how stupid is that? I don't need her anyway. I've got Tomi (¤7,500.00), Zoë (¤5,000.00), Katrina (¤1,000.00) and now Olivia (¤6,000.00) in my pocket. And I know they're doing right by me because Champagne said there's been a lot of talk about me, and when I asked if it was good talk she said Pandora seemed to think so.

The Sufis remain the unknown element. I sense money doesn't mean much to them, so instead of paying them I've just been trying to be nice. The little girl doesn't want much to do with me, but a smile at Ngozi seems to go a long way, and Haji finds me interesting. But then, he seems to find everything interesting, so who knows?

Olivia says there may be yet another piece on the chessboard.

I don't talk about Olivia much because she's pretty forgettable, but I'll take all the help I can get. She is literally a train-spotter. While I've been building an homage to a timeless work of fiction, all she's done is collect trains and train stations—how nerdy is that?—and she's hooked them all up together as a mechanism to go from domain to domain. So from Tomi's domain you can hop on an elevated Japanese bullet train and by the time it reaches mine everything around you will have morphed into a French or British train, say the 300-kilometer-per-hour TGV or the Flying Scotsman. It's a bit stupid, really, because why simulate a trip somewhere when you can go there instantly? Maybe it's some kind of experimental art project, because Champagne seems to like it, but I don't get it. Not my problem, thankfully, but what's Olivia going to do with her life, be a travel agent? Good luck.

I met her in her home of Grand Central Terminal, circa 1917, with soldiers and sailors saying goodbye to their loved ones. She had Ngozi on her arm and I dare say he's smitten with her, apparently poisoned with hormones telling him to breed with her—again, good luck—but he got the hint and gave us some privacy, which gave me a chance to discreetly buy her support.

We boarded a train with red, white and blue bunting on the caboose and rode together past flag-waving crowds, and past an-archists in their shabby clothes with crudely painted signs that screamed, "American Boys Belong in America!" "No European Expansion!" and "Impeach Wilson!" Everyone wore hats back then—that's a look I hope comes back in style.

Upon taking my money, Olivia said she'd do all she could, but that if I really wanted to win Pandora over I should get Malachi on my side.

"He's just a program," I said.

"So what if he is? Say you were a painter and you wanted to be van Gogh's apprentice, what better endorsement could you get than from his finest brush?"

"Why not get all the programs, then? Einstein, Aristotle, Dar-win, van Gogh, why not Genghis Khan? I can ask them all to speak on my behalf along with the conductor who took our tickets, but none of them are real. I'll look silly—it won't help my cause."

She chewed that over and said, "You could try Halloween."

I tried very hard not to laugh at her. "He's dead."

"As good as dead," she said, suggesting a difference that I couldn't see.

"Have you ever talked to him? I sure haven't. Except for Pan-dora, no one's heard from him in years. It's like he doesn't even exist."

"That's my point," she said. "For us he doesn't exist, but you better believe he does for her."

"Lovelorn despair?"

"She'd do anything for him."

"You're exaggerating," I said.

"Go to the shrines," she told me. "Listen to how she talks about him. And then imagine if you could get him on your side. How could she say no?"

So I went. Picture a palatial temple atop Mount Olympus, white Corinthian columns holding up the lattice ceiling, and cerulean sky beyond. Completely empty, except for a circle of ceremonial urns—six of these—on raised platforms in the center. That's the domain Pandora set up to honor our great pantheon's dead and missing. We call it the shrines.

Four shadows—Lazarus, Tyler, Simone and Mercutio—assumed room temperature years before I was born, but the last two—Fantasia and Halloween—still live, presumably, though it's an arguable point. No urn for Hessa yet, which I take as a good sign—that the shrines haven't been updated just shows how busy Pandora's been and how badly she needs a helping hand.

The way it works is you walk up and touch an urn and imagery pops all around you like a holoshow. They're tributes, mostly, psychedelic and sentimental glimpses at who these aunts and uncles were, the things they cared about, the domains they made their own. You can watch it with music selections from their personal collections, or with commentary from a trio of audio tracks. First is Champagne's because she always has to be first, Pandora's comes second, and the last track is Vashti's because she always has to have the last word—or maybe it's just alphabetical, I'm not sure. I don't come here much because—well, don't get me wrong, I know these people had a lot to do with how we got here—but what effect on my life do they have now? They exist without any gravitational pull, and in my book that makes them shadows.

But maybe Halloween has some influence yet.

He's one of the two murderers in my family. Mercutio's the first, and then Halloween murdered him. Possibly I make three for giving Hessa the evil eye, but let's not get into all that. My understanding of how things went is that Mercutio went crazy and killed Lazarus and Tyler, and maybe Simone, and then Halloween had to put him down like a rabid dog. I might have it wrong though.

No one can agree as to exactly why Mercutio did what he did. Champagne thinks he just went unhinged. He was always

weak and couldn't take the shock of what happened to the human race. When he discovered that he'd been lied to, that billions
were dead and only a few still lived, his moral compass broke and
he decided to settle old scores, starting with Lazarus, whom he always hated. And after your first murder, it gets easier—so I've
heard—and when he found he had a taste for killing, he just
couldn't stop. The whole kid in a candy store thing.

Pandora thinks it was a sex thing. Over the years, all the girls
rejected his advances, so when he had the chance he murdered
the boys. She says there's that old expression, "Not if you were
the last man on Earth," and he only had to kill four people to
test the theory. If he were the only boy left, the girls would have
no other choice but to pick him to repopulate the Earth. But the
joke was on him—it's eighteen years later and still no one's gotten pregnant, 'cause anti–Black Ep drugs are hell on the ovaries.

Vashti remains unconvinced that Mercutio did it at all. It's
possible, she admits, but so much of what happened comes only
from Halloween's say-so, and she doesn't trust him not to lie. If
Mercutio is guilty after all, then Gedaechtnis is to blame—that's
the corporation that genetically engineered my moms' generation.
To combat Black Ep, they designed each of them with slight variations, and in some cases those variations backfired. Fantasia, for
example, is purportedly schizophrenic. Vashti suspects that Mercutio lacked the empathy gene, and between that and runaway
testosterone he was an accident waiting to happen. Completely
treatable, she says, with proper medication—and that's the tragedy
of her generation, four people buried thanks to a genetic engi-
neer's slight miscalculation.

Last year Rashid told us my Uncle Isaac's theory, but I think
maybe Rashid was pulling our legs. He said Isaac and Mercutio
had this weird friendship they kept from everyone else. Isaac was
counseling him spiritually or something and knows Mercutio attacked the others but feels certain he never would have attacked
him. Isaac thinks Mercutio was secretly in love with him, and was

jealous of his best friend, Lazarus. So Mercutio murdered Lazarus, and when Halloween and Tyler started asking questions, he had to try to kill them too.

The other theory that gets floated around sometimes is something about angry computer programs on the Inside, and how their "emotions" spilled over into everyone's brains, Mercutio getting the worst of it because he was oldest. I don't fully understand that one, but my parents, aunts and uncles spent eighteen long years Inside without a break, and maybe when you spend that much time plugged in weird things can happen.

Who knows? Why do people do the things they do?

The guy deleted a huge amount of information before he got popped, so I expect his secret died with him. Anyhow, I think it's wonderful Halloween killed him, because I probably wouldn't be here if he hadn't.

The funny thing is I think I appreciate or don't appreciate my aunts and uncles based on their taste in music. Take Tyler, Champagne's first love. The guy was really into shock bands like Witherstick, Killer Nurse, Max BSG and my personal favorite, Lung Butter. Champagne sometimes plays those bands when she gets sad, and it's loud, energizing music I associate with her cheering up. So he's okay in my book, better than, say, Simone, who had a yen for ancient Chinese folk music—talk about your atonal ear stabbers—or Mercutio, who had a thing for Mozart (I can't stand Mozart)—but in fairness his tastes were pretty eclectic, and I like all the "Crimson and Clover" covers he's got in his collection. And I can take or leave Fantasia's jazz ragtime swing fusion or whatever you want to call it.

Vashti once told me that musical taste is a reflection of scripting. Gedaechtnis apparently wanted a "living memory" of human history, so they scripted events in her generation's childhoods to subtly push them to study specific time periods. So Fantasia's interest in early-twentieth-century music stems from a larger interest in early-twentieth-century culture, one Gedaechtnis scientists thought she should have. Halloween got the late twentieth century, Vashti the Enlightenment, Champagne the Renaissance, Isaac the Ancient World, etc. Likewise, they wanted all the major religions to be represented, which is why my Uncle Isaac's a Muslim, but they wanted the most tolerant practice of Islam they could find, and that's why he's a Sufi.

I suppose I can understand why Gedaechtnis would do it, but honestly I think it's hateful. To grow up and discover you like the things you like and believe what you believe in only because somebody tricked you? Champagne's a fantastic artist, but every time she picks up a brush or grabs some clay, she must wonder if the only reason she's doing it is because Gedaechtnis wanted an artist in the group.

Aside from the jack-o'-lantern lithographs that embellish it, Halloween's urn is too black for light to escape. When you touch it, you feel like a flock of birds are taking wing, but when you follow the sounds you see they aren't birds but these pitch-dark demon-things whipping around you too fast to see their faces. Then the lightning comes crashing down like a devil's pitchfork, and you can make out a Gothic structure under a full moon, its roof pocked with gargoyles, grotesque and forbidding. And then there's Halloween himself, shot after shot from his time Inside. There's one where he's striding through a pumpkin patch with a stubborn wind blowing in his face, tossing hair as orange as sunrise. I like that one. He doesn't really look like a murderer to me. He just looks—I don't know—lonely, mostly. Brooding. There's something a little dangerous about him, but it's a good dangerous, I think.

I skipped over to Pandora's commentary and listened. I'd never bothered with it before, but wow. Olivia's right. It's not so much what Pandora says about him, it's how she says it. Like she's falling and he's the only one who can catch her. He owns her, that's how much in love she is, and even though I made fun of it with Olivia, I think there's something beautiful about it too. I can only wonder if I'll ever feel that way about someone. On the one hand love sounds like a perfect way to ruin your life, but without it what do you really have? That catch-22 might be my favorite part of *The Scarlet Pimpernel*—his relationship with Marguerite, his estranged wife. They despise each other, and the English nobles are always commenting on what a tragedy that is, and he just shakes his head and says no, the tragedy is that his love for her never stopped, that he'll always love her no matter what she does, love her 'til her dying day.

So let's see if Halloween wants to help me. I doubt he'll respond, but like Olivia says—if he does, I'm golden.

Time to shoot him a letter. Just on the off chance.

Lock and load.

Entry #308: The Princess and the Off Chance –locked–

haji

In one of Nymphenburg's many butler pantries, we are snacking on fifty-year-old soy cheese and vitamin-enhanced whole-wheat crackers, my brother fox, sister frog and I. We would normally enjoy it, but after Inside fare like chocolate-covered cherries, almond croissants and black-olive pizza, this meal suffers by comparison, and the acrid, chalky taste of ultrapreservatives hits my tongue sharper than I have ever noticed before.

Does this taste different to you?

Ngozi nods as Dalila makes a sour face.

Maybe this is what Mu'tazz meant by glitter, Ngozi says. No more cheese and crackers for us.

We share a smile, but the realization that our attitudes are changing hangs over us. Even as minor a change as this carries weight, for it is but symptomatic of something larger that we can feel but not quite define.

Ngozi decides he has had enough and forages about, returning with three spoons, a bowl of strawberries from Champagne's garden and a carton of synthetic cream.

Dalila puts her elbows on the counter and a hand on her forehead, gingerly stroking the space between her eyes. I pass her the pain medication and her blue eyes flash with gratitude. The headaches we have been promised have arrived. Vashti has assured us that they will dissipate sooner rather than later. I remind Dalila of this as she takes the medication with a spoonful of cream.

It isn't just the headaches, I feel different somehow, she says.

Good different or bad different?

Don't know yet, she says, and Ngozi nods, agreeing.

My siblings have been having a wonderful time here, but between the culture shock and exposure to the Inside they are starting to feel like strangers in their own skin. We said as much to our father this morning when we called him. This is to be expected, he replied, perfectly normal. And compared to his childhood, I suppose it is. I can scarcely imagine what a wrenching shock it was for him to discover that the world he knew and loved was only the Inside. How rich and populous that imaginal realm seems to us, and how bereft of life the real world must have seemed to him. To have come through that experience as unscathed as he has, and emerge even stronger for it, impresses me as a powerful testament to his resilience and virtue. Without his wisdom, where would we be?

I had a strange dream last night, Ngozi reports, almost a fever dream. I can't remember much about it, just a feeling of distance.

Distance? Emotionally?

Like I was outside of myself, watching the dream even as I was dreaming it. I remember the sky. Pictures of the sky, I was taking them and I felt afraid. Real fear. And I'm never afraid, not like that. Crazy, huh?

Just a side effect of our first trip Inside, I suggest. We have seen so much in such a short time and our minds now struggle to make sense of it all.

Maybe the human brain isn't meant for IVR, Ngozi says. Maybe it's just for jinn.

I ruminate. I feel breathless. I have spilled water on the counter and am now tracing a pattern in the drops with my straw. Rashid's words echo in my memory. Your dreams will change, he said, though from his point of view, change is positive. Did I have dreamless sleep last night? I cannot remember. I wish my head hurt less.

My sister did dream, a disconnected fantasy about a tribe of people living beneath purple snowcapped mountains, all the men and women with brightly painted faces stretched into delighted smiles. Despite the smiles they took offense at everything they saw, particularly each other, which Dalila found strangely humorous. Not a nightmare, but certainly an odd dream. She says she told Katrina about it, and Katrina said she had one like that once, but different, and the more she described it, the more it sounded like *Alice in Wonderland*.

What are you drawing?

In the spill I have sketched a key, and on its face a numerical code. This is what I found in my Inside pocket. I tell my siblings this and they understand it no better than I. The more I think about it, the more I believe that it is a message. Someone wants to tell me something, and believe me I am listening.

It may be a clue to how our sister died.

Dalila squints at me, searching my face. Hessa got sick, she says.

As simple as that? Why did she get sick? Why not Mu'tazz or Rashid? Why not us? Have we ever received a clear answer? Maybe the answer is in the code.

More likely someone playing a practical joke on you, Ngozi says. Olivia tells me sometimes they do that here.

I think practical jokes are neither, Dalila snorts.

Just then, a black-and-white football rolls into the room, and Penny breezes in after it, eager to invite us to a match. I'm trying to get enough people together to make it interesting, she says, and if you three come aboard I'm sure my sisters will follow.

Sure, I'm always up for a game, Ngozi agrees. Dalila uses her headache as an excuse to beg off, though I sense she might not play with Penny under the best of circumstances. As for me, last year I had a great time playing three-on-three matches against Brigit, Olivia and Tomi, so I am excited to play.

I should warn you I'm pretty good, Penny tells us, showing off with a little keepy-uppy by bouncing the ball from knee to knee.

I doubt you're as good as Haji, counters Dalila.

Goalkeeper is a position I play rather well, I admit, clarifying and downplaying my sister's praise. My legs won't let me run around for very long, but I like the game, so I've compensated by learning how to stop a kick.

Then between the two of us, we've got the unstoppable force against the immovable object, Penny smiles. Might be fun to see which wins out.

Right as she says this, she loses control of the ball, and it goes from keepy-uppy to smashy-bowly, scattering the strawberries and splashing us all with cream.

Oh, crapping hell, Penny frets, swiping a paper towel to blot up the mess. She dabs the table gingerly, as if she does not wish to get her hands dirty. Ngozi is collecting the ball and I am collecting shards of porcelain when Penny shoves the damp towel at me and asks if I will please gather up the strawberries as well.

They make me sick, she explains. I don't even want to touch them.

So the children of Isaac wind up cleaning the bulk of her

mess as she heads off with the ball, promising to find more play-
ers. But she never returns with any, leading my siblings to specu-
late that either she could not find any or she was too embarrassed
after smashing the bowl to go through with the actual game.

She's probably not even allergic to strawberries, she just didn't
want to do any work, Dalila complains, and this may well be true
but for now I am inclined to give Penny the benefit of the doubt.

An hour later, Tomi links to me, and I find her out by the
fountain with the swans. A rustling of feathers, and a little gosling
pokes its head out from under its mother's wing. I would stare at
it longer but something in Tomi's gaze pulls me to her and pushes
all other thoughts aside.

Come with me, she says.

I fall into step with her. I have a kite-making workshop starting in just minutes, and already I know I will be late for it. I have
a faint inkling that I will not attend at all.

Is this about the number?

She stays silent, but nods yes. We stop in front of a building in
which I have never set foot before, and she presses the elevator but-
ton down. The doors open and I am not certain I want to enter.

Does it have to do with Hessa's death?

No, Haji, she says, it has to do with you.

pandora

Isaac and I are on wildlife control, establishing a safe perimeter for
our camp by defacing the rainforest floor with an Argos security
filament spray. The inky, ropy streaks we paint the foliage with

looks about as natural as a scorpion teaching yoga, but it's biodegradable and we need it to keep the jaguars and boa constrictors away.

Manu, Peru. I've never been to this part of the Amazon before, either here in the big, wide world or in the IVR I maintain. It's breathtaking, and I'd probably enjoy it as a vacation if I didn't have a job to do, and if I wasn't so lightheaded and flushed with sweat. It isn't the air or the heat that's bothering me—it's the sad fact that I'm closer to home than I've been in eighteen years. The proximity has my stomach in knots.

I hit IVR Brazil with some frequency, instinctively drawn to it the way a salmon feels the need to return to the stream of her birth. Rio is fun for a nice distraction, but São Paulo is my home. I spent the first five years of my life there, and nearly all my vacations and holidays. None of it's real, but I feel safe there, cradled, carefree. Like Dorothy in the poppy field, without any wicked witch.

My parents are there. My father, the crown prince in Grandpa's kingdom, devoted to beautifying all the women of the world—he's the kind of suave, sophisticated fashion plate who would have made a fine diplomat or spy. And my mother, his former patient, the model-turned-activist, living a life of dinner parties and protest marches, always focused on the next worthy cause. I like visiting them, even if we can't talk about any of the important things, and even if they do still treat me as a teenager because no one at Gedaechtnis ever programmed them to interact with me as a full-grown adult.

When I discovered they were AI programs, and recognized how calculated Gedaechtnis was in raising me—nourishing my teenage rebellion against the family business by subtly channeling it into traditional medicine—so many arguments with my father and grandfather about their vision, how I was damn sure going to save people's lives, and not just prettify them—the whole thing left me with a rotten taste in my mouth, but I've moved past it and can appreciate my IVR family and friends for who and what they are.

Are they based on real people? At eighteen I got the chance to find out, newly freed by Halloween and dropped fresh into the world. Once we divided the continents and I took South America, I had to go to São Paulo, the real São Paulo, not only because a Gedaechtnis lab was based there, but also because I had to see it with my eyes and compare it to the artificial city I hold dear.

The São Paulo I know is warm laughter and piranha soup. It's fun and freedom, with just a little splash of danger. In the real world, that city no longer exists. My São Paulo boasts a skyline dotted with endless skyscrapers. That São Paulo has been demolished, high building after high building pauperized to debris. Vast sections of the city have buckled and burned, crevasses in the earth gaping open like wounds. My São Paulo sports the beautiful Parque do Ibirapuera, where I played football poorly but enthusiastically as a child, and coached it cleverly as a teen. The real Parque do Ibirapuera has swallowed itself, its paths and roads engulfed by unchecked flora. It belongs to the rats now, and they belong to the lancehead vipers. My people are gone. So many dead, and I will never get used to seeing the skeletons of unburied children, the wreckage of boys and girls like the ones I grew up with, the ones I used to teach. The entire world feels haunted but not like this. Not like my home. Between the riots, Black Ep and a cataclysmic earthquake, the largest and best city in South America has become a hell to me.

The Gedaechtnis lab there is a scarred mound of rubble someone could spend years picking through. But that someone won't be me. I won't ever go back. It's too painful, seeing my homestead raped like that. I prefer the simulation. It's now a kind of memorial for the real city. I can go there and light candles with my father in an IVR church, or with my mother in an IVR synagogue, and despite my agnosticism and their essential unreality, together we can pray for the souls of the dead.

Isaac prayed with me once. In the real world, since he won't set foot back in the IVR. I won't go back to Brazil, he won't go back to IVR, and Halloween won't leave North America. I suppose it's funny, all our little phobias. Only in their case I don't think it's fear that's stopping them but principle.

"Ten o'clock," says Isaac, pointing ahead and left, not to a pygmy marmoset, but to a giant anteater feasting on a nest of leaf cutter ants, his pink, sticky tongue catching several at a time. We make eye contact with the gray and toothless creature, and though it tenses with caution, it seems curious and affectionate to me, as if it would like nothing better than to become our domesticated pet. Before that can happen, we give it a wide berth, completing our security perimeter without seeing sign one of anything resembling a monkey.

They won't be easy to spot. "They're tiny things," Isaac tells me, as he sweeps the horizon with an infrared lens. "Smallest monkeys known to man. Four ounces, maybe. You can fit one in the palm of your hand."

"A shame they're no bigger."

"Bigger might be harder to bring down."

"Let's just hope they're here."

With the perimeter established, we return to my copter to let out the kids. We left my nieces working on Life History projects, homework downloads from StoryCorps, but now I find them in discourse with Mu'tazz, the three girls entreating him to be the cheerful sort they remember from the start of his visit last year, before Hessa died, and not the dour zealot he became after. And Mu'tazz is smiling, almost apologetically replying that if nothing else Hessa's death proved that we aren't safe from God's wrath— He killed billions and still we don't fear Him enough to obey His laws.

"I hate to break this up," I say, "but we could really use your help out here."

They grab supplies and hop out, excited to see Peru ("Amazons in the Amazon!" Izzy happily exclaims), and the urge to call the love of my life again strikes me with cyclone force, but I fight it off, and when I catch Isaac's eyes I realize how similar in color they are to Halloween's. He looks back at me, questioning, but then pixielike Zoë is clamoring for my attention, telling me how wonderful her sister Penny is, which strikes me as odd because Izzy and Lulu—Penny's supposed best friends—have been bad-mouthing her all trip. I assure Zo that Penny's on my short list of candidates for private instruction, which seems to satisfy her, but I feel a little insulted that Penny would send others to do her bidding instead of coming to me herself. I love all my nieces, but from Penny I always get a ruthless feeling, bad wishes behind the smile, fueled by what I'd guess is just plain loneliness. I don't like it and I don't see her improving. Still, she's not a bad little IVR designer, and she can't be any less disciplined than Rashid.

"Monkey!" Izzy shouts, and we snap into action, eagerly scanning the treetops, but it's just a joke—the only monkeys are those of us who believed her.

haji

The elevator doors part to reveal a corporate drop. Wall-to-wall supplies. The multinationals established hideaways like this all over the world for prospective survivors such as we. Tomi leads me past products from Founder, Coca-Cola, Procter & Gamble, Ningworks, Argos, Sony, Smartin! and Nike. Her sunkissed legs take long, loping strides through the maze of consumables and I must struggle to catch up.

Hurry, she says. We're short on time and I want you to see this. See what?

This way, she says, pushing open the far door to lead me down a cold gray hallway, the walls and ceiling reinforced with steel. To my right I see what may be a prep room for surgery, but I do not dawdle because Tomi has turned left, stopping abruptly at an impregnable-looking security door, which she opens via fingerprint lock. I follow her into a great cube of a room, in architectural style not that dissimilar from the ectogenesis lab I saw on the Nymphenburg tour, only here instead of the artificial wombs which bore my cousins, I see rows upon rows of upright plastic coffins.

Eighty-one bodies perfectly preserved. Dead now, but maybe death isn't forever. This is what I do, Tomi says. I help Vashti maintain the cryonic suspension chambers. Popsicles are what she calls the people inside but that's not how I think of them.

Frozen flowers, I say.

My garden, she agrees.

I ask her what this has to do with me, and as the question leaves my lips, the answer awakens in my head. So this is where I come from.

I knew that code looked familiar. It's the type of code we use for the chambers and when you showed it to me I had to see which one it unlocked. And what I found was you, Tomi says.

She brings me to a suspension chamber near the back. The man inside is older than me, vitrified, brain-dead, his skin and organs ravaged by disease. He is less of a man and more a collection of body parts. Still, I can see myself in him. This is where my DNA came from. He is my biological ancestor and I am his clone.

The marker reads Dr. James Hyoguchi.

Do you know who that is?

One of the Gedaechtnis scientists, I reply. My father has mentioned his name in the past, and always with reverence.

He's one of the greats, she tells me. A pioneer in Immersive Virtual Reality. He and his team of programmers built the Inside as we know it.

I have wondered about my origin, and have asked my father about it many times. While he has offered to tell me if I insist upon it, I have not done so, and he has preferred to stay silent, cautioning that where I come from is not nearly as important as who I am and where I am going. I can see the wisdom in this, and so cannot help feeling like I have disobeyed him here. And yet, guilt cannot spoil my delight. I owe a debt to Tomi and to whoever put that key in my pocket. They have introduced me to a new member of my family, and answered a question that has plagued my imagination for so very long.

Beneath the marker, I see a case with seven discs. I take the first and drop it into the accompanying player, my anticipation satisfied as a hologram appears. The image of Dr. Hyoguchi stands before us to talk about his life, biographical information spawning about him in luminous text. We learn about his family history, his formative years in the United Kingdom and Japan, and about his turbulent youth in the private schools. His professional repertoire is wonderful if dizzying, and I can scarcely imagine accomplishing but a small fraction of what he did. Last year and over the past few days, I have seen my cousins do Life History assignments and now this is my chance to cull meaning from someone's experiences in the time before the plague.

It is like meeting another version of myself, one from a parallel universe. Where I have my faith, he carries a lifelong fascination with simulated reality, approximate humanity and altered states of consciousness. I begin to see him as a brilliant hedonist, stronger for his passions, but slave to them as well.

I notice that Tomi is hugging herself. It occurs to me that the temperature is too cold in here for her, even with her fall blazer. I offer her all I am wearing but she refuses, regarding me with a level of concern I find mystifying.

There's something else, she says when the Life History comes to an end. He wants to talk to you.

He wants to talk to me?

Disc six, she says and I swap as she directs.

Okay, I laid out most of the tech specs on the last two discs, but as long as I'm recording here I want to talk to the man who's saving my life. The man who shares my DNA, my twin, I want to talk to him personally.

Well, hello there, handsome stranger. Konnichiwa. If you can see this recording, then you exist. Which means, amazingly, all the pieces came together. Which means all this work we've been doing wasn't in vain.

I wish I could meet you in person. Maybe I will, in a sense, in that midpoint when everything's perfectly balanced. What will that be like? I wonder. Most of all, I want to say thank you. Seriously, you have no idea. I'd hug you if I could.

You don't know how much I wish there was another way to do this.

Ideally, I'd love to be thawed out and be that caveman you wake up from the glacier. If you can successfully warm me up, pump blood back into this tired body and get my heart and brain going again, I'll be ecstatic. But the thawing process doesn't look so good to all the experts here, because even minor fractures can make Swiss cheese of my organs, and then you have to fix the cells on a molecular level. We've got scientists working on the nanotechnology you'd want for that, but it's slow going, especially with the kind of damage this horrible-as-fuck disease can do. That's one big problem. The other problem is, according to Stasi, the only ones who have a chance at surviving Black Ep are kids who've been taking medicine their entire lives. So even if you did manage to resuscitate my body, the disease would probably just top me in a couple of days.

So we're left with this. Retrieval.

Have you been to Arizona? Hot as hell, isn't it? Beautiful though. There's a city called Holbrook, near this park, this American national park where they have these terrific badlands. The hills are striped from bone white to chocolate brown, all natural, all sedimentary rock. They call it the Painted Desert. And the park itself is a petrified forest, all that wood fossilizing over time, dissolved minerals gradually replacing all the organic matter. It's quite fascinating how it works, petrifaction. If you look at this procedure as a new kind of petrifaction, it might not seem so scary.

We've mapped my brain, and uploaded every neuron into electronic storage. That's me, the real me with all my knowledge, instincts and quirks, truer than any simulation I've ever made. And with your help, if we're lucky, out of storage I'll come. In the animal trials it's worked astoundingly well: disassembler nanites dissolving the organics, the assemblers replacing each vanished natural neuron with a new artificial neuron. In this case, my artificial neurons. So over time, one personality fades while a new one emerges. You'll gradually forget you and come to remember me.

Now it has to be a clone with identical DNA or the body won't work with the brain. And the clone has to come to adulthood first, so the brain can fully develop and reach a comparable size. The good news is the procedure is virtually painless, because the assemblers and disassemblers will be swapping out your neurons at a nearly imperceptible rate, and all the problems we've had with cephalic cybernetic implants, brain tumors and whatnot shouldn't be a problem. It's safe and it's doable, even if it hasn't been tested as much as we'd all like.

Now I'm sure this flies in the face of every survival instinct you have. And I know it's unfair to ask it of you. Everyone deserves a chance at life. Without a doubt. But this is necessary. Your family needs me. I'm extremely well suited for the kind of challenges you're facing. The fact that you're even here to play this message is proof that my team and I have done a wonderful job.

In short, I'm asking you to be a hero. Not just my hero, but also a hero for all humanity, willing to sacrifice himself for the greater good. So will you do it? Will you step up and download my soul? Will you set me free?

I feel like there is no air in my lungs. I look to Tomi and see compassion swimming in her eyes but nothing more. There is nothing she can do.

I am startled by Vashti's voice. She has been standing behind us, but I do not know for how long.

What are you doing here? she asks.

It is an excellent question and I am unable to find words with which to answer.

deuce

See? Do you see where he is? You pushed with your invisible hand and he just glided into place. Zing, right where you wanted him. Right there.

Slicker than a polar bear in a vat full of seal blubber, that's what you are. Why, you'd be practically diabolical if you weren't fighting for such a righteous cause.

Truth! Justice! Liberation! That's the side of the angels and always will be. So if you want to shed a tear for the poor guy because he ate from the tree of knowledge, go ahead and let that bad boy roll off your cheek, because you get one tear, just one. But don't you dare kid yourself about it—without the apple, Adam and Eve would have motherfucking starved.

No one lives a lie while you're on watch.

Years from now imagine it. This comrade-in-arms has become your dearest friend and the world is open and true. You sit with him and you drink together. And you talk the way people do. And you look at him. And you say how funny it is that things have changed. And he doesn't understand, but he asks you to go on because he really wants to know. And you tell him it's funny because you used to feel like such an abomination. You used to be so terribly empty, too frightened to think, an infant shadow lost in a world of fire. So many times you wanted to reach out to someone your age, to make a friend, and see yourself through new eyes. But you couldn't. You'd panic every time you'd try. You'd retreat so deep into the fear, and feel around all zenlike for a sense of nothingness to hang on to, so you could pull yourself up and try again.

And your comrade-in-arms? He laughs. Not a cruel laugh, not a disparaging one, not the kind of humorless jagged vanguard to calling you pathetic, as has happened so many times already in your mind, but the kind of laugh best friends save for each other when they hear one hell of a joke. It's funny. And when he sees you're serious, he says he can't believe it. You? Of all people, you were afraid?

You tell him that for years something was wrong with you. You tell him you would always imagine the worst and never the best. You would feel like you were sitting outside yourself, watching your hopes wither and rot. And you knew you had to do something. You had to level the playing field. You had to make a sword of the truth. And so even though what you did, you did for them, you had to do it for you. Or you would have never had the courage to introduce yourself.

And the confession comes with some shame, and you feel a pinprick of the old fear again because maybe he'll reject you now, and call you pathetic, and blame you for exposing his old life as a poisonous lie. But he just smiles at you, and punches you on the chin with the force of a whisper, and hugs you without hesitation.

And he tells you that you must be joking because you saved him. You gave him the key. You brought him the light and let him see for the first time ever. He's grateful to you. He always will be.

That's your best friend, Haji. Your buddy. The one who makes you feel like your own man, not a shadow, not a freak. Because he understands you.

But not like she does. Not like she will.

If you can win her heart.

Can you imagine that? Can you possibly imagine?

No time to get complacent. The first thunderbolt's thrown. Time to dust the sparks off your fingers and grab the next.

haji

Why can't I get a straight answer, Haji? Is it too much to ask for? Have I set my hopes too high? In the time it would take to get the truth out of you, I could probably beat a whale to death with a rolled-up newspaper.

I am not used to interrogations. I am finding that I do not particularly like them.

Couldn't I, she asks, pressing it, hungry for me to answer her hypothetical question, her eyes like winter and her voice like flowing silk. There is something agreeable in her tone that makes me want to answer truthfully, and I must remind myself that I have been nothing but truthful, and still she does not believe me.

I go through it again for her. It comes pouring out of me. Halfway through my recountal, I notice that the chair behind her desk rests upon a raised platform while mine does not. Vashti has become taller while I have shrunk.

Yes, yes, fine, but who gave you the key?

I can only guess.

Haji, for good reason, the cryonics lab is off-limits. No kids allowed. Tomi is the singular exception to that rule, and she knows she's not to take anyone there without my express permission. I don't suppose she told you that before she took you?

Vashti suspects that I am trying to protect Tomi. That Tomi instigated the trespass all on her own and that I am now fabricating a story about a mysterious key in order to minimize her responsibility for this affair.

You don't want to get her in trouble, is that it?

She takes my silence as a yes, lets out a long sigh, and tells me how sweet and chivalrous I am. My loyalty to Tomi impresses her though she lectures me that I should never spin lies for someone else's sake.

My expression does not waver. I remain in a black, faltering daze. I am not thinking about Tomi. I am not thinking about my siblings. I am not even thinking about God. I am, for the first time in living memory, thinking only about myself. Vashti must recognize this on some level, because she gets up from her desk to pour hot Assam tea into a silver filigree cup, and sweetens it with honey. Honey contains worker-bee enzymes, and never spoils. It can last forever. She passes me the cup, her eyes winter no longer. Along with the tea, she is offering me kindness and understanding. I have been through quite an ordeal after all. Would I like a mild sedative to calm me down?

No, I would not.

The tea is sweet and smooth and too hot to drink comfortably, though I drink it just the same. Vashti pours herself a cup and hops up on the edge of her desk, her legs dangling. She blows on her tea and sips, eyeing me throughout like a magpie on a perch.

So what are you going to do, Haji?

I shake my head.

I didn't think I'd be having this conversation with you for a few years, but since you were so eager to break into cryonics, I suppose we'll have it now. How old are you, anyway?

Fifteen.

So three years for you, a little less for Rashid and Mu'tazz. Yes, the brain grows until you're eighteen or so, though certain synapses and neurotransmitters keep developing in complexity for some time after that.

What about my brothers?

She hesitates and says, Well, naturally, their DNA comes from Gedaechtnis employees. Just like you. All Isaac's children are Gedaechtnis clones.

Are we all sacrifices then?

Sacrifices is not a word I'm comfortable with, she frowns.

Do you have a better one?

She does not, and acknowledges the point with a small tilt of her head. In the silence between us I reflect how sacrifice in one form or another has always gone hand in hand with worship. I have read that for a beloved ideal no sacrifice can be too great. I have a great belief in sacrifice. I believe in purifying my soul, and sacrificing all that keeps me from knowing God.

These are the lessons of Isaac, the lessons that he has taught. I know they are true, but I wonder now why he has taught them. Never before have I felt this way. It is a terrible feeling, not to know your father's heart.

Empty vessels, I say, answering my own question. Perhaps that is what we are.

The phrase has a spiritual connotation, for it is said that the best teacher is merely an empty vessel, through whom God makes His presence felt. To learn a student must become like the teacher, unburdening, releasing, freeing, until he is empty as well. Teacher and student become no one, and in that empty space there is God. But I am not certain I mean it spiritually. My siblings and I are empty vessels, it would seem, in that the essence of who we are may as well be hollow, for we are to be obliterated and replaced with those who came before us.

I do not know how to feel.

Is this really what my father wants for me?

Vashti shrugs. I can't speak for Isaac, she says. Wouldn't presume. But it certainly looks that way to me. Listen, it's no secret your father and I don't agree on much. He must have told you about all those wonderful debates we had before you were born. We tried to work together, honestly we tried as hard as we could until we realized how different our values and methodologies were. Until we agreed to disagree. So I don't know what he wants for you, but this is just the kind of thing he does that drives me crazy.

She falls silent, thinking. I watch her make perfectly controlled circles with her cup, quick, tight orbits to cool the tea inside. Do you mind if I speak candidly? she asks.

I make an open gesture with my hand.

Your father is a backwards person, she says. That may be hard for you to hear, but it's true. I look forward. He looks back. That's why you're human, Haji. Here we are fighting a war against Black Ep, and Isaac wants kids who are, forgive me, genetic liabilities. Here we have a chance to build a new and improved tomorrow, and he wants to set things back to the way they were. There's no reason you shouldn't be as strong and as healthy as my girls are. There's no reason your sister should have died. With a decent immune system, Hessa would still be here today. The man clings to the past like a security blanket, and it's the kind of mistake that costs. And it looks like you're part of that cost, Haji, and I'm sorry.

penny

Entry #309: The Princess and the Unfinished Entry -open-

Bad language can get expensive, and in more ways than one. First of all, you can't swear in front of moms since they'll fine you for it. Much better to do that in private. I try not to do it at all, because I don't want to get in the habit. But it's also expensive in that we're not exposed to a lot of swears—everything Inside runs through a language filter, and if you want something unabridged it costs a lot more. So I only know a handful of dirty words—hell, damn, crap, ass, and a couple of Portuguese swears Pandora taught us once when she was drunk—but there have to be a lot more out there because I've seen the language filter block words that can't be the ones I know.

I've thought about combining them, but mostly they just sound silly. (Except for "crapping hell." That's fun to say when you bang your knee.)

Anyway, I bring it up because during study hall today Sloane thought no one was watching and went into a cursing fit over some stupid thing or other, but Champagne was right behind her, and the look on her face when—

Sorry, Vashti's calling me. I'll be back in a sec.

Lock for now.

Entry #309: The Princess and the Unfinished Entry
-locked-

haji

When I make the call, I can hear my cousins singing in the background. It is a song my father sang to me when I was small, a simple piece about finding joy in the smallest chore. I can see them gathering fruit from a towering, wildly twisting tree I have never seen before, its long hanging vines draping down to kiss the Peruvian rainforest floor. In the foreground, I can see my father. He is pleased to see me and says he wishes that I were there.

I learn they are gathering bait for a tiny monkey, which may or may not exist. He says the satellite photo is indistinct, and while the animal seen leaping from a branch may in fact be a pygmy marmoset, it is impossible to say with certainty.

Good luck, I say. Do you love me?

Of course I love you, Haji.

Really? What is it about me that you love?

Is something troubling you?

You once told me that no man loves his son so much as God loves those who walk in His path. Is that true?

You know that it is.

Then would it be fair to say you love me less than God?

It would be fair to say that we both walk in His path, that we both follow Him, and that the love He has for us is reflected in how we love each other.

I stare mutely at him, my feelings entwined like knots of tangled string.

I think I know what this is about, he says.

Do you?

You've discovered a new way of life, the path your cousins

walk, and you prefer it, or envy it, or feel confused by it, and you have questions, and perhaps you blame me for keeping you from it for so many years. If you feel this way, I may owe you an apology, but please know I protected you from Nymphenburg for as long as I have, not out of my own selfishness but because I thought you needed the tools to see it clearly, to make up your own mind about it without inescapably succumbing to its many lures.

I am not Mu'tazz. I am not Rashid. Coming here has made me wise. Leaving here will make me wiser. I do not blame you for keeping me from this place.

Then I have misread you, he says.

And perhaps I you, I reply.

Haji, please, speak plainly, he says, his jaw tightening, a fatherly look of concern settling into his eyes. I am frightened to speak. I must take a moment to breathe deeply and slow the scurry of words jackknifing in my mind.

Vashti told me not to let you do it, I hear myself say. She said you could not make me and I should stand up to you.

About what? What's happening over there?

Will you tell me about James Hyoguchi?

A long-tailed macaw with bright red wings, the tips tinged with yellow and blue, swoops past to steal a treat from the growing stockpile of fruit. We ignore it. I search my father's face. He reveals nothing.

This is not how I wanted you to find out.

But I have.

And now you feel unsettled?

Unsettled?

Dr. Hyoguchi was a great man, and a visionary with many accomplishments to his name. But he's simply the source of your genetic material. I certainly don't want you to feel like you have to compete with him or worry about how you measure up. It's much better for you to focus on your own accomplishments, your own future.

What possible future is that? Being a host for a dead man's soul?

Now I see, he says, a glimmer of light in the obsidian of his eyes. You played all his discs. Oh, Haji, you've got the wrong idea.

Explain it to me then.

The scientists at Gedaechtnis are heroes of mine, he says. Without them, none of us would exist today. What better way to honor them than by using their DNA?

But on the disc, I cut in, the rest of my sentence faltering when my father points his index finger skyward. I am interrupting him. This is not something I normally do.

Before I took genetic samples, I wanted to know them, he says, so I watched their discs. Yes, a fraction of the scientists expressed an interest in being cloned, and yes, a fraction of that fraction wanted their clones to serve as boxes. Son, when a man knows he is dying and he has faith in God, there is peace in his heart, but when he lacks faith, in those final days what most commonly happens?

Despair becomes his bread and desperation his butter, I recite, which pleases him.

Such was the case with Dr. Hyoguchi, he says. But consider me. I am not a despairing man, and these are not desperate times.

His words have weight and I feel increasingly foolish for jumping to conclusions.

So I am not a sacrifice?

No more so than anyone else, he smiles.

I did not understand. I thought I had learned my true purpose.

Your true purpose is the same as ever. To follow God and accept whatever plan He has for you.

I say, But what if this is God's plan? What if the world is better off with Hyoguchi instead of me?

What if? There is no time for what if, Haji. There is only time for what is. Keep to the path of love, human kindness and compassion. Whatever will happen will happen, and you must embrace it unafraid.

He is right as always, and I apologize for my folly, an apology he graciously accepts. The tension is broken between us, though something still gnaws at me, a tiny unpleasant worry scratching away at a part of myself I cannot define.

Now why do you think Vashti stirred this up in you? he asks.

He thinks Vashti simply took me to her cryonics lab, so I explain what really happened, my words bringing a calculating expression to his face.

Vashti sent you that key, he says. She wanted you to play the disc.

I have not considered this. It is possible, I suppose, and more possible the longer I play it out in my mind. Reluctantly, I tell him what Vashti said about him being backward in his thinking, and he tells me he has heard much worse from her.

She has no love for where she comes from, he says, and she takes no lesson from the past. She's an absolutist in a progressive's mask, and though she plays at decency, it rarely enters her heart. She loves to create *fitnah,* he says, using the Arabic word that means mischief and the testing of faith. She turned Champagne against me, he says, and now she hopes to do the same with my children.

Then why do you send us here?

So you can see for yourself, he says, and make up your own mind. Besides, she's family.

Before he goes, he puts me on the phone with my three cousins. We talk for a time, and Zoë, who hopes to be an ecologist, tells me about the great sinuous tree from which she has been gathering fruit. It is not one tree but two, I learn, which explains its many twists. She does not know the name of the first tree, the support tree, but the one that bears fruit is a strangler fig. She tells me how it has contorted itself tightly around its host, its gangling vines rooting into the soil to steal water and nutrients, the essence of life. It is a parasite. And it lives a long time, she says. Hundreds and hundreds of years.

pandora

So I'm watching Mu'tazz retreat from a collared peccary, the grunting, snorting animal hot on his heels. Just a few steps past the perimeter, he ran afoul of this wild, tusked, rank-smelling bristly pig, its neck ringed with snow-white fur. Here it's defending its territory and maybe its young, aggressively charging, but upon crossing the filament spray, it gives up the chase, the sudden light show and ultrasonic frequency disorienting it and sending it panicked in the opposite direction.

Mu'tazz doubles over, catching his breath. "I have become a cliché," he frowns, "a Muslim running away from pork."

"I'm glad to see humor isn't *haram*." I smile.

"Definitely *halal*," he replies. "God enjoys a good laugh as much as anyone."

"I've long suspected that myself."

He sits on a blanket I lay out for him, and gladly accepts my bottled water. I watch him for a bit, listening to his breath and mine, and the sounds of nature, and the throaty cries of a pygmy marmoset resounding off the trees. But this is our trick marmoset, a holographic ghost image of a female long dead, the recorded call outliving her by decades. Any cheeky monkey who comes to investigate gets a blast of anesthetic—that's the plan anyway. But Mu'tazz has also scattered his own traps throughout the rainforest: hollowed-out coconut shells with slices of fruit inside.

"This is an old trick," he explained, while unloading them from my copter. "The monkey reaches into the hole to grab the treat but cannot pull his paw free without letting go. Because he is unwilling to let go, he is trapped by the force of his greed."

Though they are low-tech contraptions, my nieces and I find them wonderfully resourceful, the kind of outdoor-savvy skill set Isaac's kids have inherited, and Vashti and Champagne's kids have not. And Mu'tazz is Isaac's son in another respect as well, using the event as an opportunity to teach. "We all carry coconuts," he told the curious girls. "They are our problems, our woes, and we drag them around, shortsighted, too proud to let go and welcome God into our lives."

I leave him now to check on the others, and find Isaac in a state. His détente with Vashti just took a major hit—she's been manipulating his kids, he complains, saying things they should only hear from him, which tempts him to do the same with her kids—turnabout being fair play—but he's committed to rising above it and keeping himself pure. I don't agree with everything Isaac does, but he takes the high road far more often than Vashti does and I have to give him credit for that.

Over those first few months the tension between them brewed and brewed, and I was useless as peacemaker. It all finally bubbled over, with Isaac and Champagne insisting on having natural children, boys and girls, and Vashti insisting only upon girls via an artificial womb.

No natural children were born. Champagne's part of the story is a sad one, so let's leave it at that. But Vashti—she chose girls because girls are slightly more resistant to Black Ep than boys, with ever so slightly stronger immunodefenses, and with the disease just one bad mutation from putting us up against the knifepoint of extinction, that was reason enough to proclaim, "No boys allowed."

"This is a war," she said. "Black Ep has declared war upon us, and what use can we have for second-rate soldiers?"

She further justified it with the very problems Isaac and Champagne were having—not much luck returning us back to the kind of sexual reproduction our ancestors enjoyed for eons. But there's more to it than that. Vashti thinks all boys suffer from "testosterone poisoning"—that's her diagnosis for Mercutio, by the way—and likes to point to the vast majority of killers and war makers in the course of civilization being male. "Just being practical," she'll say, and, "If we're serious about preventing violence in the future, why not start society off as a matriarchy?" But then I remember Vashti feeling dispossessed back in school, sniping at the boys for showing off and disrupting the learning environment. She used to talk about matriarchies back then, arguing how they were the natural state of things once upon a time, and how patriarchies took over by hijacking the very first magic trick— giving birth—by having male gods like Zeus getting knocked up in the myths.

Considering the only births we've had over the past few decades have involved artificial wombs in ectogenesis labs, it's safe to say that playing field's been leveled. Then there's the old debate about Lazarus and Simone. Had they lived, whose side would they have taken? Neither, I say, because there wouldn't be any sides— we'd all be working together. Halloween too. Laz would have kept us all "on message" with his basic goodness, and Simone would have inspired us with her brilliance and enthusiasm. Even Tyler might have made a huge difference. We just aren't enough people here. We needed a critical mass, but never got it, and if I weren't such a hopeful person, I'd say it looks like we never will.

Years ago I tried to bridge the gap, truly settle the ideological differences between them, and when Vashti brushed me off with her usual, "Biological limitations are to be overcome—end of story," I pressed on and argued the need for diversity of opinion, not just diversity of genetic material. When you consider the extent of Isaac's knowledge and skills, every day she refused to compromise with him was a day she hamstrung her life's work. Like Champagne used to say, sometimes the most important step you can take in life is the step to meet someone halfway.

"I am a Transhumanist," Vashti replied, eyes flashing with the force of her convictions. "Unapologetically so. Isaac is, by comparison, a Humanist. Though I use that word loosely, given the life-after-death pabulum he feeds his children. He embraces the frailty of the human condition. I refuse to let suffering have the last word."

The tilt of her head and the curve of her lip said she was right and he was wrong and only a fool couldn't see it. "Just because he's religious," I said, which was all she needed to shout me down.

"Religion causes a kind of brain damage! It's kryptonite to reason. We are not fallen angels. We are not cut off from our higher selves. That's bullshit, absolute bullshit, Pandora. 'God' and 'Nature' are foolish words said by foolish people to explain events they don't understand. You want a word? Try 'evolution.' 'Acceleration.' 'Extropy.' 'Immortality.' Why pray to God when we can become gods? Hell, why stop there? We can even become Nature."

"Don't you think that's a little arrogant?"

"That's not arrogance, it's optimism!" she laughed. "Arrogance would be to assume we can't!"

Isaac received my argument less impolitely, but with no greater enthusiasm. "She thinks she has all the answers," he sighed, "and she'll take any risk to prove she's right. She doesn't think through the consequences. It took millions of years to reach this point in human evolution—all the credit for that goes to Nature, Time and God, not a shred to us—and to think we can blithely pick up where those three left off? Dangerous."

It reminded me of something Hal said to me once: "For such a fan of matriarchies, Vashti sure enjoys bitch-slapping Mother Nature."

"Maybe self-evolution is the way to go," Isaac hedged, "but there's only a few of us left on this planet. We're much better off restoring things back to the way they were, not remaking the world in our image."

I don't know who's right, Isaac, Vashti, both or neither. That's why I stick to maintenance and repair. Fewer headaches and I get to stay neutral.

Patently ridiculous. You've never been neutral, Pandy.

I've always tried to be.

Wouldn't you say over the years you've been more in Isaac's camp than Vashti's? From the day Champagne went over to Vashti's side, you became increasingly sympathetic to Isaac's point of view.

Well, that's neutral—two against two, I'm acting as a counter-balance.

That's your definition of neutrality?

Standing there in Peru, thinking about how we all got to this point, a thought creeps back into my mind. Something Halloween said back in that first year of freedom. Something he only said once. "You're the only good one left," he said, "but you spend so much time with them, I bet they'll rub off on you. As the years go by, you'll become more and more like them, and frankly I don't want to see it."

I must have blocked it out. I can't remember what I said in reply. Something like, "I think you're judging them too harshly." And that's still how I feel—Hal's the biggest grudge-holder of anyone I know. But maybe that's why he won't return my calls now. Have I changed over time? Am I no longer who I once was?

"Monkey!" Izzy shouts, and I yell back, "It wasn't funny the first time!" but then I hear Lulu shriek—sure enough, a little yellowish-brown creature has descended from the trees and gotten himself caught, not by the holographic trap, but with his hand locked in a coconut. I'm not even sure what it is when I aim the tranquilizer, and there's no time to find out—it's on the run, paw free now as I draw a bead on it—whatever it is, I don't want to hurt it, but it's no bigger than a housecat, and I'm just as likely to catch it in the back of the head as the rump, and far more likely to miss it entirely.

Except I don't. It's the luckiest shot of my life, catching him square in the tush as if that tiny, furry target were the size of an elephant.

He shrieks, high-pitched like a frightened, furious birdcall, as he scampers off, dashing like a squirrel, but drunk now, stumbling, the knockout inevitable. He flops stiffly over onto his side, and I'm afraid I've killed him—but no, he's breathing still, little pink tongue lolling out of his mouth, poor guy, and he's one hundred percent monkey, all he needs are the hat, the vest and the cymbals.

The girls are practically screaming in jubilation, Isaac congratulating me on my aim, while I just stupidly keep saying, "Is he okay?" until everyone assures me that he is.

Everyone except Isaac's oldest son, curiously, so while Isaac and Zoë collect the pygmy marmoset, Izzy, Lulu and I double back to find Mu'tazz there on the blanket, pale as I've ever seen him, and clutching his stomach in terrible pain.

penny

Entry #310: The Princess and the Suffering –open–

This is the worst news I've ever had to write. I feel like a thousand bricks are crashing down on me at once.

Vashti wanted to see me, so I went down to her office. She gave me a pep talk. Told me how great I was doing. Raised my allowance.

Olivia is Pandora's new assistant—not me.

When she said it, I got cold all over. Olivia? I mean, really, Olivia? I said, "That's just unfair!" and, "But I'm better qualified!" Yeah? So? Apparently better doesn't matter.

It's the trains. The stupid trains did me in. Pandora "appreciates" everything I've constructed Inside, but my *Scarlet Pimpernel* is "all for Penny's enjoyment" while Olivia's transportation system "can be used and enjoyed by everyone, and one of the most important qualities in this line of work is what a person can do for other people."

I don't do things for people? Who the hell did I give my money to, porcupines? I'm flat broke because I gave away all my money. To who else but people—the ones who were supposedly putting in good words for me? What a ridiculous joke.

Vashti told me there were so many other jobs I could do, but no, there aren't, not the kind where I'll be able to call my own shots. Not the kind where the people who hate me won't be able to push me around for days and weeks and months and years, keeping me underneath their heels until all the qualities that make me special disintegrate into nothingness. This was my stand. I made it. I refuse to give it up. When I told her Pandora made a big mistake, she handed me pills, telling me how stressed I seemed, and how these might help me relax. Honestly, is this any time to relax?

"You don't understand," I told her, "you never do."

I tracked Champagne down in the botanical garden, and when I told her what Vashti had told me, she threw her arms around my shoulders and stroked my hair like when I was a little girl.

"Oh, Penny, I know you're disappointed," she said, "but it's not your time to do this. It's Olivia's."

I said, "Didn't you tell Pandora I was the best for the job, didn't you tell her I was the only one who could do it right?"

She swore she did and said she was truly sorry that Pandora had decided to go with Olivia instead. I begged her to go to Pandora and make her reconsider, or to tell Olivia not to take the job, and she just held me until I knew that wasn't going to happen. I felt something cold and brittle spreading through my chest, like ice crystals gathering in a storm drain. Can no one see that Olivia is nothing compared to me?

No matter what I said to Champagne, all I got was more stupid hugs, more empty reassurances, and dopey words about how maybe, just maybe, in time Pandora might feel the need to hire another apprentice. Number two isn't good enough. I'd probably have to take orders from Olivia, and that's too awful to even consider.

Champagne was no more help than Vashti and it just about killed me. Why didn't I see it before—moms were just playing good cop, bad cop with me all along. Champagne is just sugar-coated Vashti. Don't they care about me? Is my life really going to be lots of tea and sympathy from family members unwilling to help me get what I want and need?

"What you're telling me," I said, "is even though I should be working with Pandora, I'm not because of politics. Because she likes Olivia more than me."

Champagne looked more useless than I'd ever seen her. I didn't even listen to what she said—I just started to run. She called after me, asking me where I was going, but I just pretended I couldn't hear her.

She linked me, "Penny, I love you, everyone does," but I killed the volume so I wouldn't have to suffer any more lies.

I found Olivia dusting the porcelain room, which was perfect because I was in the mood to break something.

"You have to tell her no," I said.

She tried, "What are you talking about?" like I'm one of our stupid cousins—but I had her number and told her it wasn't fair. She knew how much I wanted it. She gave me advice and said she'd help, and then stole it out from under me.

"You can't do this," I said. "It's not right."

"Why are you blaming me?" she whined. "It's not up to me, it's always been up to Pandora."

"Don't give me that," I said. "You played me. But that's fine because you can make it right. You can say no. They can't force you to do anything, and when you tell them that as much as you'd like to do it, it wouldn't be right, they'll have to listen to you."

She just stared at me, and when I told her I was the best, she didn't have any comeback at all, just hemming and hawing about "the way things worked out."

"Nothing worked out," I told her, and she laughed (!) into her hand, saying, "No, Penny, nothing worked out *for you.*"

Jealousy. The perfectly average, boring, forgettable girl happy to see the top scholar, the star athlete and the virtuoso musician not get her due.

I told her this was the kind of thing people do that makes others not like them, and that sooner or later someone wasn't going to stand for it, but apparently that wasn't specific enough for her, so I said if she didn't help me right now karma would catch up with her, and quick, and in ways she wouldn't want.

"I'm not scared of you," she said. But she said it so quietly, the liar. So I picked a doll up by the face and swung it against the wall, and it shattered, little pieces of porcelain flying everywhere, and when I looked down at my hand I saw it was cut up pretty bad. I squeezed the biggest fragment, all jagged and bloody, and Olivia shrank back against the wall.

"You'd be amazed at how resourceful karma can be," I told her, then got out of there before it went from scaring her to hurting her, because the thought was in my head and I didn't like how it kept pulling at me.

God, I hope that did it. I really hope it scared her enough to drop out. I don't want this to go any farther, but what if it does? What if I broke her like the doll? And got caught? Is the risk greater than the reward?

There has to be another way to get what I want. Think, Penny, think.

My hand hurts.

Lock.

Entry #310: The Princess and the Suffering
-locked-

haji

I have never made a black kite before. Always I have sought bold colors to lend my creations vibrancy and magic. Not this time. This one will be black as the Black Stone. Black as my father's eyes.

My heart is restless, and so I do this for meditation, not leisure, though the two are often one and the same. As I connect a lark's head to a knotted loop, I picture myself as a single dot in the fabric, envisioning the rest of the kite as infinite space about me, a universe unto itself. I can almost feel the enormity of it when my concentration is cut by the soft purr of the autoclean's motor as it sweeps dutifully across the floor. I must look up to link to it, willing it to please come back another time.

I call the Black Light, vainly perhaps, but with all the force I can muster. Many years ago, my father taught me that it is the color of enlightenment, the last step on the Sufi path. We call it *fana*. This is where the ego dies, in the blackness, where one can become empty and find union with the divine. It is an Arabic word, *fana,* meaning extinction or annihilation. Annihilation of everything but God.

After fearing that my father brought me into this world only to destroy me, only to reach Dr. James Hyoguchi, I am now seeking self-annihilation to reach the love and wisdom of God. The irony is not lost on me, but it is precisely what I must do. I am off balance. I do not feel holy. I must move through this turmoil to find answers and peace.

May this kite be God's kite, and when He flies it may my soul lift!

My father has taught me so very much over the years, but the construction of kites I learned from a book. I found it in Egypt, in one of the libraries we sought to restore, when I must have been half the age Dalila is now. I remember how my eyes danced over the racks, a kaleidoscope of color from spine to spine, and I wanted that one, the high one I could not reach. Hessa stood up on tiptoe and got it for me, reading it with me at the little table, delighted to see my imagination so captured. Every time I make a kite, I return to that first moment of joyful innocence, of awe and wonder at what I might create.

Thought I might find you here, says a voice. This is Penny stalking into my sanctuary, a phone in her left hand, her right wrapped tightly in gauze.

She has discovered me in the Magdalenenklause chapel, Nymphenburg's "place of penitence," designed for solitude and prayer. Of little interest to my aunts and cousins, this grotto is one of the few structures in the palace that have not been altered in recent years. Though the outside looks ruined, the inside is clean and well maintained.

Will you please help me? she asks.

I am in the midst of something but will gladly help if you but wait a moment, I say, but she does not understand, sitting next to me on the pew saying, You're making a kite, that's terrific, but I need you now.

I have come here seeking quiet refuge, I explain, and I stop explaining when I see the heartsick look on her face. Whatever she needs must be important and perhaps it truly cannot wait. I set the black kite down.

Call Pandora, she says.

She wants me to speak on her behalf, to convince my aunt that she should receive special instruction while the girl of my brother Ngozi's affection, Olivia, should not. This is doubly wrong. First, I have already complimented Penny to Pandora. Second, I am not in a position to judge Penny's merits relative to Olivia's. The Inside remains a mystery to me, and if she is asking me which domain I most prefer, the answer is Tomi's.

I don't care if you've already called her, she says. Call her again.

What good would it do?

She'll listen to you, Haji. She may not like me but she's definitely sweet on you. I'm counting on that.

What can I say to her that has not been said?

Tell her Olivia doesn't have the maturity to handle that kind of responsibility.

How do I know that?

Because she insulted you. Because she made fun of your religion. I don't know, because she ripped up one of your kites, how's that?

You want me to make something up?

Right, make something up. Whatever you think she'll believe.

I sigh and tilt my head back. Scenes from Mary Magdalene's life stare down at me from the frescoes above.

What? You won't help me?

Not if it involves lying.

I'm not asking you to make a habit of it. I'm asking you to slant the truth, just this once, as a favor to me. As a tiny kindness to someone who desperately needs it.

Penny, you are banging a drum.

She does not know what I mean. I explain:

Once upon a time, there was a young boy who liked nothing better than to bang on a drum. He would joyfully bang it all day long, no matter how much the noise irritated those around him. No matter what his parents tried, he would not stop, and in desperation they turned to learned men who called themselves Sufis.

The first alleged Sufi tried reasoning with the boy, arguing that so much drumming would damage his eardrums. The second professed that drums were sacred instruments and should only be beaten on special occasions. The third distributed earplugs. The fourth tried to distract the boy with books. The fifth offered to teach the boy's parents and neighbors how to live with the noise. The sixth introduced the boy to meditation and claimed that the drum was merely a figment of his imagination. But none of these men were true Sufis and none of the remedies worked.

Finally, a real Sufi arrived. He took stock of the situation, sat next to the boy and handed him a hammer and chisel. I wonder what is inside the drum, the Sufi said.

Penny stares intensely at me, saying nothing. She clears her throat. She frowns. She says, You're saying there's a simple solution to my problem?

Of course.

Tell me, she whispers.

Stop caring about it, I tell her. She shakes her head as if I have suggested something unconscionable. Stop caring, I repeat. Let it go. Some things are not meant to be, and we must press on, finding new dreams when the old ones have been destroyed.

That's your advice? she says.

Perhaps God has another plan for you. Will you resist it or accept the embrace?

Do you hate me? she asks. Is that what's going on?

I hate no one.

Well, when you look at me, what do you see?

I have no ready answer, and so she fills the silence with all the triumphs in her life, a litany of virtues both perceived and imagined. For all her achievements, she is the unhappiest girl I have ever met, and the feeling I absorb from her tells me she would only do a good deed if she thought someone was watching. Pity rises in me and I try to take her hand, but she is too agitated for such a gesture.

Is it money? she cries. I don't have any left but I swear I'll get some if you call.

I do not want your money.

Here, she says, I know what you want. She whips off her blazer, tossing it aside. The tie is next and by the time she gets to the shirt I tell her to stop, but my words mean nothing to her, and I avert my eyes. I know what you want, she says, again and again, voice rising, a furious, anguished girl offering sex she cannot even feel.

I will not be a party to her abasement. I tell her this and I leave.

Outside, I can hear her shaking the pews, kicking them. I can hear the wood splinter. She is crying. Not in great heaving sobs, but in sudden tremors and tiny chokes. There is nothing I can give her, and nothing she can give me. I wait until the fit of temper has been tempered, until she is quiet again, and when she emerges I am relieved to see that she is dressed once more.

You're too holy, she says, the gauze bandage on her hand unraveled and dangling until she rips it off with her teeth. How nice for you to be so holy and enlightened when I'm losing everything I ever had.

She leaves me, and when I reenter the chapel I see my black kite in tatters, stomped irreparably beneath her heel.

God breaks the heart again and again until it stays open, I mutter.

I fear Penny is right. Maybe I am too holy. Were I less so, maybe she would have listened to me. If I spoke like her, thought like her. Maybe the way to find enlightenment is to give up on it completely.

As the autoclean disposes of the debris, I take measured breaths and collect my thoughts, pushing the unpleasant ones aside. My work is ruined, but Champagne may have materials I need to start it anew. But not now. Tomi and I have a date Inside in less than an hour and I do not want to be late for it.

Haji?

Someone is linking to me, and I recognize the voice as Malachi's.

I heard you found out, he says. Who you are, I mean. Where you come from.

Where my DNA comes from, I correct him.

That's more accurate, he agrees.

For several minutes we discuss Dr. Hyoguchi, to whom Malachi owes his existence. The source of my DNA is not so much a programmer as a patriarch, where Malachi is concerned.

Am I anything like him?

Not so much. Since meeting you, I've been curious to see if you might spark to some of the things to which he sparked. But as I say, not so much with you.

A disappointment, then?

In a sense.

So would you rather that I go through with the procedure? So your father might return to you?

I'd love to have him back, he admits. I miss him. But I'd never in good conscience ask you to go through with that. Eventually, I'll find another way to resurrect him, a way that won't come at your expense. You should see what Pandora and I have been working on. It's fascinating.

I think to ask him about it, and behind that thought another follows. Could Malachi have sent me the key? And if so, to what end?

But he has gone back to talking about Hyoguchi, and as I wait for a pause in his speech to voice my questions, the sound of interference begins to build until an abrupt click ends the conversation, removing Malachi in mid-sentence.

I call his name, once, twice, but I am once again alone.

penny

Entry #311: The Princess and the Sad Thing -open-

I've made a list. Let's not call it an enemies list. Let's call it a list of people who need to be sorry for what they've done.

The trouble with lists is who to put up at the top. That's part of the fun of it too, but I don't want to make those choices yet so I'll do it alphabetically: Brigit, Haji, Izzy, Lulu, Olivia, Pandora, Sloane. That's seven. I'd make it nine and put my moms on the list too, but there's sorry and then there's sorry, and I have to cut a little slack to the people who brought me into the world.

I've been thinking of making a chart where I tie each of the seven to one of the so-called seven deadly sins, but they're all guilty of more than one, and it'd be unfair to peg just Olivia with envy when frankly they all envy me. Wall-to-wall envy, wall-to-wall pride, and they're too damn slothful to get up off their butts to help someone in need. To hell with them. If they think I'm not worth fighting for, maybe they should see what I'm like to fight against.

The new name on the list is Haji, because getting help from Haji is like asking a chipmunk to do calculus. Or begging a blind man to see. Or more to the point, yelling at a cripple to stop limping—he can't. He wasted my time and energy with a stupid story about how I'm playing the drums when everyone knows my operas are part of the Baroque tradition where you use very little percussion to accentuate the melody, and the worst part is he actually thought he was helping me, the condescending fool.

Actually, he's not a fool—he's a robot. A Sufibot, that's what he is—pull his lever and he jingles and jangles and burbles out pithy, holier-than-thou fortune cookie sayings. Well, I've had it with his oh-so-pious non–contraction–using Jonny Quest ass—he's on the list!

I should probably go to the source and blame Uncle Isaac for unleashing genetic throwbacks upon the world. That's probably worse than infecting them with religious mumbo jumbo. Why create garden-variety Homo sapiens when you can have Water-babies? If you're going to bring back old hominids for nostalgia's sake, why not go all the way back to Homo erectus or Australopithecus? They might at least make interesting grunts, or discover fire or something. Let's face it—my cousins are oxygen thieves. They're just backward people taking up space, and if they all met up with an axe murderer I don't think they'd be missed.

I don't miss Hessa, that's for sure. It's a funny thing—I've been carrying around this guilt for a whole year but now I'm thinking I did the world a favor. Just one more accomplishment I won't get credit for.

Okay, I didn't just hex her. I played a joke on her. But that's all that it was, a stupid prank. It's not like I plotted her death or premeditated it, rubbing my hands together and cackling in ghoulish glee. She got on my bad side, so I hexed her, and then the joke, and then she died. Like an accident. I'd say it was an unfortunate accident, but by that I'd only mean it was unfortunate for her.

She was this silly little Sufibot who took nothing seriously—everything was just a big game to her like nothing really mattered, and she was all buddy-buddy with Sloane, and I just knew she'd turn into another Brigit if someone didn't take her down a peg. She was coming to breakfast one day, and back then my baby sister Katrina used to have this bad habit of running through the house like a crazy person—she still does it these days, just less—

and this time when she ran in, she accidentally knocked the pill-box out of Hessa's hand. Everything went flying and Katrina apologized, but Hessa just laughed like it wasn't the least bit annoying, and we all had to get down on the black-and-white-checkered floor and crawl around on our hands and knees to help her find all her medicine. And I decided to hold on to a pill because—I don't know, I guess just because I could. She had plenty of them after all.

It wasn't until the next day when the idea for the joke came to me. I was rolling this dirty white pill between my fingers, trying to move it from knuckle to knuckle the way I've seen magicians move coins on the Inside. And I just noticed how generic the pill looked. Not very special. Just boring. So I had the idea to dip into the medicine cabinet, and going through all the different bottles, I had a nice laugh finding laxatives that looked almost exactly the same. It was too good not to do. When they all went out skating, I snuck into her pillbox and made the swap. And I hexed her. And I thought, let's see how happy-go-lucky you are after a taste of the crapping hell.

What I didn't know was how incredibly fragile she was. From an immunological perspective, she wasn't any tougher than the porcelain doll I smashed. Three days without her medicine and she got a lot more than diarrhea—we're talking vomiting, fever and worse—that tiny gap in her defense was all Black Ep needed to take hold. I'd never seen anyone get really sick before.

It was awful, honestly. It wasn't what I'd planned.

I didn't want to get caught, so I swapped the original medicine back for the laxatives before Vashti could check. They put Hessa back on the right pills, and even tried some new ones, but the damage was already done. It had become multidrug-resistant, like the worst strains of tuberculosis and HIV. Once Black Ep gets a foot in the door, it's over.

Isaac flew out, suspicious and rightly so, but no one could

prove anything. Hessa got worse and worse and when it was all over I wore my grief on my sleeve so no one would suspect and that was pretty much that.

I've been carrying this for so long, it feels good to finally write about it. I can't really talk about it with anyone. They might not understand—they might think I'm responsible when no one told me how vulnerable she was. Call it what you will, it was a joke, an accident, a tragedy I'll admit, but not murder.

I didn't mean to do it then but today I realized that never in my life have I wanted to kill someone more than I do right now. Take your pick of anyone on the list and I can picture a dozen different ways of doing them in, each more satisfying than the last. But you want to know the sad thing?

I don't think I can do it.

I just don't have it in me. Believe me, I wish I did—I'd be beautifying my environment—but every time I try to psyche myself up for it, I wind up with some awful memory popping into my head that messes everything up. As much as I hate Brigit and Sloane—and I can't stand either of them—I can remember learning how to read with them, or skipping rope and playing double Dutch. One time when they tried to get me in trouble, Olivia stood up for me and kept moms from fining me. Even Haji made me laugh once—that time I beat Tomi in the Louvre.

Why can't I get these thoughts out of my head?

Haikubot?

Troubled though I am
Happy moments in my past
Bar me from madness

Okay, Haikubot, you just made the list.

I'm going back Inside now to think of the worst thing I can possibly do to Olivia. Even if I don't have the nerve to kill her, I bet I can make her life a living hell. And maybe I'll find another present from my mystery friend. So far, I've got half a yin-yang symbol, half a heart-shaped locket, half a long-stemmed rose and half a playing card. All I need is half a plan to get the life I deserve back and maybe I'm in business. Wish me luck.

Lock this.

Entry #311: The Princess and the Sad Thing –locked–

haji

I am anticipating Tomi's sprite when Rashid sends me his, a glowing silver and gold light that serves as both a call and a calling card. When I answer it, I am transported to the domain in which he sojourns. He is stretched out on a bench in the Ancol Dreamland, a science-and-technology-themed recreational park, which is to Jakarta what Epcot is to Florida. I am surrounded by ghosts, computer-generated vacationers rushing from one attraction to the next, their voices occasionally overpowered by the noisy rattle of *bajajs*, three-wheeled motorized rickshaws.

Rashid scooches over on the bench and beckons me to sit, offering me my choice of coconut scones, tuna *chapati* or *kuping gajah*. I select the *kuping gajah* because it is made of chocolate and is shaped like elephant ears.

This is one of the places she visited, he says, squinting from the sunlight.

I shield my eyes as I glance about, taking in the lagoon, the souvenir shops, the dance clubs. Off in the distance I can see white-crested waves crashing into honey-colored sand. Before she died, Hessa told me some of the girls were teaching her how to surf. Maybe that was here.

Rashid suddenly coughs, spitting up a piece of coconut scone. It lands on the sidewalk in a wet gob. He frowns and rubs his mouth with the back of his hand.

Are you okay?

Never better, little brother, he says with a smile just this side of grimace, then hands me a stack of numbered postcards. Everywhere Hessa went. I riffle through the images, beautiful and exotic, pausing at the vistas I know she would have especially enjoyed.

Have you found anything out? he asks.

Nothing.

You seem different, he says. Something eating you?

I stare at him. I am tempted to tell him where his DNA originates. Doing so would disrespect my father. I do not like keeping secrets but I must honor his request.

Why are you looking at me like that? he asks.

I reach out to put a hand on his forehead. He swipes it away.

I'm sick, he admits.

How sick?

Sick, he shrugs. Don't tell anyone. They'll kick me Outside, and I have a whole day planned in here.

Why not hold off until you feel better?

Why not mind your own business, he snipes, coughing violently again before leaving my sight in a flash of sparkling light, teleporting off to a new domain.

Pandora is not online, I learn, so I send her mail suggesting that she might want to look in on Rashid. I do not use the word *sick*.

The postcards make useful shortcuts. I tap the top one, my virtual fingertip conceding its artificiality by stretching into an emerald-green display menu when it makes contact with the call number. A twitch whisks me off to the domain itself, a cash register's accompanying chime announcing that my bank account has been drained a nominal fee.

I visit a dozen domains in all. I am looking for some kind of pattern, some clue as to how my sister died. I find nothing.

I may never know the truth. Not every question has an answer. Can I live with that? Can I simply let her go?

When the heart weeps for what it has lost, the soul rejoices for what it has found. And so I resolve to honor Hessa with the way I live my life. I will start with a gift for Tomi, I decide, something whimsical that will make her smile. A stuffed animal? A panda bear or a rabbit, perhaps in samurai costume. When I tap into my account to see how much there is to spend, I see a row of nines stretching across the display.

It is from Pandora. To the left of her name, under *service,* is the word *liberty.* Why she would grant me such a liberty, I do not know. I have enough money to fill an entire domain with stuffed animals. Perhaps it is a mistake, but if it is a mistake that brings Tomi joy, I welcome it with open arms.

Unfortunately, a maze of choices encumbers my shopping spree. With so much money at my disposal, there are simply too many choices. It seems I can go anywhere and do anything and I have no idea where to begin.

Tomi rescues me from cognitive overload, and when I greet her I discover that she has a present for me as well. Look, she says, leading me to a tower window and drawing my attention to the horizon with a delighted sweep of her hand.

Since last I came here, she has made significant additions to her domain. I see castles and armies, shrines, temples, shops and homes, a land bursting with life and color with all the splendor and pageantry fit for an emperor. The streets and the fields are teeming with citizens, and the sky is flush with kites.

Do you love it? she asks.

How did you do it?

I'm rich, she says. I can build whatever I want.

I let out an appreciative whistle. She has outdone herself.

Want to fly a kite with me?

I cannot answer. She asks me again, but I am consumed by what I see. There is a pattern in the sky, I realize, a familiarity in the motions of the kites. I can see them moving closer and closer to an image in my mind. From nowhere, an intense hyperawareness washes over me, déjà vu followed by incomparable bliss. I have been picturing the design I sketched in bathwater on the ceramic tile floor back in Saqqara and it is identical to what I see now. It is like I am living the past and present at the exact same time. In that instant I cease to exist, my physical body dispersing to the winds, and my soul is up with the kites, a single point in the pattern, and that pattern is God.

Worlds rush past me, and time and space and wonder and love.

I have known moments of higher consciousness before, moments of sublime connection with the universe, but none like this. This dwarfs everything. Laughter escapes me in a magnificent rush and all my troubles are borne away.

When the moment passes, as it must, when I turn to Tomi, I can tell from the look on her resplendent, perfectly symmetrical face that as quick as she is, she was too slow to see my transformation. She did not see me join the kites. But it does not matter. I have had a religious epiphany, or gone mad, or both. Whatever it is, I have never felt more alive, and I realize now that whatever happens to me from this point on, nothing can take away the pure, unadulterated ecstasy that has come to blossom within my soul.

penny

Something's wrong here. I have all the money in the world and can buy whatever I want. No, really. My bank account says I have nine trillion nine-hundred-ninety-nine billion nine-hundred-ninety-nine million nine-hundred-ninety-nine thousand nine-hundred-ninety-nine big ones. And ninety-nine little ones. That should be a good thing, but it's not. I can already tell.

Something's really, really wrong.

Lock.

pandora

Diagnoses are made.

First, about Mu'tazz. I've been crossing my fingers for something like an aggressive gastrointestinal flu, but Isaac suspects Black Ep. They've quarantined themselves in the back of my copter. Mu'tazz keeps making terrible retching sounds. I'm rattled. I can only imagine what Isaac's feeling. What we went through last year with Hessa, to go through that again—God, it feels unbearable.

Second, about the monkey, it's monkeys plural—my "he" is a pregnant she. A tribe of pygmy marmosets survived Black Ep naturally all on their own, which means maybe so can we, if we can only figure out what's protected them while so many other primates bit the dust. The potential for what we can learn here practically has me dancing with joy, and maybe I would be if it weren't for Mu'tazz.

Third, Malachi's gone. I tried to raise him and he's just not there. And that's crazy, because he's always Johnny-on-the-spot when I need him. I'm running a remote diagnostic, and all it's telling me is that he's running a diagnostic too. That doesn't explain why I'm not getting any response. Maybe the glitches gobbled him up and I'll have to restore from a backup.

Before I can report to Vashti, she's called me, hurling curses at me the moment I pick up, in a completely out-of-control attack mode I call "Pit Bull." Vash rarely loses it, and when she does she usually won't go past "Rottweiler" or "Doberman," which makes the rare Pit Bull really something to see.

The only words I can catch are "cocksucker" and "massive security breach."

"Slow down," I tell her.

"Your boyfriend fucked me!" she screams, sending me scrambling for mental turpentine to erase the picture painted in my head.

"What's going on?"

"Halloween just stomped his dirty boots all over your precious security system. Everything's compromised. Universal access to all the files."

"How do you know it was Hal?"

"Who else could it be? Can you think of someone else with that special mix of venom and know-how? When the system unspoofs the address I guarantee you it'll say the attack came from America. And he promised, Pandora—that son of a bitch gave his word he'd never interfere but that's exactly what he's done!"

"Well," I say, trying to keep a cool head on the situation, "first things first—take the kids out of the IVR."

"Are you stupid? Champagne already did, but the damage's done. You can't unring a bell."

"Okay, so they learned a few dirty words and got an eyeful of violence or porn or whatever else is floating around in there." *Hey, good news, we found a monkey and listen, bad news, Mu'tazz is sick,* I want to tell her, but she's still rabid.

"Pandora," she spits, "what's floating around in there is personal. All my logs, my lab notes, my private communications. Every single file is there for the taking. He found them, he put a price on them and he pimped them out."

"That is a problem," I admit, and maybe it was Hal, because right about now I can see him laughing his ass off. And she's right—it's a sophisticated attack and he's just about the only person I know with the kind of savvy to pull this off. Encryption and programming against decryption and reprogramming—I spent months and years setting up the walls he just knocked down. I wonder how long it took him. Should I be insulted or impressed?

"Some of the girls are going to be upset," I warn Vashti, which serves only to put a muscle near her left eye into spasm. She is breathless with impotent rage.

"He has to answer for this," she says. "It's on his head."

penny

Entry #313: The Princess and the Price –open–

What do I deserve?

It's a fair question, isn't it? What exactly do I deserve? Anything at all?

Obviously I don't deserve your respect. You don't trust me, and why should you? Why trust the lowest of the low? Better not to give me even my most basic privacy, which you apparently don't, because you've been reading my journal.

I know you've been doing it for years.

You're doing it right now.

But this space is private, isn't it? Private and personal? For Penny's innermost thoughts—you said I could write whatever I wanted and it would always be secret and I always believed you— how silly when you don't care, when you can break my locks and read it like I'm beneath consideration. Like I'm nothing.

Am I nothing to you? When you look at me, is that what you see?

And when I look at the two of you, what do you suppose I see? You might want to think about that, now that the telescope has turned. Now that I've read your logs. I know what you've done, how you think, all the ways you've tricked me. How does it feel to know someone's got a finger on all your horrible lies?

Oh, did you ever put one over on me. All those times you told me how smart I am, what a great student this, what a hard worker that, when behind my back you say I'm "disappointing," an "underachiever who has yet to capitalize on her promise"? I show "signs of immaturity"? My operas are "obnoxious and derivative"? And thanks for all the extra money, Champagne. You let me think I was rich when all told I barely make more than Katrina. Katrina's nine goddamn years old!

You let me think I was best—the alpha—when really you think I'm the omega. I'm the one you worry about. The one you feel sorry for. Poor Penny.

This is my true state? Should I just lay down and die? Do you have any idea what kind of monstrous betrayal this is, you filthy fucking bitches?

Vashti, let's talk about my "psychological instability." I'm a narcissist, am I? With "magical thinking" and a "self-induced sense of superiority"? And I'm a "growing problem"? You don't know the half.

You wrote you sometimes doubt I have "feelings of any kind." That's just brilliant! Sure, I'm a block of ice. I don't feel anything, so you can do whatever you want to me and it just won't matter. That's your big analysis? That's what you believe? Then why am I so hurt? Did you ever stop to think that in my heart I might feel things more deeply than you ever could, you degenerate piece of shit?

I was incredibly arrogant, wasn't I? So arrogant that an hour ago I thought I had nothing left to lose. Now I see I was wrong—all the things I took for granted were things I never had. Gone now, everything's gone. Can you explain it? Can you explain how you could do this to me? I may not be a human being, but I always assumed you'd treat me with human decency.

How could you?

I always stood up for you. I loved you. Last spring when you decided to crack down on the rules, Brigit and Sloane thought it would be funny to call you the Vichy instead of the V.C. and I said they'd better stop or I'd tell. But they're right, you made them right—you are the Vichy—you're Nazis, Vashti in charge, and Champagne "only following orders."

"We're at war with Black Ep," so you wanted focused and obedient soldiers.

You had Pandora string the Inside with subliminal messages.

You made us take mood-altering drugs and said they were immunogens.

You gave us pills to inhibit our libidos, and blamed it on our physiologies. No distractions from our studies. Even if I can't give birth, don't you think I deserve to feel like a woman? Is the plague so important you'd deny me even that?

I'm not a lab rat. Fuck you for the liberties you took.

Vashti—

You can't lie anymore.

You can't control me with drugs.

You can't control me with money.

You can't control me with love.

You can't make me into something I'm not.

You can't kill my free will.

You never really cared about me.

You only pretended.

Champagne—

I used to feel safe when you held me.

I used to feel loved.

I treasured the time we spent finger-painting.

Blowing the soap bubbles together.

Letting me braid your hair.

I used to call you Mommy.

And you stood by.

You did nothing.

You let this happen.

Listen closely, you hideous cunts: I have something you don't. It's beating fiercely in my chest, and if you saw it you'd wither. You don't know the first thing about love, and the hate you've spread will come back to you with teeth. That's fair warning. If you take away nothing else from this, fucking understand this: The next hex I put out is going to make you shriek.

Everything you did to me has a price and I'm going to collect it.

pandora

I'm five hundred miles from Cape Verde when Malachi comes back from the dead. His hologram flickers in so silently, without warning, that I jump in my seat, banging my knees against the console. From the wild look in his steel-gray eyes, I can tell he's shaken and spooked, all his fight-or-flight flags triggered.

"Reset your flags," I tell him, and even though he could instantly drop his mood back to Buddha-like calm if he wanted to, it's not in his nature to do it. He shakes his head violently, puffs out a breath, brushes his hair back with his fingers and looks at me.

"Someone took me out," he says.

"Do you know who?"

"Pandy, it was a skillful trap. Reminded me of the attacks Mercutio made against me years ago. Not the same signature, but the same level of sophistication."

"Was it Halloween?"

"It came from Michigan. So unless you think Fantasia did it—which I don't."

And I don't think that either—in my head, pieces of the puzzle are snapping into place. Halloween wants to humiliate Vashti but can't reach her with Malachi intact, so he traps Malachi first.

Wounding the security guard to rob the bank. I share the theory with Mal and he suspects I'm right.

"He took out Pace three seconds later—it looks like we were simply alarm wires he had to snip. Which, it goes without saying, I consider an insult."

"So now he's wounded both our egos. Do you think he was trying to destroy you or just keep you tied up for a while?"

"I won't hazard a guess. Either way, it's pretty callous."

"Callous," I agree. "Especially since you left things with him on good terms."

"Better than you know," he says.

"What does that mean?"

He throws me a conscience-stricken look and tells me he's glad I'm sitting down. "For years, I've had a deal with Halloween. I've worked for him. But this tears it—he's just burned through the last of my loyalty."

"You work for me," I say.

"No, I work with you. I worked for him."

"So you've been lying to me?"

"Oh yes," he says mournfully. "Do you remember seventeen years ago? When you first started spying on him?"

Of course I do. In that first year of freedom, Halloween was trying to kill himself. Not directly, but the effect would have been the same. He went to Pennsylvania to restore a rusted deathtrap of a roller coaster by the name of Breaking Point. Malachi furnished me with the satellite photos and I knew I had to try and reel him in.

"He figured out what you were doing and put a stop to it," Malachi says. "The satellites aren't under my full control—in fact, for the past seventeen years, I haven't been able to take a picture of any part of the United States at all."

"So the pictures you've been sending me? They're fakes?"

"All of them," he says. "Halloween put me up to it. I owed him a favor for saving me from Mercutio's tender mercies, and for not deleting me when he could. That's the arrangement we struck."

My stony silence forces an apology from him.

You didn't force an apology from me—it was freely given.
You just wanted to drop your regret flag.
I still regret it. Though the decision made sense at the time.

"Do you still talk to him?" I ask.

"Not in years. I honestly don't know what's been happening to him, or why he'd do a thing like this. Perhaps he just snapped. Isolation can do funny things."

"Well, by betraying me you helped keep him isolated," I snap. "Whatever your reasons for doing it, you might have done a world of harm."

"I'll do whatever I can to fix things," he promises. "What can I do to help?"

"Take the wheel," I say, disgustedly leaving my chair and storming to the back.

My head may be spinning, but one thing is perfectly clear. No matter what Hal wants, I'm going to pay him a visit. He has to answer to Vashti, he has to answer to Malachi, but more than anyone else he has to answer to me.

I come to the three girls, who are still excitedly debating names for our sedated pregnant marmoset, their rapid-fire chatter pausing when they see me.

"Is Mu'tazz okay?" they ask, and I have no answer, but I tell them that I'm on my way to check. And so into the quarantine I go.

My sixteen-year-old nephew is sprawled out on the blankets, covered with sweat, eyes closed and mouth open. "He's delirious," Isaac tells me, lines of worry etched into his face. "He keeps fading in and out of consciousness. I wish he'd just sleep."

Mu'tazz mumbles something I can't understand in a language I don't speak. I kneel down to see his eyes open ever so slightly, but they focus on nothing, and then close once again. I take Isaac's hand.

"Is it what you think it is?" I ask.

"Worse," he says.

"How can it be worse than Black Ep?"

"I have a course of treatment for Black Ep," he says. "Not for this. I've never seen this before."

"Something will work," I assure him, but I realize, quietly, that I'm not so sure. I speak not from knowledge but from hope.

Mu'tazz repeats what he said, muscles thrashing, his hands grinding into the blankets and squeezing as hard as he can.

"Is that Arabic?"

"Aramaic," Isaac says. "I've been teaching him Aramaic."

"What is he saying?"

Isaac does not look at me. He looks at his son and shakes his head, as if he could somehow save him with that one simple negation. A teardrop escapes him, rolling down his cheek to splash upon the blanket.

"'It is the End of the World,'" he says.

part three

the devil

halloween

I always knew it couldn't last.

You can hole yourself up for years, but you can't keep the world away forever. Forever is just too fucking long.

Goodbye, American isolationism. Hello, Pandora.

pandora

He knows I'm coming. He actually had the gall to try to call me when he spotted me over the eastern seaboard. Oh, now you want to talk? Enjoy a little radio silence—you can wait until I'm on the ground.

Outside, a hard autumn rain makes the approach trickier than it should. "Raining open pocketknives," as my grandfather might say.

Ever closer my heart to Halloween, and the poison-munching monarch butterflies he uses as his standard seem to have taken residence in my stomach. I drown them with Munich's finest Chardonnay, a finder's fee for delivering a certain monkey. I shouldn't fly intoxicated and actually I'm not—every time I veer off course Malachi pulls me back, guiding the craft with an invisible hand.

"Take it easy with that," he suggests when I try another swallow. "You don't want to marinate yourself, do you?"

"Are you talking to me, Malachi?"

"Are you still *not* talking to me?"

I answer by not answering. Really, I'm glad I have him and Halloween to focus my anger on. It's a welcome distraction from worrying about Isaac's kids.

I'm past the bay now—I can see the 10 freeway beneath me as I follow it west, tracking the one ray of sunset that hasn't been suffocated by storm clouds. Coming back here isn't easy. It's not quite as bad as going back to São Paulo, but it's still a ghost town, a parody of the flourishing (if unreal) community where I went to school. I can go most anywhere in the world and take in as much loss, destruction and desolation as you please without losing it, but seeing the places I remember warmly from childhood laid so low makes me jittery and sick. Granted, the alcohol probably isn't helping with sick, but it's working wonders for jittery.

Idlewild sits right in the heart of Manistee National Forest. The town's protected by five hundred thousand acres of unspoiled wilderness, but I see now that a good fraction of it has been spoiled—burned and toppled trees lay evidence to what must have been one hell of a fire. It wasn't like this when I visited eighteen years ago.

While I am wistfully recalling nature hikes, contests to see who can gather the most pine cones, and foolhardy attempts to climb fifty-foot balsam firs, I notice that some of the town has been scorched as well. Among the casualties, I see what used to be Twain's, the retro coffee shop my schoolmates and I always used to invade after classes. It's where Hal poured his heart out to me back when we were sixteen. We held hands across the table and played the kind of music no one can stand except sad people in love. We talked for hours about Simone and went out bowling, and broke into an empty lakeside mansion to have ourselves a one-night stand. So Twain's is sentimental to me, and when I see it burned to the ground like this I have to remind myself that it isn't the Twain's we went to—it's just the prototype for the computer-generated Twain's we knew in the IVR. It's funny when an illusion becomes more dear to you than fact.

I'm trying to psych myself up to mention the night we spent together, because I've always thought if he can remember that everything might change between us. But there's also the chance that he already does remember it, that it's a memory Mercutio didn't rob him of. If that's the case, then he doesn't talk about it because it doesn't mean anything to him: and that's why I haven't been able to bring it up over the years—I'm too scared to find out.

I swoop over recreational parks and technology parks, the funny mix that makes up this part of Michigan. I set the copter down in a grassy field flanked by streets with religious names—Joy, Miracle, Creation—and I take a long look at the corner of Grandeur and Forman Road. This is the one part of the town the programmers fictionalized. They created a school for us to come of age, but here in the real world, this address belongs to Gedaechtnis Headquarters.

It's a massive building, much bigger than our tiny boarding school. It doesn't look like it belongs here any more than it did the last time I saw it. My poor brain keeps looking for my alma mater, for a gorgeous green campus, for any signs at all of the "progressive learning environment" I remember. And to see it replaced with this vaultlike monstrosity—all the Gedaechtnis buildings make me nervous, and if I didn't have to work in one, I wouldn't, but this one is the creepiest of the lot.

Which makes it perfect for Hal, of course.

As I power down and step out into the rain, I have to wonder what he looks like now. It's been so long since I've seen him in person. Maybe something happened to him. Maybe he's hideously scarred and he doesn't want me to see. Or burned, I wonder, the terrible thought logical but unwelcome—maybe he got caught in a forest fire and he's blistered and charred. Everything I know about how to treat burns rushes through my mind, but there's so much I've forgotten. These days I typically store my medical knowledge in Isaac's head or Vashti's head, going to them for this kind of problem just as they come to me when a problem is mechanical or digital in nature.

Of course, he's no more burned than I am. He strides through the door as handsome as ever, fit and lean, clean-shaven with natural orange hair and charcoal eyes. The only difference is he's a man now, even if he does still have the dangerous boyish quality I fell in love with. It's a long time to hold a crush, but my shaking knees and gently pounding heart tell me it's worth it.

He's so beautiful, and if only he wasn't so broken! Alas, as my mother tells me whenever I mope about him, *não há bela sem senão,* there's no beauty without an "if."

"I don't remember inviting you here," he scowls.

"You don't remember a lot of things."

"Yeah, ain't that the truth? Now before I go and lose my temper, I suppose you've got good reason to storm my castle?"

"*You* lose *your* temper? That's a laugh!"

"Answer my question."

"You know I have reason. Don't even pretend."

Time seems to stop, the storm drenching us, thunder punctuating the pause. Then he turns about, black raincoat swirling, and he grabs the steel door, holding it open for me.

"All right," he says. "This ought to be good."

halloween

I'm a mythology geek. I used to have these illustrated books of myths and legends from around the world. One had a terrific picture of a succubus: that's a demoness who steals men's souls by fucking them while they sleep. Lovely, guilt-free way to explain wet dreams. The picture showed a tall, tanned, sexy creature with eyes as green as envy and long inky-black hair falling around her in curls. When I saw Pandora in the rain, that's what I thought of—the succubus—except she was missing the horns, the bat wings and the devil tail. And she was dressed.

I took her in, took her coat, and took a look at her. Back in school she was stuck in an awkward tomboy phase for—honestly, for just about all of it—but she grew out of it by the time we flew the coop. She never looked this good though. That's the not-completely-unbiased perspective of a man who hasn't seen an actual real live woman in almost two decades. Absence can make more than the heart grow fonder, but it doesn't help me to be attracted to someone I don't trust.

"I really like what you've done with the place," she said, eyebrows raised.

"No need to get nasty," I said.

I led her through the kind of mess I might have bothered to clean up if I'd actually invited her. The lobby always looks like a bomb hit it. That's how I like it. The debris keeps me mindful of what happened here—how I killed my friend Mercutio, and how he almost killed me—not the sort of thing you'd be quick to sweep up and kiss off.

In the elevator, we didn't look at each other. When the doors slid open I made a jaunty *after you* gesture with my hand, and she hurried out without giving me a glance.

The tiger gave her pause.

I'd been keeping him in one of the conference rooms. It was big enough to house him comfortably and the glass was reinforced. He lifted his head up long enough to shoot us a predatory look before going back to licking his injured paw. I'd practically doused the entire bandage in bitter apple and still he kept after it.

Pandora gave me a concerned look.

"I caught a tiger by the toe," I told her, "but now that he's hollered, I'm letting him go. Tomorrow I'll take out the stitches and it's back to the wild for him."

"You shot him?"

"He confused me with lunch. But he's far too beautiful to kill."

"And until then, he's your pet? You have a pet tiger?"

"So? You have a pet monkey, don't you?"

"How is it you know that?" she asked, a flash of anger in her voice. "Are you spying on me?"

"Not lately," I said.

"You've been getting information from Malachi?"

"Over the years, some," I admitted. "Is that why you're here? You want to know what I'm doing, but not the other way around?"

That pissed her off. She lit into me for pushing her little AI friend into feeding her false information, calling me an "emotional blackmailer," which confused me, as I couldn't make out whether she thought I was blackmailing Malachi or herself.

"He's paid whatever debt he owes you," she added. "It's over."

"The only thing I ever asked of you is privacy," I snapped, "and you couldn't even give me that."

"Oh, your precious privacy! I haven't been here in eighteen years!"

"No, but you started snapping off satellite photos in that very first year. Did you really think I wouldn't find out?"

She flushed with guilt, but not contrition. She looked like she wanted to take a swing at me. She said, "I thought you were going to die, Hal."

"And how is that any business of yours?"

Balefully, she stared at me, and I turned away.

"Look," I said, "we're friends, and in a lot of ways we always will be, but I'm better off not worrying about you, and you'd be better off not worrying about me. That's really all I have to say about it."

She let out a short and hollow laugh. "Every time I see you, you turn your back. Do you know that?"

"I've done my good deed. Two bullets in Merc. Now I'm retired and the rest is up to you," I told her, turning back to give her a forced smile.

"So you've said. But it's not up to us if you interfere," she replied.

"Name one time when I interfered."

"Yesterday. You hacked."

She claimed I knocked out Malachi and disrupted the IVR. That's when I got it. That's when it all became clear. I knew she had come for one of two reasons, and if it wasn't the romantic fixation, it had to be the other one—the one I was dreading and hoping for all along.

"Okay, slow it down," I told her, leading her to the sofa and offering her a place to sit. "Tell me what you think I did."

"You're denying it?"

"Just tell me what happened."

I wasn't thrilled with the frying-Malachi-like-bacon part of the story—the skill it takes to do that impresses me, but Mal's a valuable piece of programming, and I'd no sooner see him dead than I would an endangered Michigan tiger—but I loved the part where Vashti and Champagne got exposed for the villains they are.

"Sweets to the sweet," I smirked, and she pushed me with both hands.

"It's not a game!"

"Tell me those two don't deserve whatever they get."

"You might think so, but what about their kids? Do you even know what's going on over there? Some of those girls are angry and frightened, confused, even outraged."

"With good reason," I noted.

"Maybe so, but you've turned them against their mothers, and that might be fair if they were adults, but they're not adults, they're children who need parents, and like it or not, Vash and Cham are the only ones they have."

She had a point.

"Now comes the part where you tell me you don't give a damn about them," she fumed. "You don't care about them, you obviously don't care about me, and we both know you don't care about the future. All you can see is what's in front of you. Just yourself and your little wild kingdom here, just the things that made you suffer."

"That sounds about right," I agreed.

"So why did you do it, Hal? What were you trying to prove?"

"Keep an eye on Big Whisper," I said, winking.

"Big Whisper?"

I pointed at the tiger, then got up and left.

"Where are you going?"

"To look for an answer," I said.

deuce

You're shaving off all the wood that doesn't look like a swan when he knocks on your door saying he needs to talk to you. You let him in and he's all about the honesty. Did you or didn't you? Yes or no? You put your hands up and tell the officer you'll come along quietly, which doesn't make him smile.

You're happy to tell him the who, the what, the where and the why but not the how because four out of five is plenty. Let him guess the how. He's mostly interested in the why, anyway, and that's the best part of it, the part where right is on your side.

He hears you out, empathizing, but only to a point. "You shouldn't have done it," he says. "Sending them gifts is one thing, but turning their lives upside down is a whole other story."

"It's what they needed."

"And?"

"And they're not the only ones who needed it to happen," you admit.

"Right."

"Are you disappointed?"

"I can't fault you for wanting to help," he says, turning your hat so the number faces the front, "and I'd be lying if I said I wasn't proud of you for putting frauds and tyrants back in their places. But you didn't think it through."

"Don't be so sure."

"Too much offense, not enough defense."

"Is this another chess lesson?"

"You spent too much time plotting an attack, and not enough

time figuring out how to cover your tracks," he says. "You won't be able to hide after this."

"That's why I did it," you tell him.

"Is that right?"

You nod your head up and down.

"So you did think it through. You're ready, then?"

Again, you nod, your smile stretching to mirror his own. He hugs you. He's been waiting a long time for this day, but no longer than you have.

You tell him you had to make an impact. You had to show the kids that you were on their side, and now that you've done it, they're not so scary anymore. They'll have to like you now—they'll treat you like a comrade and so much more—how could they not when you just cut them out of a monster's belly? You're practically Zeus, king of the gods, and what could Zeus possibly have to fear?

"Shall I bring Pandora?"

"Why not?" You shrug.

You're ready to take responsibility and he is so proud.

pandora

For far too long, Halloween leaves me just a glass partition away from a four-hundred-pound carnivore. When he returns, I'm only too happy to follow him back to the executive offices, where I find myself staring at another untamed creature, one that makes the tiger seem comparatively normal.

"*Oi, Pandora. Muito prazer em conhecê-la,*" he says without quite meeting my eyes. His Portuguese isn't bad, and it doesn't sound completely insincere, but it definitely sounds rehearsed.

"Nice to meet you too," I say.

I'm facing a nervous teenage boy, one with orange hair and charcoal eyes. The physical resemblance is incredible; it's as if I've stepped back in time and found a fourteen-year-old Hal—and in many ways that's exactly what I've done.

"This is my son, Deuce," Hal says, and by son I know he means clone.

"Deuce," I repeat, at a momentary loss for what else to say. The boy's hair is much longer than Hal's, I notice, swinging down past his shoulders, and he's covering most of it with a navy blue ski hat stitched with a white number 2 in the front. As if Hal should be wearing a matching hat with a number 1—which he isn't.

"I'm not used to visitors," Deuce apologizes, "so the odds are I'm going to offend you by doing something I shouldn't, or not doing something I should. Uh, do you want something to drink?" He steps back to indicate the mini-fridge.

"Maybe later," I tell him, my eyes drinking in the other contents of his room, especially the woodcarvings.

"That's all hand-carved," Hal points out. "He's gifted at it."

They usher me in, directing me to a pine chess set, one side stained black and the other side stained purple. The Black King is Halloween, protected by an army of nightgaunts. The Violet Queen is our missing friend, Fantasia, leading an army of Smileys. Beautiful workmanship, perfectly capturing the kind of war games Hal, Fan, Merc and Ty used to play. But I'm more interested in a carving of my transport copter.

"Oh, that. Do you want it?" Deuce asks.

"How long have you been watching me?"

It doesn't take much prodding for him to admit to major surveillance over the years. Apparently, Hal taught him how to put hooks into everything—spy satellites, intercepted transmissions and some deep hooks in the IVR, which explains many of the anomalies I've seen over the years. Father and son have been winning the intelligence war, and I can't help but feel a righteous anger rising within me, though most of it's aimed at myself for being so thoroughly hoodwinked for so long.

"You certainly know a lot more about me than I know about you," I tell them, with my arms folded defensively across my chest. "And here I thought you didn't care."

"It's not what you think," Deuce mumbles, staring down at his hiking boots. "It's a fear thing, not a sex thing. I'm not a peeping tom."

"What do you mean, a fear thing?"

He gives Hal a frustrated look—would he please explain it to me?

"He's shy," Hal says, putting an arm around the boy. "Anxiety disorder. He wants to meet people but it's not easy for him. He's been watching from afar to try and build up his confidence."

So far I'm not exactly thrilled with Hal's parenting style, but I resolve to keep that to myself while his son is within earshot. Son—he engineered a son—unbelievable.

"We don't bite," I tell Deuce.

"I don't like some of the things you do," is Deuce's reply.

"Me, personally?"

"See, I knew I'd offend you," he says, turning to Hal for reassurance before looking around me but not at me. "No, I mostly mean in general. Like what's been happening in Germany. Lying to the girls and overmedicating them—do you approve of that?" he asks, as close to meeting my eyes as he'll ever get.

"Not completely."

"Well, okay. The longer I watched, the more I wanted to do something. I couldn't just sit by the way he can," he says with a nod at Hal, "or the way you can. I mean, those kids are my peers."

"You don't even know them."

"Actually, I do. They just don't know me." He smiles. "But I'm ready to meet them now—now that I've liberated them."

"I'm not sure 'liberated' is the right word for what you did," Hal sighs.

"'Traumatized' might be closer," I say. Despite their varied means of surveillance, neither father nor son has a clear idea of what Nymphenburg is like, nor what exactly is going on over there right now. They have incomplete pictures of the situation, Hal filling in the rest with his childhood jaundices and Deuce with what seem to be unrealistic fantasies. As I explain the kind of chaos this "liberation" has wrought, I watch the boy's face crease with concern.

"I didn't want to hurt anyone," he says, flustered. "But truth can be painful. My comrades and—uh—my peers, their trust was being betrayed! It wasn't right for them not to know. Shouldn't you be yelling at Vashti instead of me?"

"Who's yelling?"

No one, so he slips his hands into his pockets and sulks.

"Look," Hal tells me, "we all feel bad about what those girls are going through, but at the end of the day all we're talking about is a little hacking. It's not such a big deal. How about I make him fix the IVR, I help you tighten online security, and to-gether we take care of Malachi so something like this can never happen to him again?"

I suspect it's the best deal I can get from them, but I keep my mouth shut to see if he'll offer anything more.

"Is that fair?" he asks Deuce.

"Sure, Dad," the boy agrees.

"We should talk about it," I tell Hal when he looks to me for an accord. Meaning we should talk about it alone.

He gets the hint and tells Deuce as much. Deuce turns back to me to say, *"Foi um prazer conhecê-la,"* in that rehearsed way of his.

"You too," I say. *"Até logo."*

Proud and pleased, Hal smiles at his son, playfully tugging the boy's hat down over his eyes. To this, Deuce laughs, closing the door behind us as we exit his room.

We walk the halls for a little privacy, Hal pointing out a Gedaechtnis conference room that has yet to be converted into a tiger pit or teenager's bedroom.

"What do you think?" he says.

"You fucking hypocrite," I fire at him, the barb unable to penetrate his well-practiced look of innocence until I back it up with, "All these years you've been Lord High King of Bullshit Mountain. What happened to the man who told me he wouldn't help repopulate the world because the world was better off without us? What happened to the last great nihilist?"

Now I see his eyes darken and his anger flare.

"Why didn't you tell me you had a son?"

"Why should I tell you anything?" he snaps, banging the door shut so we can have this out.

"Because we're friends, supposedly! What did I ever do to become so unworthy of your trust?"

"You got yourself tainted. Laid down with dogs and woke up with fleas."

"So this is about my 'despicable friends'?"

"No," he sneers, "it's about the way your despicable friends have rubbed off on you. The way I said they would and you promised they wouldn't."

"You want me to say I'm sorry because I wanted to make sure you weren't trying to kill yourself? I won't apologize for that. You don't like what Vashti's doing or what Isaac's doing or even what Champagne's doing and you think I haven't done enough to stand up to them? Fuck you, it's an enormous task and we're all trying to do the best we can—and when you decided you were just going to hole yourself up instead of helping, you gave up all right to complain!"

"So says the Prime Mover."

"You're so wrong, Hal," I insist. "You're wrong about me."

He shakes his head, confident, arrogantly so. "I'm dead-on

and if you had a shred of introspection left, you could see it for yourself."

"And if you had a shred of— Hang on, what was that Prime Mover crack?"

"That's what you are, aren't you? Vashti's little tool to worm subliminal messages into the IVR? I'll have to check, but I think there's a special circle of Hell for people who brainwash kids."

"Mind telling me where you got that information?"

"One of Vashti's journals. Deuce found it."

"And that's good enough for you?"

"Of course. He's my eyes these days. With him keeping tabs on what you jokers are doing, I'm free to work on more important things. Like putting all this behind me."

I mouth the words, "All this," seething with resentment. "Is that why you cloned yourself and had a kid?" I snipe. "To kill your childhood? To pretend it never happened?"

"I don't have to justify myself to you," he snarls.

I jerk toward him, and he holds his ground, so our faces are but inches apart. *"Vai peidar na água pra ver se sai bolinhas,"* I tell him. "I never put any subliminal messages anywhere. Vashti isn't the boss of IVR—I am."

"What about her journal then?"

"What about it? You think I do whatever she wants?" Oh, I could hit him. "Hal, I told her I'd do it to shut her up. I put on a show for her. That's why it's in her journal. Sometimes it's easier lying to her than fighting about it—you know how she gets when she wants something."

He tells me he doesn't believe me, and without hesitation I tell him he's welcome to check. So he tries to break me down with his eyes, searching for the sign that will confirm I'm the nasty sort of person he's convinced I am—but there is no ridiculous goddamn sign—and after another moment that seems to stretch into eternity, I see a flicker of anxiety subsuming righteous indignation, and from the anxiety an expression of what might just be regret.

"If that's true," he says, "maybe I've misjudged you."

"Maybe," I agree, slapping him across the face.

He puts his palm to his cheek, staring wildly at me, and I see the smile ripping across his face right before he bursts into laughter. If I weren't so hurt and so angry I might laugh along with him, but I can't stop myself, already I'm slapping him again but this time he catches my wrist, wrestling with me, and in the back of my mind, I'm thinking about how love and hate are supposed to be similar emotions, and how we might just wrestle into a passionate kiss, but instead he pushes me back to arm's length, his arms raised defensively.

"I misjudged you," he says. "No maybe."

It's nice to hear, but I feel foolish and out of control like I might explode into tears at any moment. I put my arms down and stare at the floor. Maybe I can sink through it if I concentrate. Whatever's in my expression must worry Hal because he tries to catch my eye, and when the mortification I feel won't let me return his glance, he says, "I'm sorry, Pan. Really. I'm impossible to get along with, and you've been game to try over all these years. You're right about a lot of things. I *have* been trying to kill my past. When I see you, it brings me right back and I just don't deal with it well."

When I hear that I do start crying, and he goes to me and puts his arms about me, holding me to him until the tears are under control again.

"I'm sorry too," I tell him, as we sit together on a couch. "How's your face?"

"Hanging by a thread," he deadpans.

I tell Hal it's not just him who's got me so upset. A malignant disease has afflicted Isaac's kids. Left unchecked, it could kill them all.

"Black Ep," he sighs, but it's not Black Ep.

For years the threat has been hanging over us like a storm cloud: a mutated Black Ep coming back to finish the job. We have talked about it, we have planned for it, we have dreaded it. We saw it happen with Hessa, and we were fortunate to keep it from infecting anyone else.

And this now is indeed a mutant strain. But not of Black Ep. It's a new form of BEAR. The best defense we have against the plague has betrayed us, evolving into something with a taste for human beings.

"Detail it," he says, so I do, freaking him out more than I expected when I mention that it's an airborne threat and in my bloodstream right now.

"You can relax," I tell him, unsure whether he's concerned about my safety, his or his son's, or how exactly the percentages break down if it's a combination of all three. "I'm just a carrier. This strain can't hurt me, or you, or Deuce or any posthuman. It preys on weaknesses we lack. Human weaknesses," I add, though after I've said it, I realize the phrase has a connotation that goes beyond the purely immunological context in which I put it.

"Are you sure it's no threat to us?"

"You know I wouldn't be here if it was. Or maybe I would, but I'd be wearing a biosafety suit. Anyway, Vash is positive the symptoms only pop up in humans, and if there's one thing she knows, it's pathology."

Grudgingly, Hal nods his head, giving the much-hated Vashti her due. "Bad luck for Isaac," he notes, with an edge to it I don't appreciate. "And for you too," he adds, picking up on my mood, "since you care about those kids the way you do."

"I really do," I tell him.

"Yeah, kids," he says. "Kids can change you."

He stares off into space for a moment, thinking, then pats me on the knee. "I want to answer your question," he says, "but why don't we have a drink first?"

"What question?"

He pulls me up off the couch and grins. "The one you want to know. Why did I have a son?"

halloween

I remembered Pandora as more of a rum girl than a whisky girl, but she wanted Irish coffee and what kind of host would I be to refuse? With her whistle wet and the tears on her cheek dry, she leaned in as I opened up. By the end of it, she understood. My tale came in fits and starts—some of it I could shorthand with her, and other times I had to take the long way around. The story was essentially this:

On one level, life on my own was terrific because, miserable though I was, I knew what was real and I called the shots. No one could lie to me anymore because there was no one around left to do it. I'd made sure of that. There were only five other people on the planet and I'd pushed them all away.

Fantasia didn't need pushing—she left on her own accord.

Isaac, Vashti and Champagne were easy to push because I never liked them. They were vile pets back in school, sanctimonious, self-righteous and simpering, not to mention they were tight with Lazarus, who was dating my dream girl, Simone. That certainly didn't help my opinion of them, but I would have loathed them anyway, all so fucked up and yet so eager to save the world. Maybe that's a prerequisite. Like the warnings on a Disneyland ride, maybe there's an invisible cosmic or karmic equivalent. "You must be this fucked up to try and save the world."

Pandora was the tricky one, because I genuinely liked her. But I knew I had to push her away too. Partly for her sake—she was in love with me, while I remained in love with Simone: a sure recipe for heartbreak—but mostly for mine. I didn't want to have to worry about her, I didn't want to be reminded of all that had happened to me, and probably above all else because she wanted to save the world too. Defeat the plague. Clone humanity. Repopulate the planet. Important causes? Not to me.

No one ever proved to me why we're so fucking great. Why should we be at the top of the food chain? If we die out, some other animal just takes our place. That's as it should be. Maybe it was our turn to go. But we didn't go. Maybe our existence ruined Nature's plan.

Either way, I knew I'd be damned before doing what Gedaechtnis wanted. Not after they lied to us the way they did. It was more important to mourn my innocence, my family, my world, countless lost memories, my naïve plans for the future, my best friends and the only girl I ever loved.

And in a way I was damned, because with no one around to tell me lies, I had the green light to tell them to myself.

I told myself no one cared about me at all. Not even me.

I told myself I deserved to suffer because I'd killed the people I loved the most. Simone indirectly, true, but I felt responsible, just as I do today. And without question Mercutio died by my hand. My would-be girlfriend and my partner in crime: gone and gone thanks to me. Twin scars on my soul.

The nastiest lie came from my unconscious, where I couldn't recognize it for what it was. I told myself that suffering was not enough—I had to die.

Consciously, I hated the thought of giving in to Death because the greedy fuck had already wronged me too many times. Better to keep living out of spite. But live how? Do what? Not only had I walled myself off from other people, I'd vowed never to return to the IVR. I had to find the things that meant something to me here in the real world, and Death found me in my distractions.

Danger was my first distraction, and it came in the guise of thrill. I'd spent so much of my life testing boundaries, and after Idlewild chewed me up and spit me out, I was suddenly desperate for something new to survive. I wandered the East Coast for months before settling on an orange and black roller coaster four hundred feet high and a mile long. Breaking Point.

When working properly, Breaking Point could send a person flying at windstorm speeds: over a hundred miles an hour with G-forces snapping up to around 5.0. She could scare you so many ways—sudden curves and spirals, clothoid loops, zero gravity rolls, multiple inversions and so on—but after two decades of disrepair, she was a relic, a nonfunctioning wreck. I didn't care because she was undeniably real in a world in love with simulations, a living insult to IVR. I got it in my head to yank back on the hands of time and make her the heart-spasming, teeth-rattling beauty she once was, because if I could restore her to her former glory, maybe I could restore myself. She became my pet project, the thing that numbed me best, emotional painkiller for all the days I woke up feeling empty and alone.

The second distraction was chemical oblivion and it came in the guise of grief. Simone died from an overdose and because I wanted to know her thoughts, I started experimenting with pharmaceuticals. Part of the healing process, that's what I told myself. But really I took anything that made me feel different because if I felt different, maybe I was someone else. Anyone else. Just to be some random person who wouldn't have to think the same self-pitying thoughts and feel the same self-loathing.

I'm sure I could have handled danger or drugs fine individually, but the two together made a fool's cocktail—all the repairs I made to Breaking Point were unrealistic half-measures, and if I'd ever gotten the thing really moving, it would have ripped my limbs off the first time I tested it.

Fortunately, before that could happen, I got really high and slipped off one of the lower tracks, breaking my collarbone. Sobered me up a bit. Now I was still talking with Pandora on a regular basis back in those days, but I didn't tell her I fell because I didn't want to worry her. But she knew. I knew she knew. The kinds of questions she asked, the extra concern in her voice. So I went back to Idlewild and set up shop, calling Malachi to find out if she was secretly watching me—and, in fact, she was.

It didn't matter to me whether she was doing it for good-intentioned reasons or not—I was furious. It's a hot-button issue for me, privacy, thanks no doubt to the whole IVR thing, being kept under such heavy surveillance for so many years. I set out to make sure no one could ever spy on me again. Not only would I block them from hooking into my world, I'd turn the tables, and hook into theirs. A lot of time hacking and programming, tapping into the old skills again, a blessing in disguise ultimately, because I had a cause again, and that cause made the drugs and Breaking Point much less important in my mind.

When I had the surveillance working for me instead of against me, I found I couldn't keep from using it. I'd begun to realize how impossibly lonely I was, and seeing how the other half lived struck me as the best solution to my troubles. But what I saw only depressed me. And to make matters worse, I'd already broken a promise to myself. To test my surveillance hooks, I had to go back into the IVR. Good reason to do it, I rationalized, but in my heart I knew I'd betrayed my principles.

I started talking to myself, actually talking to myself, carrying on conversations with my devil's advocate about anything and everything. I went back into the IVR for days at a time— unhealthy stretches that always left me feeling worse about myself. It seemed like I was in an endless plummet, like my brain only existed to torture me with lost opportunities and bad choices, to cast blame, to point fingers, to find someone to hurt—and always that someone was me. In a situation like that, there comes a point when you have to do something. When your soul-searching finally comes up with an answer.

What I came up with was simple: I wasn't supposed to turn out like this.

I'd been thinking about my history, about the life I would have led if the lies I'd been fed were actually true. If the IVR had been real, and Black Ep had never wormed its way into the genome, and billions still lived. If despair had never laid claim to me, and the promise of my childhood had led to a safe and happy life. That's who I was supposed to be.

And even though I couldn't be that person anymore, that person could still exist.

I brushed up on my biology and dusted off Idlewild's ectogenesis lab. Felt a little like Dr. Frankenstein, but the carrot of that perfect me carried me through. I stole peeks along the way at what was going on in Egypt and Germany just to see if I could learn anything off the kids they were making, but in the end all I had to do was a simple clone job. When you have the right tools and the right recipe, cloning isn't much harder than baking a cake. Cook nine months in an artificial womb and season to taste.

So I dropped this other me—this better me—into an IVR pod, and ran him through "track nine," the exact same set of programs I went through: every single experience path Gedaechtnis fed me for infancy, toddler and on up.

Mercutio had killed the logs, but spared the ten tracks, so while there was no official record of the choices I'd made in my childhood, the programs that offered those choices lay ready to start anew. Like a rebooted video game—I'd lost the action replay and the high score, but the extra game was mine for the taking.

My "parents" loaded up and took over—they were celebrity doctors, or simulations thereof—they did a fine job raising me, even if I sometimes resented the times they'd stick me with babysitters so they could go off to chase viruses all over the globe.

And that was that for a while. I just let the programs go. I monitored his vitals to ensure he stayed healthy, and ran regular diagnostics on all the machines. I hid his little corner of IVR away and sealed it off so no one else could bother him.

I didn't even want to bother him. I thought, ideally, I shouldn't even watch his life unfold. Like I said, I have a thing about protecting privacy, and I didn't want to do anything to him that I didn't want done to me.

In the end, I decided I'd plug in just once every year to take a quick peek at him, always on our birthday, and always when our folks were out of the room. (There's no bad blood between me and the good doctors—I just can't stand to see them now that I know they're only computer programs. Much too painful.)

Now I may not have a lot of memories left, but the earliest one I could remember was a pretty vivid one—the first time I went out trick-or-treating. Mom and Dad had gone off filming in Botswana, so Irene took me around the neighborhood. Of all the babysitters they programmed for me—and I had a lot of them over the years (Gedaechtnis evidently wanted me to get used to people other than my parents taking care of me so I'd have an easier time with boarding school)—Irene was my favorite, a sweet-natured, round-faced college girl studying to be a veterinarian. We had yellow birthday cake with chocolate frosting, then opened presents, and then completed the sugar overload by going from house to house in our silly animal costumes in search of candy, and I remember being fascinated by all the pageantry—ghosts and goblins, cowboys and superheroes—and I would just stare at all the spooky decorations with a big smile on my face and Irene would have to move me along and prompt me to say "Thank you" every time someone dropped candy into my little plastic jack-o'-lantern bag. And then at the end of the block, the McCormick family gave us apples instead of candy, and Irene looked at me and said the most jawdroppingly gut-busting thing I'd ever heard in my short life, and maybe it was something only funny to two-year-olds, but whatever it was fled my memory a long time ago.

Now that's a memory I could have gotten back at any time. I can get it back right now if I want. I can load Irene up directly and ask her to remember what she said, or I can sift through a mountain of code for the same result. Likewise, I could load up my parents and ask them what they remember of my childhood, and those programs would tell me everything. But I won't do that. Because I don't want to know.

Over time, I've learned to embrace my amnesia. Not that I'm grateful to Mercutio for causing it, but when I look back at my early years, it's agony. The losses are unbearable and there's a lot to be said for oblivion. Honestly, I'd much rather forget the good with the bad, and just look forward to starting anew.

But even with the depth of those feelings, and as much as I didn't want to do it, I decided I had to see Irene's joke in action. It was massively important for me to see this other me laughing in my first truly happy moment. If I saw that I could hold on to it like a snapshot you keep in your breast pocket by your heart. I wanted to see this new life that was me, innocent, young, wild and free, lost in the silliness of a stupid joke.

So I did. I plugged in and put myself in ghost mode so they couldn't see or hear me. And I watched. And it never happened.

The new version of me was sitting at the old table in the old high chair, already swaddled in that ridiculous striped costume with the ears coming out of the hat, and he was looking over his shoulder to see what Irene was doing in the kitchen. "Winnie," he kept calling, because she was dressed in the costume of Winnie-the-Pooh. She came in with the cake, making a big production of it, and singing, "Happy birthday, dear Gabriel" (for it was years before I would think to change my name to Halloween), in a charmingly off-key warble. I watched her set the cake down in front of the new me, where he stared purposefully at it, staring to the exclusion of everything else, then reached out to grasp the candles. Irene pulled it away so he couldn't get burned. He tugged and squirmed to reach those two points of light, straining, immune to her explanation that fire is hot and therefore dangerous. In the end, she decided it was safer to blow the candles out— which she did—and the new me drew as much air as he could into his tiny lungs to let out a terrified and terrifying shriek, as if she'd just sliced off his big toe.

Had that happened with me? Had I just forgotten?

So I watched and waited to see how Irene would handle the situation, to see her comfort the new me so we could get on with the presents and the trick-or-treating and the hilarious joke, but the kid was inconsolable. Even when she lit new candles, he wouldn't even look at them, just crying and wailing until ever-patient Irene finally had enough and put him to bed.

So his trick-or-treating bag went unused. No apple ever dropped into it. But if I knew anything, I knew I'd gone out with Irene—it was one of the few memories I could cling on to. How could it go one way with me, and another with him?

In that moment I realized—with fascination and horror— that this other me wasn't really me at all. He might possess identical DNA and the system might be presenting him with the same semi-scripted experiences I had growing up, giving him the chance to make the exact same choices I made, but his choices and mine didn't match.

We were different people leading independent lives. And I was suddenly responsible for someone other than myself.

I agonized over what to do. Was it better to leave him in the IVR or tell him the truth about the world? I had to make a decision before he turned six. That's when I went off to boarding school. He couldn't do what I'd done, because all the kids in my class were real flesh and blood people who'd since grown up, and if he went now he'd have no peers. And I'd already deleted his teacher, Maestro. So I had to either program/reprogram artificial peers and a new teacher for him, or bring him out, and bringing him out seemed healthier.

On his fifth birthday, I plugged in and told him the painful truth. I gave him the choice, and he said he wanted to see the real world, so that's what we did.

He didn't like the real world so much, so I put him back in and gave him a way to contact me if he ever wanted to talk. And after a few months, he did. He said he tried but he just couldn't stay in a fake world anymore knowing that there's a real one, so I pulled him out again and we've been inseparable ever since.

It's a strange path to fatherhood, but what can I say?

I never found Irene's punch line, but the punch line to this story is that while I created a son for the wrong reasons, I love him for the right ones. He's made a better person of me, and he's given me something better to live for than just my spite. He may have his problems, but he's imaginative, hardworking, hopeful and good-natured. And beyond all that, he's my son. I'll do anything for him.

All my losses don't seem to matter as much because I'm not so important anymore. What's important is that he grows up happy, healthy and strong, because when I die, he'll have the future.

pandora

I listen to Hal's story and think about what might have been. But what might have been won't get us anywhere. I could drive myself mad thinking about what could have been or should have been, but the question is what do we do now?

"I'll call Vashti," I tell him, and he gives me the privacy to do it.

She keeps me waiting for a good ten minutes—but when she comes on she's actually in a pretty good mood because the pygmy marmoset has given birth.

"Twins," she says. "One male, one female. The girls are coming up with names as we speak—well, the girls who are still talking to us, I should say. Which brings us to my favorite butterfly—have you ripped his wings off yet?"

"It wasn't him," I tell her. "Not directly, at least." I give her an abbreviated version of events and at the mention of Deuce her nose wrinkles in disgust.

"Hal spawned a caterpillar, how wonderful," she scoffs.

When I tell her what they've proposed, she waves it away like a buzzing gnat about her head. "Fixing the IVR isn't enough. He's damaged my girls. How's he going to fix them?"

It's a fair question and I don't have an answer for it.

"So what do you want me to do?"

"Bring that little fucker here," she says. "I want to show him what he's done."

halloween

Deuce and I got in a few games of speed chess before Pandora emerged.

"Those take me back," she said, nodding at the clove in Deuce's hand. It was one of the brands I used to smoke in the old days, but not since—though I still don't mind the nostalgia that springs from a secondhand whiff of aromatic smoke.

"I don't know how to say 'Do you want a smoke?' in Portuguese," Deuce apologized, offering her one while overextending his queen. She let him light it for her, nodding her thanks as I forked his king and queen with my knight.

"Ugh, this one's done," he said. "Good game."

"Good game," I replied.

Pandora looked like she wanted to play winner, but shook her head when I offered, instead telling me what Vashti told her.

"Out of the question," I said. "What does she want him to do? Stand trial?"

"I suspect she just wants to give him a good talking-to."

"Ah, but not having to listen to Vashti is one of the greatest pleasures in life," I told her.

"And do you hear me contradicting you?" she replied, flashing the guilty smile of someone telling tales out of school.

"Exactly, so why inflict her on my boy?"

"I don't mind," Deuce said, snubbing his cigarette and giving me a half-shrug. "She has a point, really. If I were in her shoes, I'd want to talk to me."

"And if I were in her shoes, I'd take a good, long look in the mirror and hang myself from the highest tree," I growled.

"Dad, I know who she is," he said. "I'll pay whatever price she thinks is fair."

"Why don't I give you boys some privacy?" Pandora suggested, taking another clove for the road and making herself scarce. I noticed myself watching her curves as she left, and with mixed emotions saw Deuce doing the same.

"I'm not scared," he told me, once she'd slipped from our sight. He said he didn't like the idea of Vashti hating him, and laid out a scenario in which he would go and make amends to build a bridge between Idlewild and Nymphenburg.

"Maybe I can bring the family together," he said.

"They're not family, Deuce. We're family."

"Right, I know, I meant it like 'Family of Man.'"

We talked about the strides he'd made, and all the new people he wanted to meet. Girls, mostly—he was a powder keg of hormones—but he also wanted to meet Isaac's boys, and when I told him what was happening to them, he worried he wouldn't be able to get to know them if bad came to worse. He was so excited about the trip and I wanted to let him go, but I had to admit the thought of zipping halfway across the world to jaw at Vashti was one of the last things I wanted to do.

"She's transparent," I said. "She wants us to come out so she can try to humiliate me. Call me a bad parent, parade me in front of her kids, rake me over the coals for not getting involved. I can hear her talking up my potential so she can carp about all the things I could have done but never did."

"You're right," he agreed. "I don't want you to have to go through that."

"I will, though. In a heartbeat, if it's what you want."

"I don't," he frowned, slumping into his seat. "I guess I'll just stay here."

The selfish part of me thought *That was a close one,* and in the few seconds it took for me to beat that sentiment down, sigh and get ready to say *No, going is more important,* he shot up in his seat, pointing his index finger in a gesture of *Eureka* and said, "Wait, I can go there, but nothing says you have to!"

"You want to go without me?"

"It's the best move on the board," he said. "I do what I want and you don't give Vashti any satisfaction."

"That's a really big step." I frowned. "I don't know if you're ready."

"I'm almost fifteen."

"Almost, but Europe's a long way away, and to jump into that mess right now all by yourself—don't you think you might find it overwhelming?"

"Sure, I might. But Dad, you didn't do anything wrong—I did. When I did it, I knew I wouldn't be able to hide anymore—and if we went out there together, I'd still be hiding behind you."

There was such a sweet look of determination in his eyes, the look of someone in love with freedom. And his need to stand on his own two feet moved me, choked me up. I wondered if I'd been overprotective over the years. Maybe all the time I'd been trying to look out for him, I'd also been holding him back.

"You don't have to fight my battles for me," he pushed. "I have to do things on my own eventually, don't I?"

"You're right," I told him. "If you want to go, you can go. I'll be here to back you up if you need me. Say the word and I'll get you."

He grinned. "You don't have to say that, Dad, I already know."

I hugged him close and he hugged me back, my eyes misting on the word "proud" when I asked him if he knew how proud I was of him. "Just don't burn anything down," I said when I let him go.

He laughed, meeting my eyes, taking it as a joke, but I wasn't really joking. "I'm serious," I told him.

"Fire safety, Dad, you got it."

"And do whatever Pandora tells you."

"Okay."

"Good. Who loves you?"

"You do, Dad."

Outside, the rain had stopped, and the three of us stepped out into the cold air. I helped Pandora refuel as Deuce loaded his backpack and suitcase into the cargo hold.

"I'll run interference with Vashti," she assured me. "She's mad at me too about the IVR, so maybe I can act as a buffer."

"Good, because if you let her go crazy on him," I warned.

"You'll kill me," she said. "Understood."

"Thanks, Pan."

I gave her a hug. "Have things changed today?" she whispered.

"I don't know," I told her. "Maybe a little."

"But I shouldn't get any ideas?"

"I might be a little more willing to let you visit now. That's it."

"That's a start."

"And it's a finish too, because I still don't trust the braying jackasses you work with and it's awful hard for me to trust you while you keep ties to them. Fuck them and fuck their work. I'm not going to be responsible for their kids, and whatever global community they manage to build, you can leave me out of it."

"You could do a lot of good there," she said. "You have more influence than you think. No matter how they might feel about you, I know they'd always listen to you. And if that's not a sign of respect, I don't know what is."

"They respect me? And do you really think that street runs both ways?"

She sighed, not quite resigned, but close.

"I have something for you. I don't know how you'll feel about it, but I was thinking of you when I did it," she said, handing me a tiny, unmarked disc.

"What is it?"

"It's what you make of it. Play it and see."

So I tucked it away and said my goodbyes. The stairs went up. The engines roared. I watched them go. *Deuce might be his own person,* I thought, *but it feels like a piece of me is missing.*

Back inside, I grabbed my tranquilizer gun and plopped down in a chair outside the conference room. The time said almost midnight. I sat for a while, waiting for the hour to strike, killing time by fiddling with the disc in my pocket and thinking about all that had happened. When the sounds of growling and huffing started to get to me, I decided it was midnight already.

"All right, I'm tired of listening to you," I told the tiger. "Let's get those stitches out and set you free."

deuce

Think of him as the Bye Bye Guy. What else can you call him? He swoops in when you're an infant, and he says things you don't understand. Later when you start to learn language you try to remember what he said, but it all slips away. Except the last part. The part with him waving his fingers at you while you're there in the stroller. You look up at him. Ring finger, middle finger and index, one two three, beginning, middle and end. "Bye bye," he says. "Bye bye." And he's gone for another year.

Did he come to you in the hospital? Trace memories of the man holding you up hours after you were born, but are they real?

Is anything?

Last night you dreamt about bodychecking triceratopses and wrestling their ugly heads into the tar. The night before you lived the life of a pirate king, making men walk the plank and counting their doubloons. It seemed as real as anything.

He comes to you next when angels blink—when walls shudder—when barriers collapse—when you're building a town out of books, blocks, dice and tiny plastic racecars. You're alone in the house with him because the babysitter vanished. He walked right through the front door and found you playing in the living room. You're not scared though. Not scared because he looks like family. Not scared but you should be.

Because everything will change.

He doesn't tell you that. Not then anyway. He just wants to look at you. Listen to you. See how you're coming along.

"Who are you?" Ask him that. Better not to say anything, but too late now.

He says his name and sits down beside you. Mom told you about strangers once. You feel like you're falling from a very high tree. Where's the babysitter?

"She'll be back soon," he says, guessing the question but not answering it. He can read faces. Body language. Minds. He reaches for a book about wizards, stops, fingers frozen an inch from the cover. "May I?"

Shrug. Guess so.

He makes a nice bridge of *A Blizzard of Wizards and Their Ninety-nine Lizards,* connecting your residential street to your shopping mall. That's good. Fewer traffic jams now. Big ups from the imaginary drivers in the plastic racecars. Time stops and you build the town together, the Bye Bye Guy anticipating everything you want to do and never complaining when you change your mind and want to switch things around.

It's like he cares about you.

Bye bye and bye bye over the years, until he sprang you from your cage. Talk about your life changers! There's no greater wrecking ball than the truth.

And as thou wert liberated, so must thou liberate, because what kind of selfish prick would you be if you didn't give back? That's why you kick more ass than a spastic ostrich in a sea of donkeys. The way you shine a light on the lies just to watch them burn, they might as well call you the motherfucking magnifying glass.

Or maybe the God of Fire.

It's spirit and sex, purity, power and candy. It's the spark of life, the energy ticking at the heart of all things. Disrespect it and melt. Fire doesn't just liberate and purify, it devours. It even has the power to annihilate time, because there's nothing to which it can't bring an end.

So you have to be careful with it.

You didn't mean to burn down the forest. You underestimated it and it ran away from you like a dog off its leash. Wildfire everywhere, the wind bringing it all the way up to the tops of the trees, and stretching it into the burning face of a giant. All you could do was stare at it, mesmerized, and look to see if the face in the fire was your own.

Only when the Bye Bye Guy found you and dragged you from the smoke and the heat did you realize the amount of damage you'd done. Never had you seen him so angry. He shook you and yelled at you and asked you why.

"I had to see if I was," you stuttered, tears stinging your eyes.

"See if you were what?"

"You're the God of Death, and I can't be you. So maybe I'm the God of Fire."

When the blaze was finally out, he sat you down and told you that you could be whatever you wanted to be. You could be the God of Nothing, and he'd love you just as much. So stop worrying about where he ends and you begin. Just be yourself, and if you don't know who that is yet, take heart because you'll find out in time.

"Want to do something in the meantime? Try a little reforesting, you crazy pyro," said Halloween, God of Death, the Bye Bye Guy. And in a playful, fatherly way, he pushed you, and you laughed, rolling up your sleeves to begin the first of many days of hard work clearing and replanting trees.

Now you've gone and left him. You climbed into the copter and waved to him and he waved back. It's a strange feeling. A sad feeling. But it's good to know that someone's waiting for you to return.

And it's good to know someone's waiting for you to arrive.

pandora

I'm high over the Atlantic, flying Halloween's amazingly weird kid back to Germany. He still won't look directly at me, the little twerp, and I'm coming to grips with the fact that I'm jealous of him. It's insane, but I am. Hal may not treasure my heart, but he owns it through and through—just one of those ill-fated chemical attractions from which there's no escape—and the thought of someone spending fourteen years with him makes me more green-eyed than I already am.

I wanted to help him bury his past, and it turns out he's been doing it without me. His son's given him a reason to live, and that's phenomenal, but it's the position I wanted. I've lost out. I can't say it doesn't hurt.

The good news is what he said. He might be more willing to let me visit now. Those ten words keep running through my head, and it's pathetic how happy they make me. Christ, I feel like an abandoned pet waiting by the front door for the sound of keys.

I shouldn't have given him the disc. He'll take it wrong, I know it.

But hell, it was the only thing I could think of that had a chance of engaging him again, of bringing him back into the fold.

Sometimes I think I'm the only one who cares. Isaac doesn't get along with Vashti or Champagne. Halloween doesn't get along with anyone. I'm the only one who thinks the divisions between us can be healed. Or should be healed. Or must.

Hal says we're all control freaks while he's a chaos enthusiast. I remember the last thing he said to us the day we split up the world: "You're lost in a pipe dream, all of you. The itch you have for some happy, harmonious, orderly tomorrow will only lead to tyranny when you impose it. It doesn't matter how good your intentions are."

Maybe he was right with Vashti. She's been controlling her kids chemically more than I ever realized. I can't approve of that. Especially giving them anti-aphrodisiacs. I called her on it yesterday, right before I left to see Hal, only to have her blame me for it.

"My girls are the future," she said, "and they should be learning all they can about Black Ep and about building the best society we can build. How are they going to do that if they're always going goo-goo-eyed about their latest crush? You were the inspiration, sweetie—all I had to do was ask how much more work you'd get done if fucking Hal wasn't consuming all your thoughts."

I wonder how much Champagne knew. She said she was always happy to let Vashti worry about the types and amounts of medication, so she could focus on motherhood and on providing the girls a well-rounded education. I don't know whether to believe her or not.

And Isaac might be the kindest, most caring guy I've ever met—he's my rock, and I don't know what Hal's beef is with him. So he's been raising his kids religiously. It's what he believes. I don't see the problem. And you have to give Isaac a break—he's so worried right now. He used to have such a positive attitude about everything, but he can see what happened to Hessa happening all over again—but worse this time, so much worse. Medically, I don't know how much help I can be for his kids, but I'll do whatever I can. And Vashti's working with him, thank goodness, and if nothing else I can try to keep them from getting into loggerheads.

"How fast does this thing go?" Deuce asks, and when I tell him, he's unimpressed. "My dad has a jet that goes faster."

"Well, his is built for speed and mine's built for safety."

"Where'd you steal it?"

"Gedaechtnis left it, I co-opted it. I like to think of it as the company car."

"Can I take the controls?"

"Maybe on the way back."

"It's an interesting design, even if it is slow," he says, looking about the cockpit. "It was fun to carve."

"I like your swan," I tell him, with a nod at the wooden sculpture resting on his knee.

"Oh, thanks," he says. "I figured a swan for Nymphenburg. I've got more in my backpack. Thought maybe I should paint them first, but I don't know." He trails off, shrugs. "I figure I can give them as gifts or something."

"That's a nice thought," I tell him, because I don't expect that little trinket to mollify Vashti one bit.

haji

Dust devils can surprise you in the desert, whipping up from nowhere to sting your body with sand and grit. I remember circling around the Sphinx for a better look once when the biggest whirlwind I'd ever seen appeared before me, a twenty-meter cone staggering like a drunk, pulling me into it and throwing me out, then disappearing as mysteriously as it came.

The sickness was like that, coming so suddenly, and with such force.

We have been confined to Nymphenburg's hospital, my older brothers fighting for their lives in intensive care, the rest of us in an isolation ward. Ngozi, Dalila and I spend our time conserving energy, telling stories and playing games as giant screens on the walls and ceiling cycle through soothing imagery. Dogwood blossoms and swarms of tropical fish help us transcend the sensations of pain and rot, and where meditation falls short, my father is quick to fill the gap with the most glorious analgesics. What a blessing painkillers are.

Father conducts himself as he always has, but when I look closely at him, I see he does not wear his usual face. There are strange pulses of emotion crackling behind his eyes, emotions I have never known in him before. If only I could define them. When the others are asleep and it is just the two of us whispering, I find myself reassuring him. We remember your lessons. We embrace the future. We fight for life with every drop of blood in our veins, but the microbes that threaten us come from God, and with God what can we do but surrender completely to whatever fate He has prepared?

I tell him these things and he praises me, but still the unfamiliar look in his eyes remains. It is so painful to lose a sister. It may well be more painful to lose a daughter or son. Perhaps I cannot truly understand what it is he feels. I wish I could help him. Failing that, I wish he would guard that look around Ngozi and Dalila, as it unsettles them more than he realizes.

Our cousins visit from time to time. Not all of them, but some. Tomi does, though not as often as I would like. It hurts her to see us like this. Olivia comes most often, and I am moved by her tenderness toward and loyalty to Ngozi. She will spend hours whispering with him, trading jokes or simply holding his hand. When she is in the room, his symptoms all but disappear. Dalila enjoys special attention from all the girls. She has become like a sister to them, an honorary Waterbaby.

The ones who do not visit are too frightened or too angry over secrets that have been spilt. I am not privy to such secrets. I gather that my aunts have been mistreating my cousins in some way, but no one will tell us how. They do not wish to burden us. When we are feeling better, perhaps they will tell us then.

Whatever it is, I have heard that Penny has taken it the worst. She will neither eat, nor speak, nor come out of her room. She must be in a terrible pit. The last words she said to me were spoken in anger, and yet without them I think my rapturous trip through God's universe might never have taken place. I do not fully understand why I feel the way I feel, but I find myself strangely grateful to her. Indebted. I pray she finds what she needs to take away her pain.

halloween

Here I thought I'd seen the bottom of Pandora's bag of tricks, but you can hook the IVR in ninety-nine places and still miss the hundredth. That disc unlocked a hidden staging area when I played it, a part of the IVR she'd camouflaged for her personal use. It was a patchwork space, not a domain unto itself. Like those old "get rich quick" hacks to steal insignificant sums of money from vast numbers of bank accounts, it was populated with tiny fragments of domains no one had used for years. So when I slipped in to see what was there, I found myself in what looked like one room but it was really hundreds of slices of rooms all stitched together. And what I saw in the center of that room filled me with the sickest sense of nostalgia I've ever felt.

"Finally, you're here," she said.

The last time I saw her she'd been corrupted, standing over my virtual grave, helping two other programs bury me alive. Jasmine. I'd designed her back when I was a teenager, modeling her to the best of my ability after the girl I loved in vain, Simone. She was my fantasy girl, Jasmine, my consolation prize for losing out on the real thing.

I hated her.

She'd betrayed me when another program's personality bled into hers and I'd never really gotten over it, even if intellectually I knew the corruption wasn't her fault. The reasons why I'd originally designed her embarrassed me a bit, and beautiful as she was, it pained me to look at her—why be reminded of how close I'd come to the real Simone with a soulless parody? For Pandora to throw Jasmine back in my face like this—it was the kind of cruel joke I'm not the sort to forgive.

"I'm not laughing."

"It's not often that you do," she said.

Bitterly, I stared at her.

"Is that all you have to say to me after all these years?"

"You want more? How about: 'I still haven't forgiven you,' or would you prefer, 'I should have deleted you when I deleted Maestro'? Take your pick."

The corners of her mouth turned up in a Mona Lisa smile, and a knowing twinkle danced in her almond-shaped eyes.

"You think I'm Jasmine," she said, "but there you're wrong."

"All right, what are you calling yourself now?"

She told me and I did laugh, finding an ugly blister of mirth in the black humor of it all.

"So Pandora reprogrammed you to think you're Simone?"

She nodded her head. "In a sense."

"And am I supposed to be pleased? No, don't answer. I don't have the patience for it."

"Hal," she said, before I could slip back out, "I really am Simone Qi." And she told me about the day we first met back when we were six.

"How do you know that?"

"Because my parents were there."

She cut my answer off with, "Just go with me for a second. Pretend I'm Simone. I spent eighteen years plugged into the IVR. The system was designed to keep track of that data. And you can use that data in interesting ways."

"Mercutio wiped out the official log," I said.

"That's true—those records are gone—but some of that data can be reconstructed. I spent those eighteen years not only with you and my other flesh and blood classmates, but also with all kinds of virtual characters: my parents, my sister, Nanny, Maestro, Charles Darwin, Albert Einstein and so many others. By and large, those characters remember each and every interaction, and because Mercutio didn't bother to wipe them out along with the logs, that data's available."

"Okay, so Pandora sifted through that garbled stew of code, found some of Simone's memories, and slapped them onto Jasmine's template personality. Is that it?"

"No, that was just the beginning," she said, as the truth began to dawn on me. "Pandora had Malachi examine each and every one of those memories—every breath, every word, every gesture—and had him match the time stamp with my vital signs. Those logs are still available. So when my heart rate went up, there's a record of it, and when my blood pressure dropped, there's a record of that, and on and on. By correlating what happened to my body with what the virtual characters remember me doing at the time, Malachi has created a new artificial personality, one that he considers nearly identical to the Simone he remembers."

She put her arms out to her sides like a capital letter Y, a gesture of *C'est moi*. "And that's me," she said. "What do you think? Am I the Simone you know?"

The question left me speechless.

pandora

Champagne is the only one to greet us when we land, and when she catches sight of Deuce she rapidly goes from looking like she's seen a ghost to looking like she'd like to perform an exorcism.

"Give us a minute," she tells him, struggling for a neutral expression as she takes me aside.

"Hal raised a hippie?" she asks, with a glance at the long orange-tangerine hair spilling out of Deuce's ski hat. "He's gone from dead to Grateful Dead?"

"Cute. Where's Vashti?" I ask.

"Working."

"Just as well."

She has no news on the End of the World except to say the situation hasn't gotten any better. Before I can see for myself, she asks me when I expect to give the all clear for returning to the IVR.

"I really haven't even thought about it," I tell her, and she tells me there's a landscape she was painting that she really wants to finish.

It strikes me as an odd request right now with all that's happening, and I tell her so.

"Do you realize what's going on here?" she asks, indignation rising. "I'm the one who's been holding everything together here. Vash and Isaac are always in the hospital or the labs, and thanks to Hal junior over there, I'm stuck with a flock of sullen, resentful girls who delight in ignoring what I say, who disobey me at every turn, who ask me questions for which I don't have any answers. When I'm not with them, I'm nursing Isaac's kids, who are suffering terribly and there's nothing I can do about it—and all I want to do is take a quick break from this nightmare so I can finish something beautiful. Can you understand that?"

I suppose, so I tell her I'll do what I can. I leave Deuce in her custody and hurry to the hospital.

When I emerge, my body is in trembles. I have to lean against a wall and breathe, shutting my eyes tightly against the aftereffect of what I saw. The pessimism I've been trying to keep at bay is beginning to suck me inside out. Who couldn't be shaken by what this bloodcurdling disease is doing? The little ones are still fighting strong, but Mu'tazz and Rashid look frighteningly weak, like wilted flowers whose dry petals would float away in a light breeze.

deuce

Why does everyone want to make eye contact with you? It's fine if it's someone you trust, but Champagne's greedy peepers keep making your blood sugar spike.

"See something you like?" you ask.

She hits back with something that's supposed to be funny, but like the ancient punk refrain, you're looking for the joke with a microscope. That Iggy Pop was born in Michigan, just like you, and if he were here you bet he'd say she's the joke. Dad thinks she is and he's right about ninety percent of the time.

She's taking you into the main building, and you're digging all the murals—there's a definite vernal, pastoral, mythological thing going on with all the depictions of Flora, Roman goddess of flowers and spring. Tree nymphs and other nature spirits attend to lucky old Flora's every need. Looks like it's always spring in here, even if outside winter's sneaking up fast.

You don't hear what Champagne says because you're wondering if she sees herself as a reincarnation of Flora. That, and the giant Austrian crystal chandelier is distracting you, its lights sending hundreds of shining diamonds and sparkling colors through the refracted cut-crystal prisms.

"I said Vashti wants to talk to you, but she's busy right now, so I'm going to have to lock you in one of the guest bedrooms until she's ready."

You drop your stuff so you can cross your wrists behind your back.

"What are you doing?"

"Letting you handcuff me," you tell her. "Since you don't trust me and all."

"That won't be necessary."

You shrug and pick everything back up, following her through the maze. It's fun to compare what you see to what you saw in all the old pictures and what you imagined would be here in your mind.

One of the ladyloves peeks at you from around a corner, and you reward her curiosity by taking your hat off respectfully, then incorporating a funky dance shuffle into your step. "How's that opera coming, Lulu?" you ask her, but she doesn't answer when you pass her by. She might have been glaring at you—you can't tell—you're not about to look her in the eye.

Irritably, Champagne asks, "How much do you know about us?"

"Oh, lots of stuff, but honestly I don't remember most of it. Gets to be information overload after a while."

"No running in the halls, Katrina," she yells, upon spotting a blur racing around a corner. "Katrina!" She tsks with frustration and tells you, "You see what you've done? It's your fault they won't listen to me."

"Maybe you're not worth listening to," you suggest.

"You really are a chip off the old block," she says, unlocking a door and shaking her head in what's supposed to be pity.

You step on in to 360 the room—it's nicer than you thought. Nothing too fancy, but certainly not the holding cell you expected. You drop your suitcase on the floor, tossing your backpack on the bed and setting the swan over on the ottoman for maximum *feng shui.*

"How long do I wait here?" you ask, and she gives you a motherfucking, "We'll see," so you press and she tells you it'll be hours. Which means you need a smoke, but she grabs the clove from your mouth and confiscates your lighter.

"No smoking," she tells you, so you tell her your dad said she used to be a real beauty once and so did she get into a car wreck or something?

Zing! Internal bleeding! You just liberated her from her ego, and you get to grin and wince at the sound of the slamming door.

As she locks you in, you slump into the recliner chair and mourn the loss of your white hippo Zippo with a quiet prayer, but in the big picture it doesn't bother you—you've got plenty of other lighters in your pocket and you can reassure yourself by running your fingers over them like a poker player counting his chips. Four, five, six, seven, eight, all present and accounted for. So you yawn and stretch, then cover your face with your hair.

Now no one can see you.

pandora

Isaac won't leave intensive care and I don't blame him, but the rest of us are discussing the state of the union around a stainless-steel circular table, Champagne, Vashti and I. They're sipping from mugs brimming with hot chocolate, but I'm just swirling mine, telling them how Malachi and I managed to bring Simone back from the dead.

"I had a sense that's what you two were up to," Vashti says. "Is it really her?"

"That's hard to say," I confess. "We've created a virtual consciousness based on records of things the real Simone did and said in the IVR and correlated that data with records of her vital signs. So we know how her body reacted, and how her brain reacted chemically when, say, she first laid eyes on Lazarus, and yet we don't necessarily know how she felt. That part's guesswork."

"Can deeds supersede feelings?" Champagne muses.

"How good is the guesswork?" Vashti asks.

"Well, in talking to her, she seems like the Simone I remember, so I'd say Malachi's guesses were pretty good."

"Pretty good"? Faint praise, Pandy, faint praise.

I'd say "perfect," but there's no way to prove it definitively. There are major gaps in her experiences. How do you know she's the same Simone?

It feels like her.

And you can judge?

Don't forget how well I know her. I surfed her dreams growing up.

You surfed mine too, Mal, but you don't know me all that well.

I think I do. But if I'm wrong, I chalk it up to the fact that you're a work in progress like every other organic being. Every seven years you get a new set of cells, so since the last time I was "in your head," eighteen years ago, you've become a new person two and a half times over.

Brain cells don't turn over like that.

No, they don't, but you've generated plenty of new ones since then. And you're more than just your brain. Consider the role your hormones play. Also, cellular memory is stored throughout your body, and those cells collectively regenerate every seven years. In any case, if you're worried we've created some kind of Frankensteinian golem, you can relax. Whatever differences may exist between the new Simone and the old aren't so large for a soul to slip through.

A bit glib there, oh inorganic one.

Time will tell.

I tell them how Malachi has spent the past few weeks fine-tuning Simone, helping her adjust psychologically to life as a program, and bringing her up to speed on all that's happened. Especially on the medical advances, because the real Simone would have made a hell of a doctor, and if this one can synthesize information and theorize new solutions, she might be a valuable weapon against Black Ep.

"Might be nice to get some good help for a change," Vashti says, ignoring Champagne when she takes it personally.

"Well, it's only a program, and I rather doubt it'll be able to think outside the box. Even your Malachi doesn't impress me in that respect."

"You should get to know him better," I suggest.

"I'm just hoping your Simone can pass on a—I guess I'd call it a *human* level. Just to be able to talk to her about old times and have her really remember them. That would be incredible. It's been so long," Champagne says.

"Does Halloween know yet?" Vashti asks.

I admit he does, and we gossip about it for a bit, until Vash focuses our attention on one of the displays at the far end of the room. One among many security camera images, Deuce has sagged into a green chenille recliner chair, his fiery hair draped over his face.

deuce

So they're watching you. You don't see the camera, but you know it's there. They've stuck you here to cool your heels so they can decide what to do with you.

Talk about backward thinking.

What are you going to do with them?

pandora

"Impressions?"

"I'm not sure what to make of him," I admit.

"Well, he's a mean little beast," Champagne huffs, "but with Hal as his daddy that's to be expected. Catch that hair—he looks like Cousin It."

Vashti puzzles over the reference.

"From the Addams Family," I explain.

"Ah," she says, "and is he sleeping or merely too embarrassed to show his face?"

We watch the steady rise and fall of his chest until he abruptly scratches an itch from his ear. The itch scratched, he stretches luxuriously, then runs a hand up over his face, pushing his brilliant mane back to give us a brief glimpse at his eyes before shaking it back down again, obscuring them from view.

"How can we use him?" Vashti asks, her expression shrewd.

"Use him?"

"To restore order with the girls. How can we make an example of him?"

deuce

Who are you kidding?

You're not going to do anything to them. Why should you? They don't matter. You already proved your point with them anyway.

The only two people who matter here are your best friend and your soul mate. Unfortunately, one of them got infected, and won't be in any condition to go on a big adventure right now. It's disappointing, but your last fire augured illness so the news didn't come as much of a surprise. Haji has to get better, you think, because you're going to be blood brother comrades-in-arms. He'll be your Mercutio—except, you know, loyal and sane. When he's feeling better, you'll tell him.

But you can tell your ladylove right now . . .

"I'm here," you whisper into the tiny mouthpiece you just

switched on, and radio waves carry her voice on a stealth frequency to the earpiece you just scratched.

"You made it," she whispers back.

"Told you I would."

"I was so worried."

You soothe her and tell her not to be scared. She says her only real fear was that you wouldn't really come. That you'd disappoint her and betray her trust the way everyone else has. But would you ever do that to your heart's choice?

"Don't eat or drink anything," she warns you. "They'll put something in it. They keep trying to feed me but I'm too smart for them."

"You must be starving."

"It's worth it to be with you."

"That's how I feel. Why would we ever need anything but each other?"

"There's just one thing," she whispers. "One thing more that I need."

"Name it."

"You already gave me truth."

"You deserve it, angel."

"All I need now is freedom."

"Then you'll get that too. Does that mean what I think it means?"

"Deuce," she whispers.

"Yes?"

"The answer's yes."

You asked the question the day you broke the IVR, the day you burned away all the lies. You stealthed your way into her domain to find her hugging herself in a small corner of her mansion, the saddest Scarlet Pimpernel there ever was, just paralyzed with grief and fear until you showed her the yang to her yin, the sun to her moon, the other half of the card and the other half of your heart. You matched them all and told her that though her mothers let her down, you never would.

It was perfect. It was fated. You found her at her weakest point, and you knew she couldn't reject you. Because what else did she have? She'd lost everything but the truth. So she needed you. Desperately. And you knew it. What you thought would be the most frightening moment in your life became so incredibly easy. You offered yourself as a friend, as more than a friend, as someone who'd watched her lovingly from afar, who couldn't stand to see her deceived the way she'd been.

She wanted you to hold her, she cried on your shoulder; sooner or later she'll let you get bolder.

You spent maybe a half-hour together, and the time flew, but when it was all done and you played it back through your mind it seemed like days. You said you'd come visit her and taught her how to adjust her link to accept the frequency you'd try. She didn't have an answer to your question but she said she'd have one when you arrived.

You said you were running away from home and did she want to join you?

And now the answer's yes.

"Beautiful," you whisper. "When?"

"Don't make me wait any longer for you. Please, rescue me now, I'm begging you."

pandora

"Is he talking to himself?"

I strain at the image. Are Deuce's lips moving? It's hard to tell behind all that hair, but Vashti might just be right.

Champagne cranks the volume all the way up so I can just barely hear the whispered word, "When?" When, what?

Quick as a cricket, he's on his feet and spinning, hair whipping past the camera as he snatches the wooden swan and treats it to a jet of flame.

"That little shit," Vashti gasps, as I rise from my chair.

My eyes catch a glimpse of the lighter in his hand—I can make out a parody of Mickey Mouse, winking, laughing and flipping off the world.

With a well-practiced flick of the wrist, he flings the burning swan down at the baseboard of the door, and he's falling back on the bed now, rolling through to the other side to drop down for cover.

I don't wait to see the door get blown off its hinges. I'm already on the move.

deuce

Kick-ass acoustics in here, the satisfying boom crashing in your ears like delicious thunder. You poke your head out right as the alarm goes off, but no one's out there. Light on the structural damage, you see, opening the way without bringing everything down on your head, which means clever you used just the right-sized swan, the perfect amount of plastique encased in the hollow wood.

You grab your backpack with the rest of your explosive zoo. Off to find a Penny and pick her up, all day long you'll have good luck.

But wait, first you have to stomp out the one small flaming piece of carpet before it can spread. Fire safety, Dad, you remember.

Got it.

Here we go.

pandora

I've got frightened girls shrieking all over the place, alarm bells ringing and Vashti's voice screaming, "Stop right there!" over the loudspeaker. Champagne's calling for me to stop Deuce while she gets the girls out of danger. I'm yelling back at her, "Right, right," as we separate.

I'm not too sure how I'm going to stop him. I've got a brown belt in jiu-jitsu, but that was back in the IVR, and I don't know how those skills will fare in the real world. Probably fine, but I haven't practiced in years, and if he's armed and I'm not . . .

But I can't worry about that. My legs are pumping and I'm not about to stop.

deuce

Penny's large blue eyes are flecked with green, so fucking expressive, and glittering with excitement when she sees you coming for her. Those eyes you don't mind meeting, because they're sending tingles through your entire body and lightning right to your groin. But then there's the rest of the package: the cheeks of her perfectly symmetrical face rosy with health, her nose pert, her mouth mischievous and kissable, her short golden-brown hair touched copper by the sun. And a body beautiful enough to make her clothes an insult.

When she hugs you, all you can think about is avenging the insult by ripping them off her right now, but she's already pulling you down the hall with her. Sound judgment because you've got to get out of here first—all that good stuff has to wait.

You follow her back through the maze of hallways, snaking toward the exit when a shape lunges at you, grabbing your lady-love, wrenching her from your grasp. In a blink you see it's Brigit and she's bigger and stronger than Penny, yanking cruelly at her hair to tilt her head back, then slipping around for a choke. Your sweet soul mate tugs at the arms around her but can't break the grip and can't catch any air. You can't have that, so you dig in your pocket for the torch you call Genesis 3:24, which eats butane like a motherfucker but pumps out the most intimidating jet of eighteen-hundred-degree-Fahrenheit fire you've ever seen a lighter spit. Brigit sees that wicked jet and tries to step back, turning to position Penny in the way, as you come forward.

"Let her go, Brigit," you tell her, and even though she says she will, she doesn't break the hold. You realize it's a stalling game she's playing—she's trying to slow your escape long enough for reinforcements to arrive. And sure enough, there's her friend Sloane hobbling toward you on her crutches, screaming, "Over here!"

The best move on the board has you convincing Brigit that you'll burn her alive even if you have to set Penny on fire to do it, so you let your eyes get glassy and cold as you bring it about an inch from their faces.

"You're crazy," Brigit pants, releasing your ladylove and backing up as you hold her at bay with Genesis.

"I hadn't noticed," you tell her, and that's when the lighter starts sputtering because you forgot to refuel it before you left.

Out of the corner of your eye you can see Penny pitching herself at the approaching Sloane, struggling with her for one of the crutches and then pie-facing her so she topples back over her broken leg. By the time Genesis flickers out, she's brained Brigit with the crutch. The beaten bully falls down to her knees with a whump, her mouth making an astonished "o" as she covers up the best she can, and you do your good deed for the day by pulling your angel along before she can hit her again.

Next stop, freedom.

pandora

I catch Deuce rushing out the door hand-in-hand with one of the girls—Penny—young lovers making a break for the bicycle rack. Before I can say match made in hell, Sloane's panicked cry reaches my ears, "Somebody help!"

She's down on the floor, cradling Brigit, who's clutching her head in terrible pain. Brigit's eyes are fluttering closed and I'm thinking head trauma, and I just can't leave her like that, so I go to them and try to keep her conscious until help arrives.

A call comes in and when I grab it I think it's got to be Vashti or Champagne, but it's Isaac instead so I go to reassure him. No one got hurt in the explosion, and Brigit's down, but we're helping her. But it's not why he's calling—I know that when I see the glistening tears in his eyes.

"It's Mu'tazz," he says. "It's time."

deuce

Pump your fist in the air to leave Nymphenburg for the Bavarian countryside—that's a big mission accomplished—and all things considered, it went like a charm. You're almost disappointed they didn't cuff you. To think of all the time you put into teaching yourself how to melt a handcuff chain with a palmed jet torch behind your back. That's the kind of stunt worthy of Van Caneghem, who out-Houdinied Houdini, but you can't be that disappointed because you would've looked pretty stupid if you'd messed it up.

Anyway, handcuffs or no, the prize is yours.

You're coasting downhill with her, feet off pedals, just laughing and talking about whatever pops into your heads. She keeps telling you things you already know about her. Like how her name came from a Lung Butter song, but actually she's wrong about that because you know that song and the lyrics go "Play the melody," not "Play Penelope." You don't have the heart to tell her, though. She's been through enough.

"Is there anything you don't know about me?" she asks.

"Yeah, lots of stuff." You grin, because you've learned so much about so many people in such a short period of time that it all just jumbles in your head. So she tries to think up some good questions to see what you do and don't know, and you wind up three for five, missing her lucky number and—most embarrassingly— her birthday, which you think is sometime in January, but it's not, so you apologize.

"Think I take after my dad in the memory department," you explain, and she laughs and tells you it's okay.

"How can my stupid birthday compare to today? The day you freed me, the first day I get to spend with you?"

"We can celebrate every day together," you tell her.

She grins like sunlight, and then squeezes the brake to maneuver around a cluster of skeletons littering the road. It's almost funny how unscary they are. Maybe if they were fresh corpses there'd be a horror factor, but they've been dead longer than you've both been alive. The "stench of death" is long gone, and honestly they're about as frightening as a skeleton in a biology class or maybe an archaeological dig. Their modesty is protected by tattered clothing (synthetics, must be, because natural fibers degrade and all the poor saps who wore them are naked now), and all the little tatters are whipping in the wind like banners cheering you on.

With the obstacles negotiated, Penny looks back over her shoulder to see if you're being followed. Nothing there but you can understand her feeling jumpy about it.

"We're living by our wits now." You smile. "We have to out-think them and outrun them."

"And maybe outgun them?"

You laugh and tell her you don't think it'll come to that. Maybe they won't even bother chasing after you.

"I hope you're right," she says, looking reassured. "Do you think they remember what it was like to be in love?"

halloween

Simone turned out to be a lot of fun to talk to once I got past the initial shock and my sense that she was an abominable farce. Her memories were as shredded as mine—as it turned out, I'd short-sightedly made many of her recollections from school irretrievable the day I deleted our old teacher Maestro—but in the subset of what we both knew, there we were, like old times again. And many of the things she didn't know, Pandora had informed her about, including her time outside the IVR: the way she reacted to the real world, the kiss we'd shared and her eventual overdose on pills. She might have been counterfeit, but she was so close to the girl I remembered that I couldn't appreciate the difference. I spent hours with her—we had a lot to discuss.

And as we did, in the back of my mind, Pandora kept returning to me. She'd spent so much time and energy re-creating a woman who was not only her dead friend, but also her rival for my affection. She'd returned Simone to me in the hopes that it would help me. Of all my losses, I'd taken Simone's death the hardest, and with her born anew maybe I could follow suit. Maybe it would engage me again, and then I'd be willing to work with Pandora and her friends to make the world a better place.

That didn't quite happen. I didn't have any more desire to put up with Isaac, Vashti or Champagne after talking to Simone. But, to my absolute surprise, I did feel a little better about the world.

Two things happened.

First of all, there was Simone. I'd loved her since I was six, and since her death, I'd carried her absence with me as a reminder of what I could never have. She had been my obsession for years: the brilliant, talented, beautiful Simone, the special someone with whom I hoped to share my life.

I was over her. Like a spell had been broken, I just didn't feel the way I'd felt about her. I'd changed since the day she died. I'd grown up. Of course, I was thrilled to have her back in my life and I wanted her friendship, but beyond that she just didn't mean that much to me anymore.

I'd healed.

And second, there was Pandora. She'd loved me for years, the crazy thing—and always I'd rejected her, partly because I hadn't thought myself worthy of that kind of love, and partly because my heart had no room for her while I was mooning over Simone, and so I'd tried not to lead the girl on.

For her to resurrect Simone like this—granted, she did it for a variety of reasons—but the biggest of them all was as a gift to me. Out of love for me. It impressed me as the purest, most emotionally self-sacrificing thing she could ever do. Here she loved me enough to try to make me happy and whole again, even if it meant risking losing me forever.

I could finally see her in a new light.

And so I felt better about the world, seeing it as a place of possibility, where surprising things can happen no matter how jaded you might happen to be.

Then I slipped out of the IVR with a thought to call Pandora, only to find a message from her first. I called her back and she brought me back to the here and now with what had just happened with Deuce, how he'd blown a hole in Nymphenburg and run off with one of Vashti's girls.

"Fuck," I said.

"I'm sorry, Hal. I'm looking for them right now."

"Okay," I told her. "I'll be right there."

haji

When I tell the story about the frogs, I never tell it the same way twice. Sometimes they are green frogs, and sometimes they're brown. Sometimes I describe them with warts and other times without. They could be your common bullfrogs or Okinawan green tree frogs. They might even be toads. There could be ten, twenty or a whole army of them, but the core of the story is always the same.

A group of frogs was traveling together, when two suddenly fell into a pit. The others rushed to the edge to see how very deep it was, and they realized the pair would never be able to get out. Don't even bother, they croaked, but the two trapped frogs started hopping anyway. They jumped and they hopped but they couldn't quite reach the top. All the time the crowd kept yelling for them to quit suffering and just give up, lay down and die. Finally, one of the two did exactly that. But the other ignored his fellow frogs and kept jumping with all his might. Against all odds, he made it out.

The others were amazed. Why did you keep trying? they asked. Didn't you hear us yelling for you to quit?

Oh, is that what you were doing, said the bewildered frog. I'm afraid I'm going deaf. All the time I was down there I thought you were encouraging me.

My sister Dalila always liked that story, and these days I tell it to her a lot. These days we all have frogs on the brain. The microbes have delivered and devoured Mu'tazz, may he find peace, and only a miracle will keep Rashid from being the next to hear the call. But we must keep jumping, Ngozi, Dalila and I.

Since my religious awakening I have become fearless. The darkest of life's emotions have no traction with me. This must be God's plan. My siblings need my strength to buoy them, and I lend it with joy, exhorting them to keep hope even when they are adrift in oceans of doubt and fear.

Lately I have been thinking of my father as a kind of Darwin frog. The male of that species takes care of his young, scooping up the female's eggs with his tongue and protecting them in his vocal sac. There the eggs hatch into tadpoles, and when they become little frogs, he spits them out into the world.

What would it be like to have a mother? If my father and Champagne had been able to conceive? If we sprang from her womb, what then? I cannot help but wonder.

My father has not yet wept for Mu'tazz, or if he has, he has seen fit not to do it where we can see him.

pandora

As a resort area, Lake Starnberg reminds me of what Idlewild must have been like before it became a technology center. The shoreline and countryside are postcard pretty, signs inviting us to sail, water ski or hike along the trails. The water's calling to me, but there's no time for a swim. It isn't why we're here.

"Twenty meters," Champagne says, following Penny's link on an Argos tracker. She looks up and points. "The beach house."

Three skeletons inside, long dead, a couple tucked in together, and at the foot of the bed: the bones of their faithful dog. I always wonder at scenes like this. Was the dog unable to fend for himself or just unwilling? Was he trapped inside? Did they let him go? Did he have no place to go to? When his masters stopped moving and talking, did he simply lie down and wait for them?

A quick search finds the link down a sink drain. Clove cigarette crushed underfoot on the floor. Bicycles discarded in the garage. And fresh tire tracks—from a sport utility vehicle, I'd say— stretch off in the sand, heading down the beach, turning west.

I call Malachi with the news and he says he'll do what he can with the satellites, looking for a GPS if it's there, and if not, sweeping the area west of Starnberg in the hopes of picking them up on the fly.

Champagne draws a breath and lets it out slowly. "Not much for us to do now but go home and wait," she says.

"You sound relieved."

"I'm not so eager to find them right now," she confesses, brushing a strand of hair from her eyes. "They're going to play house for a little while and when they miss the comforts of home, they'll come back. And that'll be on our terms, not theirs."

"Then what?"

"I won't know 'til I see them. They have to be held responsible for what they've done, and while I don't give a shit about Hal's kid, Penny needs help, medication, therapy, whatever it takes. I know Brigit and Sloane have been picking on her, but to respond with that kind of violence—as a mom, I knew my kids would fight from time to time, but I never thought one would try to bash the other's brains out."

"It's a lucky thing Brigit's not seriously hurt," I say. "From what the cameras caught, it didn't look like she was holding much back."

"She needs help," Champagne repeats.

A call comes in—not from Malachi, but Vashti—and she's talking so fast I think she's slipped into Pit Bull again, but it must be a deliriously happy, excited pit bull whose mind is speeding faster than her tongue.

"You have to go back to Peru—that's imperative—drop everything to do it—I don't care what it takes, I need you there and I need you there yesterday!"

"Slow down," we tell her. "What's happening?"

She catches her breath and tells us about her breakthrough. She's finished the autopsy on Mu'tazz, and between the analyses she's been able to do on the End of the World and what she's discovered from the tests she's run on the pygmy marmosets, she thinks she might have found what we've all been looking for.

Black Ep diverts the immune system into making responses that don't clear the infection, but the marmosets have an enzyme that works wonders. It seems to be activated through the digestion process. Marmosets eat fruit and insects, but get most of their nutrition from gum they chew from trees. One of those trees— a type of jatoba that grows only in the Peruvian rainforest—

contains the enzyme, and I didn't bring her nearly enough samples when I brought the marmoset.

"I've got an idea how we can use that enzyme against Black Ep," Vashti says, "and maybe even against the End of the World. But I'm going to need a lot more gum."

And that's not all. For years Vashti has been obsessed with finding an answer via gene therapy—we've already found a nucleotide sequence complementary to Black Ep, one that can bind to the sequence and excise it with "molecular scissors," ripping the disease out of our DNA once and for all. But the devil is in the details. Every time scientists have tried to guide that sequence to its destination, those scissors have hacked up vital parts of the genome with disastrous results—that's one of the reasons Gedaechtnis designed us with auxiliary organs and redundant genetic code. Up to this point, ripping our DNA via radical gene therapy has seemed too risky to try, but now she thinks she's found a way to make it work. She even thinks she can rip the End of the World from Isaac's kids, but it's going to take months to make sure, and they don't have that long, which means that gum is critical.

"I'll leave immediately," I tell her.

Not one but two potential solutions. It's fantastic news, marred ever so slightly by Champagne bumping heads with Vashti over wanting to return to Nymphenburg.

"No, while Pandora's in Peru, I want you to keep looking for our little runaways," Vashti protests.

"I'll be more useful back at home," she says, "and frankly I don't have the energy to go chasing after Romeo and Juliet."

"Let's just hope it's not Sid and Nancy," I mutter, my mind flashing back to one of Hal's costume parties from years ago.

"No, Romeo and Juliet didn't end that happily either, as I recall," Vashti pointedly remarks. "And before you brush them off as harmless, why don't you take another look at Penny's last journal entry?"

Champagne just shrugs, telling her what she told me about the kids playing house for a while, adding, "And even if I found them, what could I do? I can't drag them back if they don't want to come."

Vashti says, "You're an adult. Try reasoning with them."

"Reason with teenagers?"

"Fine, I don't have time for this. Do what you want," Vashti snaps, abruptly hanging up.

"She always has to have the last word," Champagne complains, struggling to catch up to me as I hurry back to my copter.

"Come on, let's get you home and me to the rainforest."

halloween

"Damn your luck, you just missed Pandora," a decidedly unbubbly Champagne informed me as I climbed out of my jet.

I returned her icy non-greeting with one of my own but listened as she told me where Pandora was and about the progress Vashti had made.

"Not that you care about what we're doing though, right?"

"I don't. Where's my son?"

"How am I supposed to know? Nice psychopath you raised there."

"Why don't you take me to someone in charge?"

She reacted a bit negatively to that so I ignored her, leaving her to find Vashti on my own. But before I could get to her, someone else found me first.

"Halloween."

As kids never once had Isaac and I gotten along, the resentment compounded by our classmates puzzling over how we could dislike each other as much as we did when really we were so similar in so many ways. We ought to bond, they'd thought, because he was spiritually inclined while my interests encompassed mythology and the boundaries of life and death, but no, we never liked each other—he was always Lazarus's lapdog to me—and so we tried to make the best of a bad situation by avoiding each other the best we could.

Upon spotting him, I felt the animosity rising in me once again, but I managed to keep the barb in my throat from escaping my mouth.

"You're eighteen years late and a dollar short," he said, grabbing my arm, "but I'm so glad you're here."

He hugged me, suddenly, and after a moment of confusion what did I do but hug him back? It was something I hadn't done before, something I thought I would never do, but the poor guy had just lost his son.

He led me through the complex, past girls who regarded me with curiosity and fear, and he talked about his children in a raspy voice. *Raspy,* I thought, *from the strain of not breaking down completely.* For years I'd doubted his motivations, but here I saw a man who cared on some deep level for his sons and his daughter. I could empathize with that. He wasn't an enemy, or a rival anymore, and he wasn't looking down his nose at me. He was simply a broken man with dead and dying children, and though he might never earn my true friendship, in that moment he secured my pity.

Vashti was another story. She put her claws into me right away, as I expected she would, laying into me about the choices I'd made, my absence, my arrogance, my irresponsibility as a parent and as a man. She blamed me for wrecking the utopia she'd worked so hard to build, and I found that funny, telling her if she hadn't wanted her kids to hate her, she shouldn't have deceived them as she had.

"Gedaechtnis fed you the same lies they fed the rest of us, but I guess you swallowed them, huh? You learned the exact wrong lessons from what we went through," I said.

"And is that why you had your son attack me? To teach me a lesson?"

I told her I hadn't put Deuce up to anything, and she didn't believe me, saying I was out to get her. She said the only reason I'd had a kid was so I could find a loophole to get out of my promise never to interfere.

"Ridiculous," I said.

"What is it about me that you hate so much?" she asked, accusing me of sexism first, that I couldn't bear to see a society of strong women—but when I told her I honestly didn't care if she raised girls, boys or hermaphrodites, she said, "Then maybe it's because you think Cham and I are an item? Is that the thought that offends you so?"

I said, "Vashti, I'm all for women sleeping together, and why shouldn't you bang Champagne? Everyone else has."

"I can always count on you to sink to the lowest level," she spit.

"Make no mistake," I told her, "I have no problem with who you fuck, but I have a big problem with who you fuck over. But never did I tell Deuce to get wrapped up in any of this."

"Well, he seems pretty eager to get wrapped up in my daughter," she said. "Now he's out who knows where corrupting her. What kind of father are you?"

"Hey, I got a letter from your precious flower and she's a fucking nutcase," I replied. "I'll bet you dollars to donuts she's out there corrupting *him,* so what kind of mother are *you?*"

Back and forth we went, and she seemed perfectly willing to trade insults with me for as long as I could stand it, and with Isaac's kids sick I felt foolish keeping her from her work. So I blinked first, saying that I'd come here to find Deuce and take him home, and admitting that he wasn't quite as mature as I'd thought.

"He's a troubled kid in some ways," I said, "and maybe he's more troubled than I wanted to believe. Okay? Let's put our heads together and our feelings aside."

She nodded at that and said, "Most of the blame here goes to you and your son, but clearly Penelope was complicit too. The last entry in her journal complained that I didn't know what love was while she did, so I think it's fair to say that they both had this escape planned out since then."

"Agreed."

She told me how she'd scoured through her daughter's domain, journal, personal effects—everything she had—in a search for clues, but Penny hadn't left any.

"I assume you've been through his things?"

"No, I always respect his privacy," I said.

"That's not particularly helpful in a situation like this. If there's a clue to where they're planning to 'honeymoon,' it might be in his domain. And if you're going to be a responsible parent, like it or not, at some point you may have to spy on your kids for their own good."

Grudgingly, I saw her point. So she set me up with an IVR session, and I plugged in, using a special code to unstealth Deuce's domain. The entry point was a realm of volcanoes perpetually erupting and forked lightning slashing down through a rainless scarlet sky. In a tribute to me, my old servants, the nightgaunts, flew high overhead, but they'd been customized with auras of white-hot flame licking at their bodies, fire that would never go out.

I had no time to go exploring, so I froze everything with a wave of my hand, then decompiled it with a twitch of my finger. Volcanoes, sky, firegaunts, all design elements, all his secrets, all were reduced to code.

But I found nothing.

Like Penny, he'd left no clues, and I realized I'd betrayed my son's trust for nothing more than the pursuit of leaving no stone unturned.

deuce

You're working on the computer, hacking, which might just be your favorite thing to do. There's something so cool about perverting the system. It's another case where you take after your dad, rebels begetting rebels and all that.

She's distracting you, but in a good way. Not by putting her arms around you and nibbling on your ear the way you'd like her to, but with her gleeful laugh. She's amusing herself by defacing the walls with a magic marker—haikus mostly, five-seven-five stanzas about all the people in her life, most of them filled with the kind of language she couldn't afford to use until you freed her. Man, those girls are repressed. But you've been reading about repressed girls in school uniforms going buck wild the first moment they get a chance. Maybe she'll do that, given enough time.

For now instead of coaxing her out of her clothes, you're coaxing a virus into the network. Still fun, but will the network respect you in the morning?

The system puts up a spirited defense, but it's nothing you can't handle. You feel a little guilty, because it's not *your* virus, and you've always been taught not to take what isn't yours. But you don't think he'll mind. Or if he does mind, he'll understand you did it for a very good reason. I mean, come on, you can't have the tyrants chasing you down. He's been telling you for years what a nest of vipers they are. So you'll shut their eyes for just a little while, just long enough for you to find a paradise you can call your own.

Keystroke, keystroke, keystroke and it's done. Nighty-night.

You push off and slide across the room in your rolling chair, over to where your girl is, and when you get there she sits in your lap.

"Is it really done?" she asks.

"You better believe it. Now we can go underground and they'll never be able to find us."

halloween

Right as I'd recompiled Deuce's domain, a familiar colorless entity appeared before me.

"You broke our deal," I said.

"The moment your delightful son attacked me," Malachi replied.

"No biggie. I suppose I would have done the same if I were you."

He abruptly changed the subject: "Did you write a program called Polyphemus?"

Years ago, I'd written it, but I'd almost forgotten about it since. It was a virus I'd designed to wreak havoc on satellite networks. I'd conceived it as a last-ditch program to be used if anyone figured out how I was keeping America from Malachi's prying eyes.

"An ace up my sleeve," I said.

"It's just been played."

Deuce. Deuce played my ace. And I'd thought that file was safely out of his reach. Here I'd been protecting his privacy, but he'd gone and violated mine.

"That's an extraordinarily clever name for a virus," Malachi derided me. "Polyphemus, after the cyclops Odysseus blinds with a pointy stick. Now the satellites are down and I've lost my eye on the world."

"I can fix it," I promised him, "but it'll take time. Let me call you right back."

I slipped back out to the real world, and called him up as I hurried back toward my jet. "He's got to be in a Gedaechtnis complex," I said. "It's the only place he could have triggered the program. And that's either Berlin or Liège. He couldn't have gotten farther than that by now."

Champagne tried to intercept me as I exited, but I wouldn't stop for her.

"Malachi, I'm assuming he only targeted the spy satellites? Not the communication satellites?"

"You want to call ahead?"

"That's right," I told him, sliding my ladder up to my jet. "Patch me through."

deuce

"Deuce?"

That's your father's voice on the loudspeaker. You and Penny look at each other like fish caught in a net.

"I know you can hear me."

He's pissed at you, genuinely pissed, telling you to pick up and talk to him, and the tone in his voice changes your plans because you'd hoped to take Penny back to Idlewild so he could meet her. You thought he'd approve but apparently not, and that's worrisome. As you're debating a reach for the phone, your ladylove turns the speakers off, making the decision for you. "This is our time," she says. "No interruptions allowed."

"I was going to take you to Idlewild," you say.

"We'll make a new home," she says. "But we'd better start now—he knows we're here."

She's right, of course, so you hightail it out of there, sprinting right past the *Meru* pod where Gedaechtnis stashed Pandora and Isaac for the duration of their childhoods. It's a quick drive to the airfield to steal a plane, and as you help her into the co-pilot's seat she tells you she's always wanted to go to London.

"You can be the King and I'll be the Queen."

Sounds good to you, so Heathrow Airport it is. You take off and set a course, winging your way there as fast as you possibly can, frightened the whole time that your father's jet will come screeching overhead. You may be a skilled pilot, but you can't out-fly him any better than you can outplay him in chess.

Why can't he just be happy for you?

pandora

I'm a one-woman logging crew, chopping down jatoba trees with a laser saw and collecting gum from the stems. That's the plan, anyway. The reality is the saw conks out after the very first tree and me miles away from the backup parts I need. So it's back to basics, felling the jatobas with the fire axe I keep in my copter. I'd simply tap the trees if I could, but Vashti sent me with a tall order to fill, and I don't want to waste a second while Isaac's kids are suffering.

When I come to the part of the rainforest where I laid a blanket down for Mu'tazz, I can't help but feel like he's with me somehow, a mystical feeling I'm not able to fully embrace. I'd talk to Malachi about it, but I'm still not speaking to him very much after learning of his deception, my communications with him terse and without our usual pleasantries. I know how to hold a grudge. But even the biggest grudge-holder can let them go— I'm learning that from Halloween. The thought that he's in Germany amazes me. It's not even Oktoberfest. For so long it seemed he'd never leave his hermitage, and I just wish it were under happier circumstances than chasing after an errant son.

My teenage rebellion seemed like a big deal at the time, but it was positively tame by comparison, involving neither swinging crutches nor exploding swans. It simply involved piercings and a tattoo, a curiosity about alcohol, and far too much time trying to make myself look tougher than I was. Looking back on it, I suppose it all stemmed from my early school days, when I was known as the sweet one. The smart one, the pretty one, the quiet one and the crazy one were already taken by Simone, Champagne, Vashti and Fantasia. But I didn't want to be the sweet one—it drove me crazy after a while—so I tried to be the athletic one, and then the mysterious one.

My parents named me Naomi d'Oliveira, but when I found out Naomi means "sweet and pleasant" I just didn't want to be called that anymore. So I found a new name in Pandora. I didn't actually find it though—it was Hal who named me. This was back when he was still Gabriel. He'd become a big mythology buff and had taken to nicknaming me Pandora. When I asked him why, he told me the story of the girl who lets all the evils of the world out, and they bite and sting her, but then she releases hope, and hope heals all the places where she's been bit and stung. I reminded him of that girl, he said, but he wouldn't explain why.

He'd forgotten that he'd named me. I had to remind him a few years back and he said, "That's right. Well, it suits you. You don't look like a Naomi to me."

I think I'm not the sweet one but I am the hopeful one, and maybe that's not such a bad thing to be.

deuce

There may not be power in this part of the world, but you don't need power for a romantic candlelight dinner. Operation Love Machine got off to a rough start, but this warehouse is much better than the last—no rats, for one thing—and Fortnum & Mason is not only hermetically sealed but very upscale for the discriminating scavenger couple. She said she wanted to try meat, and you told her fresh is better than canned, but all Dad's guns are at home so no rabbit stew for now. No, you have to content yourselves with foie gras, which you've never had before either, and never will again. She likes it though, delightedly licking it off your fingertips, so you pack a couple of tins into your backpack for safekeeping. And in the candlelight she's never been more beautiful as she says, "I think we need a gun."

You don't disagree, because rabbits are mighty tasty, and you never know when you want to scare away something bigger.

"No, I think we need a gun in case they come after us," she says.

"They're not going to find us."

"What if I want to find them?"

She's joking, probably, because when you grin she grins too.

"Wouldn't it be cool to go back in there, guns blazing, and scare the shit out of them?" she asks. "Wouldn't they just shit?"

"Like they've never shit before," you agree, playing along.

"I just think they have to be taught a lesson," she says.

"Who do you mean?"

She lays out her enemies list, one name after another, and why, and when she gets to your comrade-in-arms, you wince.

"Why not Haji?"

So you have to tell her that while she's right about the others, she's misjudged Haji. He's a good guy, and she just doesn't understand him. Unfortunately, she doesn't take that well, accusing you of calling her stupid. Is she too stupid to understand Haji? But no, you didn't mean it like that, so you explain what the fire told you, the wisdom you received, how he's destined to become your best friend the way she's destined to be your lover. And when she blushes at the word "lover," you quickly throw "soul mate" into the mix.

"So if the fire said it, it has to be true?"

"If it wasn't true, you wouldn't be here right now," you tell her, explaining a little of how pyromancy works, and she listens wide-eyed, but you're not so sure she believes. And that's okay, because she will in time.

"You know Haji's really sick, right?"

"It's a sad thing," you nod, "but I'm sure he'll recover."

She says, "Okay, so if we left Haji out of it, what then? Would you go along with me?"

You shrug. It really depends on what she's talking about.

"You do something for me, and I'll do something for you," she says.

"What kind of something?"

She tells you and it sounds pretty great so you keep playing along to hear more and more of it, but after a while you have to tell her, "I just think it's dangerous to go back when we have everything we need right here. You want to teach them a lesson? Keep depriving them of your company. They don't know what they're missing."

"That's the point," she pouts. "They *don't* know. I don't have a place in their world."

"You have a big place in mine."

She sort of half smiles at that and looks like she's about to say something, but then doesn't, shaking her head, and no matter how many times you ask her what it was she won't spill it.

"What do we have for dessert?" she asks.

You loot the shelves together, swiping chocolate sauce, butterscotch topping, strawberry and blackberry preserves—anything that's fun to lick off someone's fingers or neck. And even though the ultrapreservatives make everything a little chalky to the taste, it's a sensual delight, kissing and nuzzling your beloved, and even though she won't let you take her top off ("I'm just not ready for that yet," she frowns), it's still as much fun as any fire you've ever set.

Then she's all tuckered out, so you cuddle her in your arms, lying back to spoon with her. And if you could just stay in that moment forever, you'd die a happy man.

But the fire curled back on itself. A bend, a sinister bend, always a bad omen.

Your ladylove tenses in your arms, and you know something is terribly wrong right before she starts coughing and wheezing.

"What's wrong?" you ask, but she won't tell you, just clutching her stomach and shaking her head.

You pound her on the back and get her bottled water to drink, which she does, but she can't keep it down, vomiting violently, shaking and crying when she's done.

The more you try to help her, the more despondent she becomes.

"What can I do?" you ask. You've never taken care of a sick person before.

"There's nothing you can do," she cries. "Nothing anyone can do. Oh, God. I feel like I'm going to die."

"You're not going to die," you assure her, smoothing her cheek with your hand.

"Yes, I am," she says. "You don't get better from Black Ep."

"Black Ep?"

"The End of the World," she manages, turning from you to try to vomit again, but this time it's only dry heaves.

"That can't be," you tell her.

"Deuce, it's in our blood."

"Yeah, but they said it's not Black Ep. They said it's only a threat to Isaac's kids."

"Well, of course they said that!" she cries, her perfect face twisted by despair. "They were lying to us, we all have it, and we're all going to die!"

halloween

I'd guessed wrong.

I flew to Berlin because it was closer, but Deuce was in Liège, Belgium, all along. By the time I got there he'd vanished without a trace, taking his little girlfriend with him. And he wouldn't take any of my calls, very unlike him. So I went back to Nymphenburg to repair the damage Polyphemus had done, all the while expecting him at any minute to come to his senses and call.

Killing viruses can be slow, frustrating work, whether they are biological or digital in nature. I spent long hours isolating, erasing, reconstructing and restoring, the hours stretching into days. I began to feel a kind of kinship with Isaac and even Vashti, because say what you like about them, they're hard workers. Champagne, on the other hand . . .

The little hellions Vashti designed as the next evolutionary rung wouldn't stop bothering me with their questions—why was I here, why did I stay away so long, could they come visit me in

Idlewild, did I really grow up in near-Earth orbit, was Deuce as eccentric as Penny, why did I hate Vashti so much—and I found myself asking the question many people do when bothered by kids, a question I'd never been able to say to Deuce.

"Where's your mother?"

To which they always asked me which one, but I knew Vashti was busy with her research. Wasn't Champagne supposed to be taking care of them? To which they had no answer at all.

When I had my fill of that I tracked Champagne down to find she was sequestered in the soothing unreality of IVR. She was none too pleased when I crashed her party and forcibly removed her therewith.

"Don't you think Vashti could use your help?"

"Like you're someone to talk about helping people."

"What? You're going to model yourself after me? Your kids are running around like stray fucking animals and you're retreating when there's work to be done."

She shook her head desperately, as if that could punctuate how I didn't understand what she was going through. "They get on my nerves, Hal. I'm feeling like they're sucking out all the air in the room when I'm with them. I can't breathe."

"They need you."

"I can't be around kids right now, I don't have any feelings left to give."

I listened to her as she told me about her miscarriages, about all the pain she went through with Isaac. And to see Isaac's kids dying now—it's overwhelmed her and left her hollow.

"They're all going to die," she wept.

"You don't know that. There's always hope. In the meantime why don't you suck it up and help."

She looked at me as if to say, How? What could she really do?

I softened my tone and said, "Look, Cham, if you don't want to deal with the kids, don't deal with the kids. You studied to be a doctor. Go help Vashti in the lab."

"She doesn't want me there."

"Why, don't you belong there? I remember you trying to save Tyler's life."

"Didn't do much good, did it?"

"No, but up to that point I thought you were a vapid waste of space, and the way you tried to save him showed me there was a lot more to you than meets the eye."

"I know first aid," she said, bitterly turning away from me. "If one of the girls scrapes her knee, you can come get me."

Back in school I'd always pegged her as the dumb one, the pretty blonde who was just killing time until she could find a nice husband to marry. The funny thing was how over time I'd come to reconsider that, while she came to accept it.

So many times in my life I go back to the Great Law of Unintended Consequences. I disparaged Champagne for years, never thinking she'd actually believe all those insults when I needed her to step up to the plate. I gave Deuce freedom because I couldn't stand how Gedaechtnis raised me—but it turns out I gave him too much. Things we never want to happen can spring from our missteps. We can take things too far and summon the devil we don't know simply by shunning the one that we do.

Case in point: Isaac.

When his daughter Hessa died last year, and he didn't have a clear understanding of how Black Ep took her, he increased his surviving kids' dosage of BEAR. BEAR has been a wonder drug for us, but even too much of a good thing can kill you.

Isaac came to me, bereft and benumbed, telling me in a quiet, inconsolable tone what his research had just uncovered. How the End of the World sprang simply from his increasing the dosage.

Instead of therapeutically working against the plague as it was meant to, the overdose of BEAR—through its sheer quantity— triggered billions of mutations, selective evolutionary pressure making a new disease as virulent as Black Ep ever was. Like trusting a friend to house-sit while you're away and returning to find a wild party has destroyed everything you own. The new retrovirus spread insidiously over a yearlong latency period, Isaac said, only to show itself now, immune to all our standard courses of treatment.

And he didn't need to do it. His kids would have stayed perfectly healthy with the regular dosage of BEAR. His daughter got sick from a spiteful trick, and his reaction to that, his fear, sickened the rest.

deuce

With every hour Penny's getting sicker and you don't know what to do. Should you call your father? Should you take her back home?

"No," she says, "don't you see that's not an option?"

"But you're really sick. Your mom's got state-of-the-art hospital equipment."

"If you take me home, they'll never let us see each other again."

You're afraid she's right, but maybe it's worth it to save her life?

She says, "You're not getting it. No one's life is going to be saved." She tells you she's been studying the plague for years, and she knows the End of the World when she sees it.

"Black Ep nearly killed everyone on the planet, and we only survived by the skin of our teeth. Vashti always said we were just one mutation away from getting flushed down the drain like everyone else. And this is it. This is the worst-case scenario. I always used to ask her, 'Mommy, what do we do then?' and she said, 'There's nothing we can do if that happens. So let's just hope it never does.'"

Your heart thuds in your chest. What if she's right?

"Are you sure that's what you have? Maybe you ate something, maybe it's the stomach flu."

She just puts her head in her hands, resigned. "I know the symptoms when I see them. I've got it. But if I have to die I want to be with you."

"Of course," you say, "that's what I want too."

She starts crying again and you hold her. And she kisses you—not a chaste kiss-and-make-it-better kiss but one with fire in it, as deep as she's ever kissed you before, and her fingers are digging into your thigh. It's like she's dying, but clinging to life through love.

"Do you know what I really want?" she asks. "I want us to be the last two people on earth. Adam and Eve at the end of the world, can you think of anything more romantic than that?"

You feel like the best day of your life and the worst day of your life are the same fucking day. No, you can't think of anything more romantic than that, but you can't wrap your mind around the fact that you're both going to die. You don't feel like you're sick but she is and maybe with you it's just a matter of time. Your throat is kind of sore and your heart's beating fast but that's probably just fear. And while you're thinking about yourself, she's thinking about everyone else.

She says, "Remember when I was talking about scaring people? That was wrong. Why do something as childish as that when we can actually do something noble?"

"Noble like what?"

"I was thinking about your friend Haji. You know how the fire said you're supposed to be friends and all? He's suffering right now. He's not going to live much longer, so if you're going to be his friend, I think you have to do the one thing he needs. The most difficult thing of all."

"What's that?" you ask her.

"You have to help him die."

You shake your head and tell her that's not how you pictured it. You and Haji were supposed to go on all these adventures, like King Arthur and Sir Lancelot or Robin Hood and Friar Tuck. You tell her that, but she says there's no time.

She says, "I think we're all put on this earth to learn something, and sometimes the people who are here for the shortest time can teach you the most. We help Haji die, we help everyone else die and then it's just you and me holding hands watching the sun set."

You don't think she'd lie to you—not after you freed her and all—but you can't help feeling a little suspect. To go from the anger she felt to wanting to help people—well, it's a little quick, and you tell her you're not sure if she's talking about putting people out of their misery or hers.

"I just want to make a difference with the time I have left," she protests. "I had all these hopes and dreams that are never going to be fulfilled. But here's something I can do to take people out of pain. To let them die with dignity. And then I get to be with you. Do you really want to deny me that?"

"I don't want to deny you anything," you tell her. But there are some things you just don't want to do.

She puts her hand between your legs and touches you.

"Think about it," she says.

She teases you into a frenzy. And then backs off, coughing, saying she needs to rest. You've never been more confused. She's sick and sexy in equal quantities and every course of action you look at just seems doomed. So you do what you always do when that happens. You write all your questions down, you build a fire, and you leave the answers up to the flames.

haji

Vashti used to surf. I have a hard time picturing it, but everyone assures me she did. Years ago, she filled her domain with vast silver pools that rippled and stretched however she pleased and churned about at her whim. There, on the Inside, she'd ride waves of liquid mercury, one after another, locking in to take the drops and crank the turns, in complete control of not just her body and her board but the shining ocean itself. It was she who taught my cousins to surf, the ones who were teaching Hessa. I am imagining Hessa and Mu'tazz catching a silver wave in my mind. They are laughing together, happy and free, beckoning me to come join them. I see no sand beneath me and neither sun nor sky above. I walk on a beach of floating air currents. When I enter the mercury it bubbles and boils and I am confused at how I can feel so terribly hot and so terribly cold at the same time. Then I realize I am dreaming a fever dream.

With no more logic than I can expect from my unconscious mind, I am suddenly in an impossibly vast underground cave, rowing a boat through dark silver water. Glare from a panoply of electrical lights distracts me now and again from my conversation with the goateed man in the fancy military uniform seated across from me. Except it's not really a conversation. I am reciting *The Waste Land* as I row, and he listens intently, eyes closed, in his spiked helmet with horsehair plume, occasionally holding up a hand for me to stop so he may ponder the significance of what I have said, then motioning for me to continue. In the silences I study him, and I realize the boat is shaped like a giant seashell and this must be the swan of all swans, King Ludwig the Mad.

Only the sick oyster can yield a pearl, he whispers, eyes opening to show me neither pupil nor iris but simply a cold and infinite emptiness.

Fear death by water, I reply, and with my words the boat begins to sink.

Then I am aware of my surroundings, the bed upon which I lie, and the sweat that keeps my pajamas clinging to my skin. I do not think I am dreaming, but when I wake I remember the faintest wisps of yet another dream, this one with me in some kind of market with wings upon my back, saying I know not what (to I know not who) before a wooden mallet smashes into my face.

In the waking world, Tomi has been waiting for me. Above her mask I see warm, gentle eyes that glisten with fire and tears. She changes my IV and replaces the compress on my forehead. With rubbing alcohol she cools me.

I've been dreaming, I tell her.

You were talking in your sleep.

Was it *The Waste Land*?

She shakes her head no.

Before I went to sleep, I asked God for guidance through dreams. An *istiqara*.

Did it work? she asks.

I'm not sure.

She squeezes my hand and laughs when I tell her that I love her. That's the fever talking, she says, feeding me a spoonful of ice. But I know she must love me too. To take care of me like this when it so clearly pains her. It might not be a romantic love we share, but it is a true love, a human love, and each time I see her kindness and her fierce concern, it burns brighter than any fever my body will ever know.

I fight this disease with the courage and discipline of a samurai. There are samurai in my bloodline, samurai in the Hyoguchi family tree. Like my distant ancestors, I fight on even if mortally wounded. I promise Tomi this. I do not want her to be afraid.

I am so grateful my father prepared me for battles such as this. When my cousins were growing up, they asked their mothers about the possibility of death and received assurances in return. While everyone who lives is certain to die, it is virtually guaranteed not to happen to you for a very long time, they said. But my father taught us differently. He taught us that nothing is certain, that we are but guests in this world. God may call us at any time and this is not to be feared. I am so grateful to him for stressing this. At a time like now, we are so much stronger for his teachings.

Don't be afraid, I tell my brother fox and sister frog. Dalila has been crying, and Ngozi has lost his tongue. All the people who love us are burning the midnight oil for a cure, I tell them. They are close and we must take courage no matter what.

They peek unhappily at me from their sickbeds, Ngozi to my left, Dalila to my right, and they understand the rightness of what I say.

Pray with me, Dalila asks.

Happily, I do. It helps Ngozi find his tongue. He joins in and I pray with them until they calm themselves and fall sound asleep.

I lie back in silence, lulled by the colors on the overhead screen. I watch them flow from one into the other, as my breathing grows rhythmic and deep.

The shadow that falls over me is my father's. He is weeping and I know instantly that nothing more can be done for Rashid. Hours ago, they wheeled my older brother away for emergency medical attention, and apparently he could not be saved.

Father, I whisper, as he sits and takes my hand. He says we must talk. His voice chokes as he says my name.

Haji, I want your forgiveness.

What could there possibly be to forgive?

I let you down, he says.

Never once, I assure him.

Yes, I did. I lied to you. About Dr. James Hyoguchi, Haji, I lied. I wanted you to let his thoughts consume yours. I planned it. It's why I had you, to use you. It's why I had all my kids.

I do not understand.

He takes a moment to clear his throat and wipe the tears from his eyes. Eighteen years ago when I climbed out of that accursed mirage to see what really happened to the world, I didn't know what to do, he says, anguish in his voice and in his eyes. I was just a teenager, barely older than you are now. There was so much work to be done to restore civilization, so much work just to keep ourselves alive. It was overwhelming. It still is. And I doubted my abilities. Who was I? Just a man. I had no great passion for my own ideas, but I knew enough to know that Vashti's were danger-ous. But the scientists at Gedaechtnis, they were the ones with ideas. They saved us all from extinction. And they wanted to come back. If I could just bring them back to life, then I could relax, secure that they would know exactly what to do.

So we are vessels then? We are nothing more to you?

You are so much more to me. I love you all more than I can possibly say. You are my children. As the years went by, I tried not to think about the sacrifice I would someday ask of you, but al-ways it was there in the back of my mind. I knew I could never force you to do it, I did not have that quality in my character, but I knew I could raise you in such a way so that the idea might not seem so abominable. To go to God and save the world?

Why are you telling me this?

Because it is like a knife in my conscience, he cries, almost waking my younger siblings before quieting down to whisper, I can't tell Hessa or Mu'tazz or Rashid, but it's not too late to tell you. It's not too late to ask your forgiveness.

I stare at him. I keep my jaw clenched. I do not say what I think to say. You are unburdening yourself, I finally tell him. Not for my sake but for yours.

Perhaps I am, but you must know the truth, he says. You deserve my honesty. And honestly I can tell you this, Haji: Even though I planned this cruel experiment, I don't think I could ever have gone through with it. To lose my children like this, one after another? It's monstrous. I could never conceive of such pain.

God breaks the heart again and again until it stays open. You taught me that.

He squeezes my hand tighter. Do you know why I taught you to believe? he says.

To be brave in the face of annihilation?

Yes, he says, but there's one thing more. The electrochemical activity in the brain that comes from feelings of religious epiphany? It's like a lubricant. It facilitates the work. Do you understand? It makes the process of replacing real neurons with artificial neurons that much easier. And I wanted it to be easier. For you. As for myself, I lost my faith the moment I discovered the world was a charnel house and billions of innocent people were dead.

What he says forces the air from my lungs. What he says drowns me in the truth of his lies. What he says devastates me but I will not break.

Billions dead, Haji. What kind of god allows that?

God, I tell him.

The answer dispirits him. He cannot look at me. My eyes are awash with disappointment, acceptance and pain. Will you forgive me? he asks.

Under one condition, I can.

Name it.

You never unburden yourself to Dalila or Ngozi, I tell him. You let them believe what they believe. You give them no reason to doubt.

Tears pour from his eyes. He says he humbly agrees and he thanks me from the bottom of his heart. He hugs me and I let him. After a time I hug him back.

It's fate, I tell him.

What is?

Maybe you lost your faith, maybe you were never destined to believe, but I always have and I always will. And you were God's instrument to make that happen. That is the role you played.

My father looks at me in wonderment. Then he puts his hand to my cheek, touching it tenderly, and he goes.

I hope we have reached some understanding, but my heart feels heavy and so do my eyelids. My breaths are slow and I must fight for them. I drift back into sleep. I would like to think my father's visit was just another fever dream. I know that it was not but it is so blissful to pretend that it was.

deuce

The reading the fire gave you wasn't so rosy as to assuage all your fears, but neither was it so bleak as to confirm them. So you're humoring Penny, making her happy in the time she has left. As you took her northeast to Suffolk, she seemed to get a lot better, but then right when you were thinking she was out of the woods, it all came back again, the coughing, the sneezing, the nausea and vomiting, and these nasty red splotches desecrating her skin. It made for a scary ride, and you kept looking for your father, hoping to get caught and hoping not to get caught at the same time. You've a feeling he could make all this better, even if it is the End of the World, he could make you laugh about it and put it all in perspective. But you can't go to him. She's too scared. Maybe when she's feeling a little better you can broach it then.

"RAF Lakenheath," she says, squinting at the brick-bordered

sign at the entrance. "Forty-eighth Tactical Fighter Wing." It's a U.K. base with U.S. planes and you can't help but feel just a bit patriotic.

"Now to see what we can get into and what we can't."

Your dad taught you the ins and outs of breaking into military bases when he borrowed a jet from Langley Air Force Base in Virginia. Such adrenaline-blasting fun to go roaring over towns, farms and highways, and he was right—it was so easy—actually easier in real life than it was in the IVR simulators you practiced on.

Your angel's eyes light up with every step, and she urges you to grab everything you can find. Some military bases are near impenetrable, because the soldiers there didn't panic when Black Ep came to the fore. Others, like this one, are open and unlocked, treasure troves of dangerous toys, and the most dangerous of all are the fighter planes themselves. You settle on an F-42 so you can sit side by side. Sick as she is, she's not too weak to help you load it up with your spoils, including a shoulder rocket launcher that could probably blow open the gates of Hell.

She holds up a pistol, helplessly, "Teach me how to shoot," she says.

"Okay," you tell her. "It's a lot different than fencing, but some of the principles are still the same." And you must be a great teacher because she picks it up pretty quick. Soon you're both on a shooting spree, knocking out windows, lights and a squirrel that's in the wrong place at the wrong time. She's so impressed by these slapdash military maneuvers.

She says, "I was supposed to be a soldier but this is the first training I've ever really had."

And when you tell her that it's not really training per se, it's just a couple of kids fucking around with guns, she doesn't want to hear it so she silences you by pressing up against you and thanking you with a kiss

pandora

Rashid gave me a scarab amulet when he was eight and still fascinated by Egyptology. He said when pharaohs died they were mummified, and their real hearts would be removed. A scarab could serve as a replacement heart on the other side. I remember accepting his gift with a wink and a smile, but looking back I never wore it. It was a fine-cut gem in the shape of a beetle, but the only thing I wear next to my heart is Halloween's ankh. Sometime after I bring the gum back to Nymphenburg, I'll have to go to Greece to find that amulet and wear it while I light candles, because now Rashid has joined Mu'tazz, and I have two to mourn instead of one.

Rashid was so often in a buoyant mood, while Mu'tazz was usually so serious that when the light of laughter reached his eyes the spark was dazzling. I miss them equally, and can't accept their deaths any more than I could when Lazarus, Tyler and Simone met their ends. None of Isaac's children spent enough time in the IVR for me to try doing for them what I did for Simone. It's not fair. I feel like someone's turned the houselights down on the theater of life and I'm in the back futilely shouting, "Encore!"

A warning chirp from one of the monitors, and I stare at it uncomprehendingly. Though I'm familiar with the copter's many capabilities, I don't think I've ever seen this particular light go off before.

"Malachi? I'm not alone up here, am I?"

My radar's detected another aircraft.

"It's not Halloween," Malachi warns. "He's still in Nymphenburg."

The process of elimination goes very quickly, coming to a conclusion right as another chirp turns into a prolonged, chilling tone.

"I'm being targeted," I say, but Mal has already taken the controls, trying evasive maneuvers that make my stomach rise up into my chest. He banks and rolls, and I go along for the ride, but excellent pilot though he is, Mal can't break the missile lock. It's not a question of software but hardware—my copter isn't much of a match for a fighter jet.

"Hello? What are you doing?" I call, trying every frequency as sweat pours down my brow. They don't answer me. They've already made up their minds.

Frightened, of course, I mean who wouldn't be? But more than anything else I'm angry. What a waste they are, my niece and nephew. What kind of game are they playing at? Why should I take the brunt of their wrath? Stupid fucking kids.

"Put your flight helmet on," Malachi says, his tone clear but not calm, and I look at my cockpit camera and realize how woefully unprepared I am.

"Now," he says.

deuce

It's one of those things that shouldn't be funny but is.

You've painted her copter with a laser, so you can blow her out of the sky anytime you want. It's the aviation combat equivalent of putting your hands an inch from someone's face and yelling, "I'm not touching you!" over and over again. You don't mean Pandora any harm, but it's a power trip, and your ladylove can't stop giggling as you chase your target down.

"She's freaking out," she says with joy. "Look at her run."

"Yeah, she's got to be wondering what the fuck's going on."

"I've been there."

Beneath her helmet, you wonder if she's smiling her little wistful smile, the one you love, the one that breaks and heals your heart at the same time.

"How you feeling?" you ask, as the G-forces ride up.

"Are you kidding? I'm having too much fun to be sick!" she laughs, sneaking her hand toward the trigger, then playfully yanking it away.

You see what she's doing and laugh with her, but you can hear your blood rushing in your ears. She keeps on doing it though, making a game of pretending to fire while whistling superdramatic suspense music. Then she grabs your hand and squeezes it hard.

"Okay, on the count of three, let's get her. One . . ."

"What?"

"Two . . . Three!"

Nothing happens and you just laugh at each other, relieved.

"Yeah, right," you say, "like let's *really* kill her."

"Yeah," she laughs, "because we're outlaws."

It may be the stupidest fun you've ever had, but she's having the time of her life, and there's just no arguing with that. So you squeeze her hand and say, "Okay, this time for real. One . . . two . . . three!"

It's even funnier when you say it. Your ribs hurt and you can barely fly with the tears in your eyes.

"Right," she says between giggles. "One . . . two . . ."

pandora

Laser-guided missile on the way and there's no escaping. I'm trying to pray to God even if I can't decide if I believe in Him or not, and while my brain wants to say "not like this" my lips are moving on their own accord, shouting, "shit, shit, shit, shit," like a child in the midst of a tantrum or in the thrill of learning a forbidden word.

But there's no time for any of it because on my screen the missile dot is zipping at the dot that represents me with merciless speed and as the dots become one I'm suddenly flying up in the air, up and through to the wide open sky as Mal triggers the ejection seat. I'm screaming in my helmet and it's all happening so fast because I can't tell whether I'm up or down—it's all just a catch-as-catch-can of sea, sun, sky, copter buckling and bending under the pressure, and fire so hot it feels like it's on me even when it's not. Just when I figure out how to distinguish up from down, the parachute catches and jerks me back hard, and it's such a relief to know the chute has opened that I'm dumbstruck when something metal smashes into my head and everything goes fuzzy. There's pain, but worse than the pain is the fading consciousness, and worse than that still is the dim awareness that my parachute has just been punctured, and the Mediterranean Sea is rising up to greet me faster than it should.

deuce

Charred wreckage. Spectacular explosion. When the missile screamed out of the turret all you felt was a greasy sick feeling in the pit of your stomach, letting up slightly when she ejected but coming back strong and thick, lathering your esophagus with acid as the parachute ripped and she sank beneath the waves.

You're holding Penny's hand and you each have a finger on the trigger. She turns to you in amazement and your expression is the same as hers.

"I thought you were joking."

"I was," she says.

"Then why'd you do it?"

"I didn't," she says. "You did."

"I felt your hand move."

"When you moved it."

"But I didn't want to do it," you yell.

"Well, I did, but you're the one who hit it. I don't have it in me to do something like that. I'm not that brave."

You thought she did it, but maybe it was you. You know you have an impulse control problem. So many times in your life you've gone ahead and done something you shouldn't. Impulses happen all the time and most people say no to them, but you don't like saying no. Just like you don't like saying no to Penny. But did you want to shoot Pandora? You liked her, sort of. So did Dad. What's he going to say?

"You really love me," Penny purrs. "That's why you did it."

You do love her but she's the one who pulled the trigger.

Didn't she? Or maybe it was both of you. Either way, this is so fucked. This is beyond fucked.

"Oh my God, what did we do?"

"You put her in the dirt. Or the water, in this case. Hey, don't feel so bad. It's not like she didn't deserve it," she says.

"Why, because she passed you over for Olivia?"

"Not just that! She tried to brainwash me in the IVR. She put all kinds of stuff in my head—who even knows what's in there?"

That may be true, but did she really deserve to die for it? "I don't know," you say, feeling helpless and small.

"I know," she says, stroking your trembling bicep with her fingertips. "I know you love me. Goddamn, how you love me."

You're trying to think, but your girl is telling you what she's going to do to you the moment you land. And it's so hard to concentrate when she does that. But you just start yelling, "Shut up, shut up," until she gives you a chance to think. You keep looking for a way to undo what you did, but there's just no undoing it. The only bright side you can see is that if she had the End of the World at least she's out of pain.

"Let's go to Paris," Penny whispers, "I'm hungry and I want to go to Paris."

halloween

I was close to putting the finishing touches on the repair work when Malachi called. I thought he was here to rib me about my programming speed and ask me for a status report, but fifteen words into what he had to say I was running out the door.

Champagne could have been anywhere, but it was her dumb luck to keep winding up in my path. I grabbed her arm in mid-stride and didn't let go until we reached my jet.

"Let go of me," she fumed. "What do you think you're doing?"

"Pandora needs us. Get your ass in the seat."

pandora

The water breaks me. Not completely, but enough.

I curl into a ball right before the impact because I remember it's what you're supposed to do in this situation. But when I hit water I black out and when I come to it's still black. My eyes won't work and neither will my right arm or my right leg. Excruciating pain shoots up and down my spine. I have a funny taste in my mouth and I can hear Malachi in my ear, but just barely.

"Pandora, can you hear me?"

I think I answer him, but everything's kind of sluggish. He's yelling at me because my helmet's damaged and leaking oxygen. Soon water will get into the mask unless I plug the leak. I realize then that I'm trying to stay afloat and keep my head above water, but the underwater currents keep pulling me down and I don't have the arm and leg strength to ride them the way I'd like.

He guides my fingers to the leak and helps me plug it with a scrap from my tattered parachute. How does he know what's going on? And I realize that my flight suit's emergency beacon has activated, sending Malachi information from transmitters through-out the stitching.

"I'm blind," I tell him, and he says not to worry, he's going to stay with me. He'll be my eyes as best he can and keep me from drowning until Hal comes to rescue me.

Where is the gum Vashti needs? I wonder. Did it survive the blast? Has it sunk to the bottom of the sea?

The currents keep pushing me and I want to scream and sleep but I try my hardest not to. I'll hang on because Malachi tells me everyone's working together now. My mind keeps drifting from the warm cradling lull of the sea, but what Mal says is the one thing I can hold on to. We're a group again—it's no longer just me, Isaac, Vashti and Champagne against all the problems of the world. Now that Hal's coming for me there are five of us and with five we can make a fist.

Some part of me recognizes that Malachi is telling me what I want to hear and it may be true or it may simply be a means of keeping me alive. My friends might still be divided, and maybe no one is coming for me at all. But one way or another we'll see. And I'm not going to lose hope. It's the one thing I'm not going to do.

halloween

Malachi told me how badly she was hurt, but I already had my jet pushing the limits. Champagne grabbed hold of whatever she could, white-knuckling it out of either fear for Pandora or cer-tainty that I was about to shake the plane apart getting there. We made the trip in silence and I kept racking my brain about Deuce. Why did he do what he did? How could he do what he did?

I wanted to believe that Penny did it, but that's a father talking, wanting to shield his son. I couldn't give in to that feeling. I wasn't going to live in a false paradise, because if he was in the plane that shot Pandora down, in my book he was responsible.

But if he was responsible, then so was I. There are things I could have done. I could have never taught him how to fly jets and I could have barred him from IVR flight simulators. Then he'd never have been able to do this. Still, I had a hard time reconciling this cowardly attack on Pandora with the innocent question my son posed years ago: What's it like to break the speed of sound?

Or maybe if I'd forced him to meet his cousins much earlier, against his will, no matter how much he kicked and screamed.

Or if I'd never let him out of Idlewild.

When he was nine, I'd taken him to see a small town southwest of Pittsburgh. Coal-mining country. But I hadn't taken him to Edenborn to learn the history of coal and coke production—I took him to see a roller coaster by the name of Breaking Point. I showed him my former folly and told him how I overcame it. And then we spent some time just wandering around the amusement park like friends together, talking about nothing of great importance. I made some sarcastic comment, and he laughed, saying, "No shit, Sherlock." When he said it I could close my eyes and hear someone from my past using that silly phrase. And then I realized—just as we were laughing about something or other—that I'd had the conversation before. Not the exact same conversation, but one close enough to amaze me because it was from years ago, when I'd done something similar with Mercutio.

So I had to wonder: Had I somehow been raising Deuce to be like Merc? I'd missed my crazy, funny, never particularly trustworthy friend, so maybe I'd been unconsciously shaping my son into a new version of him.

But the odd moment never repeated itself, and I had to come to the conclusion that it was a fluke and nothing more.

That was what ran through my mind until the crash site came into view. But when I saw the extent of the damage, how far and wide the debris scattered, all I could think of was Pandora.

pandora

Death is upon me, staring me in the face, impatient as a visitor in a doctor's waiting room. I can't see him but I know he's there. Malachi's voice is so soft now, I can barely hear him, and I must remember that what he's saying is important. So I strain to listen, and he is saying, "Tell me a story," and I feel like that girl from *The Arabian Nights* who must spin tales in order to stay alive.

I try to speak, and in my head I hear the words, but I don't know whether I'm actually saying anything at all. I try to describe the most perfect Sunday with Champagne, but I can't seem to keep my mind on it, and before long I'm just stringing words together, and my audience is Death.

He is a living shadow, each molecule a piece of plague. I suddenly realize he's a practical joker, sneaking up on unsuspecting people to play his pranks. So many times he could have played the prankster with me but instead he waited until I was blind, facedown in the water and running out of oxygen. I'd never invite him, but I have to admit there are worse times for him to visit me than now.

haji

Flowers blossom. White and pink. Screens flicker. Shapes and shadows blur. My brother turns away in the hope that no one will see him weeping. People hover over my bedside. Someone's fingers arrange origami animals on a medicine tray. Dalila's hand slips into my left hand. Ngozi's hand grabs my right. A mask covers me. These are the sights through half-closed eyes.

A long, low moan. Labored breathing. A complicated explanation of technology meant to give us hope. A pillow fluffed. My sister asking for something. Hydraulics. Wheels on tile. Clicks. Hissing gas. Farewell, my beautiful child. Until we meet again. These are the sounds that reach my ears.

Burning sickness. My legs cramping in agony. My arms tangled in sheets. Being moved. Lifted up. A lingering kiss. Coolness on my brow. The feeling of someone squeezing my hand tightly, then limp, then going still. Heat ebbing away. These are the sensations.

I breathe in the pungent scents of medicine, chemicals and sweat. The taste is thirst and ice and honey candy on my tongue.

It is so hard to keep things in my mind. Thoughts and feelings rush away like galaxies after the Big Bang. I wonder where they are going.

I am somewhere else. I see all and recognize nothing. It may be a long time ago, or a long time from now. I am losing all means of going home and I accept it. As much as I want to piece it all together, hanging on to the fragments will only cause pain. I am nowhere but nowhere is whatever I want it to be. I name it Eden.

What if the gates to Paradise are too heavy for me to open?

That's Dalila's voice. I don't know when she said it. I can't remember. She must be saying it now.

They will be as light as a feather for you, I told her once and tell her now. And though I cannot see her, she is holding my hand. She is pulling me forward.

They will be so light, they'll open of their own accord, I promise. That's how God will greet you.

She says in a tiny delighted voice, they are, Haji, the doors of Heaven are opening. Her little hand relaxes. Now Ngozi has my other hand. His voice comes from nowhere out of nothing. I don't want to die, he says.

I squeeze his hand and tell him Dalila has already gone through the gates. I tell him we must hurry up and catch her. We mustn't keep God waiting for us.

I'm so frightened, he says.

My brother, it's nothing to fear. It's just another journey, I tell him. How lucky we are to make it together.

His hand desperately clutches mine and I comfort him by squeezing back until I feel his hand no more.

I am alone now, nowhere, a universe unto myself. I can sense nothing but a growing coldness. They may be freezing me. Cryonic stasis. I can't remember if they said they would do that or not. I can't even remember who they are.

There is more than this darkness, this emptiness, this coldness. I am sure of it. Any moment now I will touch my foot down. I will hear wind chimes. I will see Ngozi and Dalila ahead of me racing each other up a snow-covered meadow, wildflowers thriving in winter, an explosion of glorious color bursting through the white.

They will look back over their shoulders and call to me. Come on, Haji, they will say. It's just over this hill.

And they'll run for me to chase them so I will put my hand out and say, Wait, wait, but they will be too excited to wait. So I will hobble after them only to find that God has made my legs healthy and strong. I will run without pain. My face will break into a triumphant smile because with each long stride I will be catching up to my brother and sister. My heart will beat with joy and my arms will reach them. At the top of the hill we will laugh together and watch the sun rising up to greet us.

Any moment, it will happen.

I am patient. I will wait.

halloween

Search and rescue: I put the jet in vertical, hovering over the crash site. Down below, all I could see was twisted wreckage and whipping waves, foam building on their caps. Right when I thought Champagne would be useless, she peered down to spot Pandora floating facedown, unmoving, suffocating in her suit. She pointed, and I grabbed the EMS gear. We didn't have to say anything to each other—we knew what had to be done. She attached me to the descender and I dropped down into the blue, reaching to slide Pandora's broken rag doll body onto the litter before she flickered out.

deuce

Paris is for lovers. Or is that Virginia? She wanted lobster, so you scoured the Seine. Some animal activist must have freed some restaurant's lobster tank, and dumped the little snappers in the river. Now they're thriving. You caught one with a shopping cart. Sometimes improvised traps are the best.

You push it through the lobby of the George Cinq Hotel, the only sounds your footsteps and the cart's squeaky wheel. Your ladylove wanted the honeymoon suite but without a working elevator, it was too many flights of stairs for your infected sweetie. So you make a honeymoon suite of the lobby itself.

Penny took fifteen years' worth of anti-aphrodisiacs and for a moment you thought it might take fifteen years for them to wear off. Mercifully, that's not the case and from the second you put the lobster down, she's all over you—and when she's touching you, it's the only time you're not torturing yourself for what you did to Pandora.

You have slow, delicate sex on the cushions and mean, fast sex on the stairs. Even with the pinkish-red blotches that the End of the World has kissed her with, you still find her even more exquisite than you had dreamed. You fuck her in every way you can think of and she invents a few more. You're addicted to her. A line from an old movie keeps repeating in your head: "You're a corpse, son, go get yourself buried!" So you bury yourself in her every way you can. And when you bring out Genesis to start burning the rooms down as you do it, and you can just look at her, and watch the flames rise, and watch her ride you, and the flames get higher, you think your heart might just explode along with the rest of you.

But just like any drug, coming down can drop you as low as the high rocketed you up. No matter how much you fuck her, when you're done, you can't help but feel like you've only fucked yourself.

"Maybe we should turn ourselves in," you tell her once, quietly.

She just gazes at you and says, "Go back to that world? Why?"

"Don't you miss anyone there? Anyone at all?"

"Why would I?" She measures you, shaking her head. "Why, do you?"

"My dad," you mutter.

"I thought I was enough for you," she says, getting up and turning her heel on you, even when you insist that she is.

Once you have some privacy, you try calling home.

"Dad, I love you," you say. "I'm so sorry."

"Fuck your apology, you almost killed her!" he yells, and you think you hear Penny coming back so you hang up before he can say anything else.

But no, she's just stomping around. You turn your phone off, and crouch into a ball on the sofa. On a whim you decide to cut your hair to the same length as your father's. Because maybe if you look like him, you'll be him and everything will be okay. But when you stare at yourself in the mirror, you don't know who you are anymore.

When you go to make amends with Penny, she's sicker than ever, and when her body stops shaking and she cleans herself up, she glares at you behind bloodshot, watery eyes. "You're leaving me," she says.

"Never," you tell her.

"Do you love me? Do you really, really love me? Because if you do, there's no room for anyone else. Either we're together or we're not. Either we're the only two people left on the Earth who know what love is, or we each go our separate ways."

And die, you think. Alone.

You remember what your dad told you about Simone, how all-consuming his love was, and how he'd have done anything just to spend a little more time with her before she died. You don't want to make the same mistake, but goddamn, if only you could go back in time and stop yourself from doing what you did to Pandora. Whether she deserved it or not, what you did crossed a line, and even though your dad said he'd love you no matter what, you think you just pushed that "what" further then he'd ever dreamed.

"What's it going to be?" she says.

The next morning, you're back in Munich, and she's by your side, bouncing on the tips of her toes. It's not right. "If you want to do this," you tell her, "it's a lot safer to do it from the air." And you're stalling her—you know that—but you only half realize you're saying that in the hopes of finding your father up there, so he can make it all right one way or another. You scan the sky, but it's clear. And it doesn't matter anyway, because she says no, she wants to see this at eye level.

You're just outside the Nymphenburg gates, careful not to trip the motion detectors or heat sensors. The best play on the board is higher ground, because you'll get the cleanest shot. So you climb up to an observation deck across the street from the entrance. It's a pretty day and an even prettier view. She reaches up to stroke your back, reassuring you, but it's not working, and whether it's your nerves or the End of the World, something's making you sick.

halloween

I knew they'd come back. Either to turn themselves in or to finish what they started. They were like homing pigeons—it was inevitable.

They wouldn't come by air because he'd be too afraid of me up there and she'd want to see ground zero up close. They had to come by foot, it was just a question of where. I had three locations in mind, and they chose the most obvious of the three. It was a bold move, or a foolish one, just like the way he played chess. No defense.

It seemed I'd lived a lifetime since the last time I'd worn the suit. The first time I saw it Mercutio was wearing it. State of the art, military issue, it scrambled light, refracting and reprojecting to make you seem invisible. To make you seem like a ghost. For years I'd kept it tucked away for safekeeping and practiced my marksmanship two hours a day religiously just in case something like this might happen. But out of all the people I'd thought I might have to take out, Deuce was the most painful to consider.

It was a nightmare for me, but I had to do it. I'd seen evil before and didn't believe in letting it win. I'm certainly no angel, and I've made more mistakes than I'll ever know. And if other people want to give me a second chance, that's their business, but with me there are no second chances.

I took a sniper position in the soft grass and waited.

deuce

You load the rocket launcher, feeling the heavy missile lock into the chamber with a solid click.

"Why are we doing this?" you ask her. "Mercy killing or revenge?"

"It doesn't matter. Revenge is the low road, mercy killing's the high, but ultimately we have to do this for us. Penny and Deuce—Deuce and Penny," she says sweetly into your ear.

You think of Haji in there and wonder if you're offering a better death than the one he's facing. You think of all the comrades-in-arms and ladyloves and wonder why you should get to play God like this. Are you really the God of Fire? Is it your destiny to put an end to all things? Or are you just a runaway who made a terrible mistake? Is it possible you can be both at the same time?

The questions hurt. The enormity of what you're about to do is crushing. And when she asks you if you're ready, you just stand there.

"Come on, I'll do it with you," she offers. "We'll count to three."

She counts and you look at her. You say, "I can't."

"Sure, you can. You already did it once. This time will be easier."

"Penny," you say, laying the rocket launcher on the ground, "my father might be in there and if I don't know where he is, I'm not going to do this."

"Why not?"

"Because."

"You really think he's any different?" she scowls.

"He's my dad. Without him I wouldn't be."

"Deuce," she says. "You are who you are only because of the choices you made. All he wanted was a copy of himself."

"It's more complicated than that," you say, but it doesn't matter—she isn't listening.

"It's Adam and Eve, not Adam, Eve and Adam's dad," she says.

"I won't make this choice," you say, trying hard not to fold when she gives you that wounded look.

"Okay, so you're making it clear you don't care about me. You're just like the rest of them," she says, making knives of those words, and you don't protest because maybe you are like the rest. As much as you love her, maybe you're not meant to be with her. Maybe what the fire was really trying to tell you is sometimes you can't have it all.

"Fine, *I'll* do it," she says, reaching for the rocket launcher, but you snatch it away from her, unloading it as she looks on in shock. And the misery in her eyes surprises you with its depth, like you're looking into empty wells in the midst of endless drought.

halloween

I watched them through my sights, ready to end it and praying I wouldn't have to. He loaded that rocket launcher and kept threatening to raise it, but I kept my cool, thinking *Don't you do it, don't you dare* every time it looked like he would. And in the end, he couldn't go through with it. He put the weapon down. Took it away from the girl. She went berserk, started yelling at him, completely out of control and somehow I knew that she'd been in the driver's seat all this time. My son had fallen in love with the wrong person, but now he'd come to his senses. I could understand that. I could empathize. I dropped my sight a fraction of an inch and watched. And thought *Good*. And then she pulled a gun so I had to fire.

deuce

You saw the pistol come out of her pocket and jerk up, and you did nothing, and then the shot rang out. It rang out early, and that surprised you and didn't surprise you at the exact same time, and the blood splashed out so quickly, it was like she kept fireworks in her head.

Blood pools out of her onto the pavement beneath. You could kiss your Sleeping Beauty but she would never awaken. The Bye Bye Guy has delivered her from the End of the World. Into the next.

Your dad's here, and he must think he's saved your life but in your heart you always knew you had no life to save. And you realize you were never the God of Fire because he's the God of Fire—he must be, because only he can put an end to all things.

halloween

I dropped her because I had no choice. She'd made her decision, so I had to make mine. When she fell, he knew who'd done it—I could see him whirling around, scanning the grounds for me.

I lowered my rifle, ripping off my helmet to become visible again. I called his name. There was so much to tell him and I didn't know where to begin. I wanted him to know that I was there for him, that I understood how she'd tricked him, that love wasn't always like that, and that even though she'd died, he didn't have to let his heart die with her.

The look on his face told the full story. I saw him clearly and he saw me. And we both knew the truth.

When I reached the base of the observation deck, my arms were still open, hoping to catch him. But there was no saving him. He'd made a swan dive as if he were leaping recklessly into my arms, but they weren't my arms, and he hadn't wanted me to catch him. There was no way I could have reached him in time. The odd thing is somehow I thought I could.

pandora

I wake to the sound of surf and the sight of nothing.

"You're awake," a voice says. "Welcome back."

It's Champagne's voice and I'm happy to hear it. But I still can't see her. It doesn't bother me as much as it will when the painkillers start to wear off. My broken bones are still broken— despite my hope that it was just a dream—and I've been strapped to a backboard; I can feel it beneath me.

She tells me how long I've been asleep and I groan.

"Tell me what hurts."

"We can save time if I tell you what doesn't."

I run through my injuries and she gives me her diagnosis: herniated discs, broken femur, broken ulna, blunt force trauma to the head causing blindness and concussion. Everything will be as good as new given treatment and time. The only thing she can't promise that for is the eyesight, which Vashti and she will want to examine more closely upon our return to Nymphenburg.

"Actually, considering how hard you hit the water you're lucky to be alive," Malachi chimes in. They tell me how I almost didn't make it, how Halloween rescued me and how Champagne revived me.

"You worked together?" I ask incredulously.

"I really can't stand Hal, but in some ways he brings out the best in me," Champagne acknowledges.

"Where is he now?"

So they tell me. And I expect to feel glad that Penny and Deuce are dead, but instead I just feel numb. They had so much more going for them than they ever realized and they never appreciated it. Like my mother used to say, *Dá Deus nozes a quem não tem dentes.* God gives nuts to those who don't have teeth.

It's a mystery why those two did what they did except to say it was a fatal attraction, a mixing of fire and gasoline. A strange thing, in Penny's pocket they found a broken jar of strawberry jam and no one could understand why she had it. She was allergic to it and all they could think was that either she was so rebellious she was willing to hurt herself to eat the sweets she wanted, or she was so guilty about what she'd done she wanted to poison herself.

When they've told me their story, they tell me about Haji, Ngozi and Dalila. How Isaac and Vashti weren't able to save them in time, except to cryonically freeze them. At least, thank goodness, they have a small chance, but my heart is breaking for Isaac.

Once we salvage that gum, perhaps Vashti will be able to synthesize it and eliminate Black Ep once and for all. And if that works maybe someday we can rescue so many of its victims from cryonic suspension. Isaac's children too. Maybe we can give them the tomorrow they deserve.

Always the optimist.

You say that like it's a bad thing.

No, I admire it. There's a quality certain people have to come back from adversity without being broken by it.

You mean courage.

I suppose I do.

I hear the sound of a plane landing, which means the salvage team is here. First Isaac, then Halloween. They come to my side and sit with me, and then set out to retrieve what's left of my cargo.

It's even better than old times. We're all working together. If only Fantasia were here it would be perfect, but I'll take what I can get.

halloween

I've been trying not to dream. When I do sometimes I wake up thinking Deuce is still alive. Then I spend the whole day looking for him out the corner of my eye.

I put Malachi to work on a pet project of mine. An analysis of exactly how the dream cycles work in IVR. I have a theory that there's a recursive quality. So much data gets sloshed around in there, I've reason to believe my son's generation grew up dreaming some of our old dreams. I'd never begrudge anyone Pandora's dreams, but mine can be dangerous, and I don't even want to consider what Mercutio's might be.

Dangerous, dangerous dreams.

I've made a decision, I won't do any more dreaming. I'm going to concentrate on living. And doing what needs to be done.

Everyone wanted me involved—well, now I am.

For Pandora's sake, if no one else's.

ACKNOWLEDGMENTS

First, a shout out to my talented and patient editors: Jennifer Hershey at Putnam, and Simon Taylor at Transworld (U.K.). It's my privilege to work with you.

Equally wonderful are my supportive and savvy agents. Cheers to everyone at InkWell, but especially Matthew Guma, Richard Pine and Lori Andiman, all of whom I'm lucky to have looking out for me.

Andrea Ho's and Gretchen Achilles' top-notch design sensibilities made the U.S. hardcover a work of art. Richard Carr did the same for the U.K. edition.

Katherine Pradt copyedited the manuscript, transmuting commas, parentheses and em dashes via a literary alchemy known only to an enlightened few.

Sharon Greene and Rita Calvo came through once again with sage counsel on epidemiology and molecular biology. Volker Vogt answered my virology questions, helping to shape the End of the World.

Kelly Zamudio, Steve Ellner and Richard Harrison indulged all my hypotheticals about what might happen to the planet once humanity stops taxing it.

Lee Meadows Jantz furnished me with specifics on human decomposition.

I'm also grateful to the institutions that let me borrow these experts' time: the University of Michigan (Greene), Cornell University (Calvo, Vogt, Zamudio, Ellner, and Harrison) and the University of Tennessee (Jantz).

Brandon Benepe discussed thrill rides with me, giving color to Breaking Point.

Adam Adrian Crown was kind enough to answer my questions on dueling. His *Classical Fencing: The Martial Art of Incurable Romantics* is a fantastic resource.

The epigraph comes from a band that speaks to my heart, the energizing and moving Local H. The *As Good as Dead* and *Whatever Happened to P. J. Soles?* albums are never far from my CD player. My thanks to Scott Lucas and Brian St. Clair, and special thanks to Wes Kidd of Silent Partner Management, who moved heaven and earth to get me "Heaven on the Way Down."

"Is this working?" might be the writer's most neurotic refrain; I routinely torture my friends with it. My gratitude to Dave Parks and Doselle Young, two mad skills writers who helped sharpen the book, cheerfully kicking ideas around and giving me feedback on the early pages.

John Scalzi was finishing *The Android's Dream* while I was finishing *Edenborn*. He'd call me up, tell me about his progress, and laugh like a Bond villain at mine. Having someone to race is a great motivator, even when you don't win.

Additional support, encouragement, assistance and inspiration came from Warren Betts, Nick Bortman, Rosie Brainard, Damned If I Don't Productions, Jack "Yaki" Dunietz, Rich Florest, Dan Goldman, Mozetta Hilliard, Annah Hutchings, Nathan Jarvis, David Klein, Walt McGraw, Joel McKuin, Clinton L. Minnis, Maurice and Renee Minnis, Nova Group, David Owen, G. J. Pruss, Sam Sagan, Sasha Sagan, Jerry Salzman, Tom Schneider, Raphael Spiritan, Janine Ellen Young, and everyone who came to my *Idlewild* signings and/or dropped by www.nicksagan.com to say hello.

My father's sensibilities continue to inform much of what I do, and I'm grateful to Ann Druyan and Cosmos Studios for keeping his vision of the future alive. I miss him every day. There are so many things I wish I could share with him today; this book is merely one of them.

Clinnette Minnis remains my (not so) secret weapon. Where would I be without her brilliant mind and loving heart?

Finally, my thanks to one of the world's few interplanetary artists: my mother, Linda Salzman Sagan. Yes, she designed the Pioneer plaque, but let me sing some of her other praises. When I was an infant, she took the time to nourish my intuition and imagination. When I was a toddler, she raised me on great books and on foreign films that went (mostly) over my head. When I was a kid, she sympathized with my rebellious spirit and helped channel it into my creativity. When I was a teenager, she taught me how to write (I spent years watching her write for TV), she encouraged my willingness to take risks and try new things, and she never stopped believing in me, even when I dropped out of high school. And here in my adulthood, she's been teaching me courage and an appreciation for what it takes to survive amidst adversity.

Life lessons learned, and I'm grateful for all of them.

Nick Sagan
Ithaca, New York
9 May 2004

ABOUT THE AUTHOR

NICK SAGAN is the author of the novel *Idlewild*. He is the son of the astronomer Carl Sagan and the artist/writer Linda Salzman. His greeting—"Hello from the children of planet Earth"—was recorded and placed aboard NASA's Voyager I spacecraft, which is now the most distant human-made object in the universe. Sagan graduated summa cum laude from UCLA Film School. Visit his website at www.nicksagan.com.